MOHAN RAM

Sri Lanka

The Fractured Island

PENGUIN BOOKS

Penguin Books (India) Limited, 72-B Himalaya House, 23 Kasturba Gandhi Marg,
New Delhi-110 001, India
Penguin Books Ltd., Harmondsworth, Middlesex, England
Viking Penguin Inc., 40 West 23rd Street, New York, N.Y.10010, U.S.A.
Penguin Books Australia Ltd., Ringwood, Victoria, Australia
Penguin Books Canada Ltd., 2801 John Street, Markham, Ontario, Canada L3R 1B4
Penguin Books (N.Z.) Ltd., 182-190 Wairau Road, Auckland 10, New Zealand

First published by Penguin Books India 1989

Copyright © Mohan Ram 1989

Typeset in Times Roman by Tulika Print Communication (P) Ltd., New Delhi
Made and printed in India by Ananda Offset Private Ltd., Calcutta

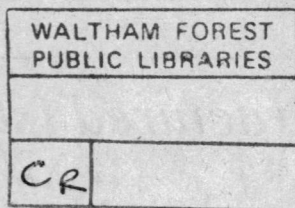

To
The People of Sri Lanka

Contents

Preface

Serendipity means the faculty of making happy and unexpected discoveries by accident. Horace Walpole coined the phrase in 1794 after *The Three Sisters of Serendip*, a fairy tale. Sri Lanka was known as Serendip then.

The anti-Tamil riots in Sri Lanka during the last week of July 1983 shattered the island's idyllic image, and the continuing violence ensured that the country would, in the immediate future, be seen as a fractured entity with little hope of becoming whole again.

Sri Lanka, known as Ceylon until 1972, began independence in 1948 as a model post-colonial democracy. Among all their colonies the British had prepared it longest for self-government but the transition was delayed by the outbreak of the Second World War. Multi-racial, multi-religious and multi-lingual Ceylon had known free and fair elections (with universal adult franchise) since 1931. With its strong political institutions, a high literacy rate and a healthy economy, it had much going for it. Yet it did not take post-independence Sinhala nationalism long to direct its hostility at the Tamil minority, perhaps out of a perceived fear of being swamped by India, the big neighbour across the Palk Straits, that had sent scores of invading armies to the island nation over the last 2,500 years. Whatever the reasons for Sinhala belligerence, the first group to be victimized was the immigrant labour, mostly Tamil-speaking, the British had brought in from India to run the island's plantations. They were disenfranchised and deprived of citizenship. Then the attack was turned on the ethnic Tamils in the northern and eastern tracts.

Successive Prime Ministers pursued policies that sharpened the ethnic conflict until the Tamils, who thought their traditions, and the victimization they had experienced, underscored the need for them to have a nation of their own, demanded self-determination in 1976. The demand was soon to be supported by guerrilla action plunging the island into civil war.

Unsurprisingly enough, India got into the act soon; and Indian mediation between the warring groups culminated in an agreement between the governments of India and Sri Lanka on 29 July 1987.

But the agreement had been worked out without Tamil participation or a Sinhala consensus, with the result that it had no real effect on the conflict. India's role therefore graduated from mediation to intervention (with tacit Sri Lankan consent). This sparked off a Sinhala backlash with ultra-nationalist militant youth challenging the regime in Colombo.

Two years after the agreement, neither a Sinhala consensus nor an end to the Indian military involvement in Sri Lanka, aimed at liquidating the Tamil secessionist guerrillas, seemed likely.

With the situation in such a flux, it would be useful to state the aim of the book. It will certainly take as its central theme the demands the various groups—Sinhala extremists, Tamil guerrillas, the Sri Lankan government, the Indian government—have put forward, and attempt to verify their validity. However I must make clear that the starting point of this book is not the statement of the right to self-determination or its refutation. I refrain (deliberately, I might add) from attempting the definition of a nation (except briefly in the last chapter) even if this means I lay myself open to the charge of trying to study something that I do not define. But to define nationhood in this context would be to prejudge a demand, undermining the whole historical basis of the study.

To clarify the point further, I would say this book will, in addition to surveying the various groups and their aspirations, seek to place the contemporary developments in Sri Lanka in a historical perspective. As for the future, one can do no more than speculate on how well or poorly the challenges to Sri Lanka's unity can be handled.

In the course of the book the following acronyms and abbreviations have been used for the various political parties and groups involved in the current crises. These are: AIADMK, All-India Anna Dravida Munnetra Kazhagam; DMK, Dravida Munnetra Kazhagam; ENDLF, Eelam National Democratic Liberation Front; EPRLF, Eelam People's Revolutionary Liberation Front; EROS, Eelam Revolutionary Organization of Students; JVP, Janatha Vimukti Peramuna; LTTE, Liberation Tigers of Tamil Eelam; PLOTE, People's Liberation Organization of Tamil Eelam; SLFP, Sri Lanka Freedom Party; SLMP, Sri Lanka Mahajana Party; TELO, Tamil Eelam Liberation Organization; TULF, Tamil United Liberation Front; UNP, United National Party; USA, United Socialist Alliance.

Another word about the problem of consistency in style. Media reports (and even official documents) describe the Rajiv Gandhi–Jayewardene accord of 29 July 1987 as the Indo-Sri Lanka Agreement, but this book refers to the document (Appendix I) as the India-Sri Lanka agreement, for that is what it is in actuality. There might be other variations in nomenclature but best efforts have been made to retain standard spellings and acronyms.

PENGUIN BOOKS

SRI LANKA: THE FRACTURED ISLAND

Mohan Ram was born in 1933 and graduated with a degree in economics from Presidency College, Madras. He took up his first newspaper job in 1960 and since then has filed reports on South Asia for several newspapers and magazines, among them the *Christian Science Monitor* and the *Far Eastern Economic Review*. He has also p...
Mohan Ram i...
the *Indian Post*...

I am indebted to friends in India and Sri Lanka (Sinhala and Tamil) for their constant and generous help which enabled me to eliminate many faults and misconceptions. For those that remain, and for all the statements and opinions, I, of course, am entirely responsible.

New Delhi   MOHAN RAM
May 1989

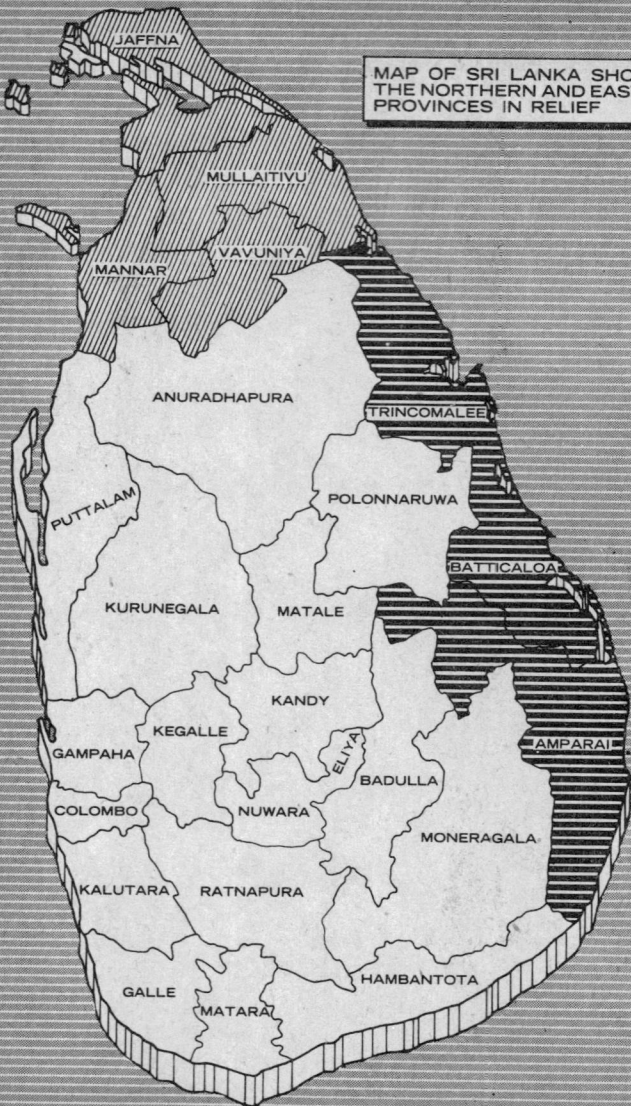

MAP OF SRI LANKA SHOWING
THE NORTHERN AND EASTERN
PROVINCES IN RELIEF

JAFFNA

MULLAITIVU

VAVUNIYA

MANNAR

ANURADHAPURA

TRINCOMALEE

PUTTALAM

POLONNARUWA

BATTICALOA

KURUNEGALA

MATALE

KANDY

KEGALLE

ELIYA

AMPARAI

GAMPAHA

BADULLA

COLOMBO

NUWARA

MONERAGALA

KALUTARA

RATNAPURA

GALLE

MATARA

HAMBANTOTA

LEGEND

Northern Province   Eastern Province

The Northern and Eastern Provinces, together claimed to be
the traditional Tamil homeland, were merged to constitute the
North-Eastern province, subject to a referendum in the
Eastern Province to ratify or reject the merger.

Full Circle: A Diary

1987

23 July   It is a no-win war in Sri Lanka, wearing into its fifth year today. The battle for the Jaffna peninsula (population 830,000), the last bastion of the Tamil secessionist guerrillas fighting for a homeland of over 2 million people, is stalemated. Sri Lankan forces which launched a major offensive on 25 May have stopped short of their decisive assault on Jaffna city (pop. 200,000).

After an Indian flotilla of fragile fishing boats flying Red Cross flags and carrying food and medicines for the beleaguered people is turned away by the Sri Lankan navy on 3 June, five Indian Air Force transport planes escorted by two Mirage-2000 combat aircraft drop twenty-five tonnes of relief supplies. The sortie is a technical violation of Sri Lanka's air space.

There is a lull in the fighting amidst speculation that India, having got the message across to Sri Lanka that it can rain bombs down on the country with impunity if it chooses to, is engaged in quiet diplomacy. Indian and Sri Lankan newspapers report a political settlement is round the corner and the two countries might sign an agreement in the next few days.

24 July   A dramatic development. Velupillai Prabhakaran, the charismatic thirty-three-year-old President and Commander of the Liberation Tigers of Tamil Eelam (LTTE), who has been directing the guerrilla campaign in Sri Lanka since late 1986 from his hideout in Jaffna, is flown, with his aides, into New Delhi to meet Prime Minister Rajiv Gandhi who wants to discuss the proposed agreement with him. This is a sensible move as the LTTE, the most significant Tamil militant group, will have a veto on any settlement. Significantly, till now, the LTTE has not been a party to the negotiations between India and Sri Lanka.

26 July   Talks between Indian government representatives and the LTTE leaders, held incommunicado in New Delhi's plush Ashoka Hotel, and guarded by the elite Black Cat commandos, continue.

28 July   Prabhakaran has a ninety-minute meeting with Prime Minister Rajiv Gandhi, and media reports based on Indian official briefings, suggest that the LTTE intends to go along with the agreement and its reservations are limited to the time-table for the surrender of arms.

But the LTTE leader does not endorse the agreement. He merely says he is satisfied that Rajiv Gandhi has understood Tamil fears and aspirations.

Meanwhile, Sinhala opposition to the proposed agreement (its contents have been leaked) has been building up. The agreement is seen as capitulation to Tamil secessionism. Curfew is imposed on Colombo, the Sri Lankan capital, after riots the previous day. Curfew is then extended to the whole island so that the agreement is signed on 29 July.

Violence continues in Sri Lanka (nineteen are killed in Colombo as police fire on mobs). There is uncertainty in New Delhi about Rajiv Gandhi's two-day visit to Colombo to sign the agreement. The general feeling is: why not wait till the Sri Lankan President, J.R. Jayewardene, overcomes opposition to the agreement and restores normalcy in the island?

The Political Affairs Committee of Rajiv Gandhi's cabinet meets to evaluate reports from Colombo. It thinks cancellation of the Prime Minister's visit would add to Jayewardene's problems and the agreement should be signed to schedule.

29 July   Colombo under curfew is eerily silent. Black crows fly in formation over the city's roof-tops and empty streets, a tableau reminiscent of Alfred Hitchcock's film *The Birds*. About 10,000 Sinhalas, including Buddhist monks in saffron robes, gather on the city's outskirts to march to the airport and demonstrate when Rajiv Gandhi arrives. They break the police cordon and five die as the police open fire.

Rajiv Gandhi and his wife Sonia, along with a bullet-proof limousine for their use, and a large contingent of officials and New Delhi-based media persons arrive in a chartered jet. They are whisked away from the airport to Galle Face Green, the vast open space overlooking the sea in the heart of the city, for the ceremonial reception. Not to be seen on the welcoming committee are Prime Minister Ranasinghe Premadasa and six other members of the twenty-seven-member cabinet. They are known to oppose the agreement*, which is signed later in the day in the panelled audience hall of the seventeenth century Presidential palace, once the private residence of the last Dutch Governor of Ceylon, Johan Cerard Van Vandelbeak.

30 July   The government-owned *Daily News* has the following quote from Shakespeare's *Henry IV* for its customary 'Thought for the Day'

> A peace of the nature of conquest
> For then both the parties are nobly subdued
> And neither party loser

A couple of hours after the newspaper is delivered in hotel rooms, Rajiv Gandhi survives an assassination attempt while inspecting a guard of honour. A naval guard slams his rifle at him but misses the Indian Prime Minister's head. (There is perhaps no precedent in contemporary world history of an attack on a visiting dignitary reviewing a guard of honour. The closest parallel is the assassination of President Anwar Sadat of Egypt while taking the salute at the national day parade.) President Jayewardene apologizes for the outrage. Rajiv Gandhi flies back to New Delhi.

Indian troops begin landing in Sri Lanka, at Jayewardene's request, on a peace-keeping mission.

31 July   Two frigates of the Indian navy carrying a crack commando force, and helicopters in support, anchor off Galle Face Green in readiness to rescue Jayewardene and India's High Commissioner, Jyotindra Nath Dixit, in the event of a coup.

An unknown assailant kills a ruling United National Party Member of Parliament Jayadasa Weerasinghe despite the

---

*For the complete text of the India-Sri Lanka Agreement see Appendix I.

curfew to contain the violence. There are fears of an insurrection by the Janatha Vimukti Peramuna (JVP), a Sinhala nationalist youth group outlawed since the July 1983 anti-Tamil riots which were largely responsible for escalating the ethnic conflict.

The arrival of the Indian Peace-Keeping Force (IPKF) is officially announced. The Indian military presence, limited to the two Tamil majority northern and eastern provinces, relieves pressure on Sri Lanka's armed forces. The Sri Lankan army is redeployed in the Sinhala areas to thwart the JVP threat.

4 Aug. Prabhakaran, who has rejected the 29 July India-Sri Lanka agreement, returns to Jaffna. (He had insisted in New Delhi that he be taken back to his home base.) News that he would be addressing a public meeting (he has been living 'underground' or has been in exile since 1973) eases tensions because people in Jaffna fear that he is being held captive in New Delhi (the jeep of the officer commanding the IPKF is rocked, in one incident, by an irate mob demanding that their leader be restored to them).

Prabhakaran speaks in Tamil from a prepared text. The English translation is made available by the LTTE.* It is significant for the content and the nuances because it contradicts India's version of the LTTE's attitude to the agreement.

The points he makes:

- The agreement was concluded without consulting the LTTE
- When confronted with the draft of the agreement, the LTTE told India that the agreement was no permanent solution to the Tamil problem
- The agreement primarily concerned India-Sri Lanka relations and contained 'stipulations for binding Sri Lanka within India's big power orbit'
- The agreement put a stop to the armed struggle the LTTE had built up over fifteen years, and disarmed the organization without getting the consent of its fighters or without working out a guarantee of the people's safety and protection (because of this the LTTE would not surrender its arms)

*For the English translation of the speech see Appendix II.

- If the LTTE did not hand over its weapons to the Indian Peace-Keeping Force, it would be in the 'calamitous' situation of having to clash with it
- The monster of Sinhala racism would devour the agreement soon
- Only an independent Tamil Eelam could be a permanent solution to the Tamil problem.

5 Aug. A sullen, grim-looking Dileep Yogi (his real name is a secret), a political aide to Prabhakaran, whips out a Mauser pistol and drops it on the table at a ceremony organized for the LTTE's surrender of its weaponry. Sri Lanka's defence secretary, Gen. A.S. Attiyagalle, touches the weapon to symbolize his acceptance of the 'surrender'. The bespectacled Yogi refuses to repeat the act for cameramen who missed it in the first instance. Nor does he shake hands with the official who hands him the letter of amnesty.

All in all, it is a reluctant farewell to arms for a proud band of fighters at the Palaly airbase near Jaffna. India would like it to be seen as a 'surrender' of arms but this concept is too humiliating for the LTTE to bear and it is for this reason that they have rejected the idea of turning in their weapons at a grand public spectacle near Jaffna railway station. The media notes that Prabhakaran is represented at the ceremony by a political aide, Dileep Yogi, and not a military leader of the LTTE.

18 Aug. President Jayewardene survives an assassination attempt in which grenades are hurled at a meeting of United National Party (UNP) MPs that he is presiding over. Prime Minister R. Premadasa and National Security Minister Lalith Athulathmudali are among those who escape with injuries.

14 Sept. Peace is under seige. The IPKF, after securing the disengagement between the Tamil militants and the Sri Lankan forces, is yet to disarm the groups completely. Clashes between the LTTE and the Eelam People's Revolutionary Liberation Front (EPRLF), another militant organization, leave eighty dead in Batticaloa district in the eastern province. The EPRLF says that the LTTE attacked its cadres while the Indian soldiers looked on. It demands that the IPKF maintain peace or return the arms it surrendered so it could defend itself against the LTTE which has said on 1 September that it is taking over the civil administration in the Tamil province to curb 'anti-social activities' (which means, once the persiflage is stripped away, that it is trying to assert its primacy in the eastern province, which it doesn't yet control).

15 Sept. It is unusual for a militant group to try fasting as a political weapon, though the extremist groups in Ireland have tried it on occasion. Amirthalingam Thileepan, 23, chief of the LTTE's propaganda wing, begins a fast unto death to press for a charter of five demands including the release of all political prisoners and detenus held under anti-terrorist laws, an end to Sinhala colonization of Tamil areas, the disarming of the Home Guards (a predominantly Sinhala paramilitary force used against the Tamils in the past) and the closure of all army and police camps in the Tamil areas.

20 Sept. The LTTE backs Thileepan's fast with peaceful picketing of government offices (this has been going on since 16 September) while India warns the militant groups against sabotaging the peace process. The LTTE is specifically blamed for the Batticaloa killings and its political campaign is seen as being aimed at diverting attention from 'fratricidal' killings. Meanwhile Thileepan is reported 'near death'.

24 Sept. The IPKF, earlier welcomed by Tamils as saviours, fires on a violent Tamil mob in front of its camp in Mannar* killing one. India warns that its troops will be compelled to respond with even stronger measures if the LTTE provokes violence.

25 Sept. Thileepan dies rousing strong Tamil emotions even as India's High Commissioner in Colombo, J.N. Dixit, goes to Jaffna to persuade the LTTE to co-operate with the peace agreement.

28 Sept. The LTTE is offered seven places in the twelve-member Interim Administrative Council proposed for the unified Tamil province (comprising the northern and eastern provinces).

* Also called Munnar.

2 Oct.   There are widespread Sinhala-Tamil clashes followed by Sinhala mob attacks on the IPKF in Trincomalee in the eastern province. Serious doubts are raised about India's military role and the future of the tenuous agreement. Are the Indian forces getting bogged down in a law-and-order role which they disdain to play even at home?

5 Oct.   LTTE fighters are known to carry ampoules of potassium cyanide slung down the neck. All the LTTE activists held by a Sri Lankan naval patrol off Point Pedro (and lodged in Palaly camp) on 3 October attempt suicide by swallowing cyanide because they refuse to be taken to Colombo for interrogation (and torture?). Twelve of them, including two ranking military leaders Kumarappa and Puleendran, die immediately.

6 Oct.   The LTTE charges India with failure to avert the cyanide deaths and to protect its cadres in general. Prabhakaran declares the cease-fire does not bind them any more. In gruesome retaliation, the LTTE executes eight Sri Lankan soldiers it has been holding hostage for six months. Two policemen are burnt alive and another killed in Jaffna. The interrupted war resumes.

7 Oct.   The LTTE goes on a spree of reprisal killings in the eastern province and 150 Sinhalas are reported killed.

8 Oct.   More killings, curfew in Jaffna. The IPKF is ordered to shoot at sight after India's army chief Gen. K. Sunderji visits Sri Lanka to assess the situation. (This was necessitated when Jayewardene had threatened to withdraw the IPKF from Trincomalee if it failed to keep peace there.)

9 Oct.   India's Defence Minister K.C. Pant rushes to Colombo for talks with Jayewardene. Both declare that the India-Sri Lanka agreement will be implemented.

11 Oct.   Jayewardene's amnesty to the Tamils is off since 9 October, when a price of a million rupees is put on Prabhakaran's head. ·

    Indian forces launch a massive offensive, raiding LTTE camps, seizing their radio and TV stations and closing two Tamil dailies (*Eelamurasu and Murasoli*) from Jaffna after their printing presses are destroyed by shelling.

The strength of the IPKF is raised to 15,000 against the LTTE's force of under 2,500.

India is fighting Sri Lanka's war.

14 Oct. A pincer movement on Jaffna city by the IPKF is supported by airdropped para commandos.

25 Oct. The IPKF takes Jaffna with heavy casualties on both sides.

13 Nov. Prime Minister Premadasa charges the IPKF with genocide in the Jaffna peninsula.

18 Nov. The LTTE frees eighteen IPKF prisoners, after repeated postponement. There are hopes of a cease-fire after intermittent clashes and the recovery of LTTE arms caches by the IPKF.

20 Nov. India announces a unilateral forty-eight-hour cease-fire to enable the LTTE to surrender arms amidst pressure in India for a political initiative and an end to military operations. The LTTE ignores the cease-fire and there is no surrender of arms.

23 Nov. India rejects the LTTE demand for an IPKF pull back to the 9 October positions as the condition for the laying down of arms.

2 Dec. Jayewardene says the IPKF is 'on top' of the situation and will complete its mission 'very soon', wiping out terrorism from the Tamil provinces because the LTTE is no position to confront its adversary.

As a riposte to Jayewardene, Maj.-Gen. Harkirat Singh, an IPKF commander, says his men take orders from the Indian government and no one else and they will not leave the island 'until the Tamils are satisfied and their aspirations are met'. Sri Lanka's press takes exception to this statement.

9 Dec. Gen. K. Sunderji, India's army chief, says there is no question of an IPKF withdrawal until the LTTE lays down arms—withdrawal now would only demoralize the Indian army and reduce its credibility.

13 Dec.   The IPKF goes on 'red alert' amidst reports that the LTTE plans to crush rival groups.

19 Dec.   Jayewardene vows to crush the Tamil militants in the north and the east and the JVP 'subversives' in the south.

21 Dec.   Rajiv Gandhi says in Madras that a long-term solution of the Sri Lanka problem is in sight and the LTTE should not be allowed to sabotage it.

23 Dec.   Harsha Abeywardene, chairman of Jayewardene's UNP, and three others, are killed in Colombo by unidentified JVP men.

25 Dec.   M.G. Ramachandran (MGR), Chief Minister of Tamil Nadu, dies in Madras. Though a supporter of the India-Sri Lanka agreement, his sympathies were with the LTTE. He had tried to arrange a Christmas truce in Sri Lanka which Rajiv Gandhi vetoed.

31 Dec.   As Tamil Nadu mourns the death of its Chief Minister, a fierce succession struggle ensues in MGR's All-India Anna Dravida Munnetra Kazhagam (AIADMK) Party and the Sri Lankan ethnic issue takes a back seat.

1988

15 Jan.   LTTE leader Prabhakaran promises a surrender of arms 'as previously agreed' on 28 September with India, appeals for an end to the IPKF operations and asks for it to pull back to 9–10 October positions.

19 Jan.   India's Defence Minister K.C. Pant rules out the possibility of a phased IPKF withdrawal in the near future. He wants the LTTE to lay down arms first and then enter the political process.

          There is a daring LTTE jailbreak in Batticaloa in the eastern province.

21 Jan.   A severe indictment of the IPKF takes place in Sri Lanka's Parliament from government and opposition benches. Prime Minister R. Premadasa leads the attack ('the world's fourth largest army has failed to contain the terrorists') followed by another critic of the India-Sri Lanka agreement, National Security Minister Lalith Athulathmudali ('the people of Sri Lanka want the IPKF to leave and it is the same feeling in India'). Anura Bandaranaike of the Sri Lanka Freedom Party (SLFP) says three premises of the India-Sri Lanka agreement have not been fulfilled: the terrorists have not laid down arms, the IPKF has not withdrawn, and there is no peace in the north and the east.

22 Jan.   Sirimavo Bandaranaike, the SLFP leader, calls upon the Indian people, government and Parliament to realize that supporting Jayewardene means propping up a 'puppet regime'.

25 Jan.   Jayewardene arrives in New Delhi as a guest at the Republic Day festivities much to the resentment of India's Tamils. There is talk of a Sri Lanka-India treaty pertaining to defence and security. A draft circulated in Colombo (while New Delhi denies knowledge of it) is broadly similar to the 1971 Indo-Soviet friendship treaty which has strategic implications.

Sirimavo Bandaranaike says the India-Sri Lanka agreement was hatched in secrecy and signed in undignified haste without genuine consultation with the people.

26 Jan.   The LTTE calls for a general strike to mark India's Republic Day.

30 Jan.   Jayewardene's visit to India ends with both sides reiterating their resolve to implement the agreement. Treaty proposal recedes because India thinks it is too premature and wants time to study the proposal.

10 Feb.   There is a spurt in violence in the eastern province where the LTTE cadres seem to have regrouped after the fall of Jaffna. Curfew is imposed on Batticaloa as the IPKF launches a major operation to disarm the Tamil militants. This is an extension of the October offensive in the Jaffna peninsula and the northern province.

15 Feb.   India says it is not averse to a compromise with the LTTE as long as it is within the framework of the 29 July agreement.

Vijaya Kumaranatunga, son-in-law of Sirimavo
Bandaranaike and a leader of the Sri Lanka Mahajana Party
(the breakaway chapter of her SLFP), is shot dead in
Colombo. Deshapremi Janatha Paraya, a front organization
of the JVP, claims responsibility for the murder. Earlier it
had claimed credit for the assault on Rajiv Gandhi on 30
July 1987.

18 Feb. Jayewardene says elections to provincial councils, through
which the devolution of power is to be carried out, in terms
of the 29 July agreement, will be held soon. Sri Lanka's
Parliament has already enacted the legislation and amended
the constitution to create the councils. His obligation over,
it is for India to secure the implementation of the
agreement by getting the Tamils to join the political
process, Jayewardene holds. But the devolution package
offered does not satisfy even the moderate Tamil United
Liberation Front (TULF), which is a middle-of-the-road
party.

The SLFP decides not to contest the elections in the
absence of a referendum on the setting up of the provincial
councils. Its own priority is a general election, which was
last held in 1977.

20 Feb. The LTTE offers unconditional talks with India but says it
cannot lay down arms without securing the protection of
the Tamils.

26 Feb. Lalith Athulathmudali states that the LTTE is having
informal talks with the Indians as well as with the Sri
Lankan government in Colombo.

India's High Commissioner J.N. Dixit meets Jayewardene
and says both the countries stand committed to the 29 July
agreement and there cannot be any unilateral declaration. He
also states that all the parties to the agreement will have to
jointly end the fighting.

12 Mar. Prabhakaran says the LTTE is 'morally and spiritually'
opposed to the conflict and demands that the 29 July
agreement should safeguard Tamil interests.

15 Mar. Gamini Dissanayake, a known supporter of the 29 July
agreement among Jayewardene's ministers, arrives in New

Delhi, reportedly to plead for joint India-Sri Lanka operations in the Tamil areas.

The Indian Minister of State for External Affairs, K. Natwar Singh, tells India's Parliament there is no sign of the LTTE's willingness to give up arms. He wants Parliament to understand the 'geopolitical compulsions' under which the IPKF went to Sri Lanka.

20 Mar Dissanayake, back in Colombo, says Sri Lankan troops confined to the barracks in the Tamil provinces are to be deployed in the eastern region with India's consent because of the escalating violence there. The conflict in the region is between the Sinhalas and the Tamils.

25 May A major IPKF offensive codenamed 'Operation Checkmate' is mounted while secret talks between the LTTE's political wing and the Research and Analysis Wing (RAW), which is India's equivalent of the CIA, are on in Madras.

7 June There is a token IPKF withdrawal following Defence Minister K.C. Pant's talks in Colombo. The highly publicized pull-out by some 3,000 military personnel (while close to 70,000 stay on) is a sop to Sinhalese critics of the IPKF's continued stay.

Beginning in April, provincial councils have been elected in six of the seven Sinhala-majority provinces, the ruling UNP winning all of them with the new four-party leftist compact called the United Socialist Alliance (of the Communist Party of Sri Lanka, the Lanka Sama Samaj Party, the Sri Lanka Mahajana Party and the Nava Sama Samaj Party) offering a close fight. The SLFP has boycotted the elections while the JVP, illegal and functioning underground, has tried to enforce the boycott with a terror campaign.

10 June The southern province, stronghold of the JVP, elects its council amidst strict security arrangements and a low voter turn-out of thirty per cent, which underlines the effectiveness of the boycott call.

Though the councils were devised essentially to transfer power to the Tamil areas, elections have not been held in the Tamil-majority northern and eastern provinces because of the continued disturbances there. At the end of May,

India's Defence Minister K.C. Pant had said the IPKF hoped to create the physical conditions for holding elections in these provinces. The question that is asked, however, is: without the LTTE's participation, would the elections have any legitimacy?

30 June   Indian and Sri Lankan newspapers have been confidently predicting an imminent accord between the LTTE and India ending the conflict. It has been a two-track approach on India's part—stepped up military pressure on the LTTE and negotiations with it at the political level.

Jayewardene promises a merger of the two Tamil provinces and elections to a composite council for the 'north-eastern' province. But the merger will be subject to ratification at a later date by the people of the eastern province.

9 July   The LTTE threatens to terminate its peace talks with India if the IPKF offensive continues. Its political committee based in Madras declares that it will be forced to prepare for a 'permanent' battle against alien occupation of the Tamil areas if the IPKF is not withdrawn.

The Indian media has been reporting that the LTTE leadership is divided and its military wing might have vetoed the agreement its political wing has reached with India.

29 July   The India-Sri Lanka agreement is a year old. A forty-eight-hour curfew is imposed on Colombo to pre-empt the JVP's call for protest against the India-Sri Lanka agreement. A similar curfew is clamped on Jaffna after the LTTE and other Tamil organizations call a protest in the northern and eastern provinces with good response. There are demonstrations in Tamil Nadu state demanding an end to the IPKF operations and negotiations with the LTTE.

India's military involvement in Sri Lanka enters its second year, with no end to it in sight. Sinhala criticism holds that the IPKF has failed to force the LTTE to the conference table or marginalize it militarily. The critics claim that until July 1987 India had cautioned Sri Lanka against attempting a military solution of the ethnic conflict, but it was now doing exactly the same thing it had inveighed against and without success.

31 July India decides on elections in the northern and eastern provinces even as the military pressure on the LTTE is to continue.

8 Aug. Amidst reports that the IPKF resents New Delhi's dialogue with the LTTE, operations carry on. 150 LTTE men are held in a swoop in Madras.

Is it the end of the two-track approach—military pressure alongside political negotiations?

India has not decided to eliminate the LTTE but it does not want a protracted fight either.

18 Aug. The LTTE rejects India's offer of a settlement and prepares for a prolonged war.

21 Aug. The IPKF steps up its offensive against the LTTE as four months of political negotiations with the latter fail.

29 Aug. India's stand hardens. There will be talks only if the LTTE accepts the India-Sri Lanka accord and lays down arms.

10 Sept. The two Tamil provinces are merged to create the north-eastern province though hostilities have not ceased. India and Sri Lanka have been working on a comprehensive plan for elections in Tamil areas.

12 Sept. President J.R. Jayewardene orders elections in the north-eastern province. In Madras, Sadasivam Krishna Kumar, alias Kittu, of the LTTE, through whom India has been holding talks, is held under the National Security Act along with fourteen others, ostensibly to facilitate smooth elections.

14 Sept. The IPKF announces a unilateral five-day cease-fire. This is the last opportunity for the LTTE to surrender.

15 Sept. Sri Lanka invokes Emergency laws to tackle the JVP challenge in the form of strikes.

17 Sept. Offers of talks by India to the LTTE meet with no response. The LTTE cites the arrest and detention of Kittu as a hindrance to any negotiations. It holds out for a permanent cease-fire.

19 Sept.   The cease-fire is extended by five days without a single surrender.

23 Sept.   The cease-fire ends, and an extension is ruled out by New Delhi. Jayewardene says polls will be held in early 1989.

26 Sept.   The LTTE announces its resolve to carry on the struggle and sets three conditions for talks: an extended cease-fire, the release of its leaders held by India, and direct talks at the highest level without conditions.

27 Sept.   India is wary of the LTTE offer. It thinks the LTTE is determined to disrupt elections.

2 Oct.   Nominations begin in the north-eastern province but offices to receive the papers are not open. The LTTE leader Prabhakaran spells out his stand: no referendum on the merger of the two Tamil provinces; the devolution package to be improved; and safeguards against the dissolution of the provincial councils.

4 Oct.   Kittu, in letter to Rajiv Gandhi, the Indian Prime Minister, recalls that (in a letter to the PM) in July the LTTE had promised to lay down arms if an accord was reached. It had also promised to participate in elections, and support the agreement if it met Tamil demands. The LTTE had also suggested a cease-fire in a specified area anywhere in the north-east, so that Kittu could meet Prabhakaran.

Kittu threatens a fast unto death on 10 October if he is not freed and returned to Sri Lanka.

9 Oct.   Big rallies against the India-Sri Lanka agreement in three Sinhala towns of Sri Lanka.

Kittu and others flown to Jaffna to be freed later. Nominations close in the north-eastern province. The Eelam People's Revolutionary Liberation Front (EPRLF) and the Eelam National Democratic Liberation Front (ENDLF) win all the thirty-six seats in the north without contests because there are no nominations from the other groups. But it will be a triangular contest for all the thirty-five seats in the east.

23 Oct.   The JVP campaigns for the dissolution of Parliament with strikes and street demonstrations. The Buddhist clergy backs the JVP. Four Mahanayakas (Buddhist high-priests) want presidential and parliamentary elections to be held together. Jayewardene makes a conditional offer to dissolve Parliament and have an interim government if the JVP abjures violence and participates in the elections. The JVP rebuffs the offer and continues its campaign.

6 Nov. Jayewardene meets Sirimavo Bandaranaike, the SLFP leader and presidential candidate opposing Prime Minister R. Premadasa of the UNP to seek her help in the 'national crisis'.

7 Nov. Jayewardene says India will come to his help if the JVP tries to topple his government.

10 Nov. Continuing strikes paralyze Sri Lanka for the fourth day.

17 Nov. Jayewardene invites the JVP for talks without response.

19 Nov. Elections to the North-Eastern Provincial Council completed. The EPRLF–ENDLF combine gets an absolute majority in the seventy-one member council.

23 Nov. The SLFP-led five party alliance vows to abrogate India-Sri Lanka agreement if its candidate Sirimavo Bandaranaike is elected President. Her main rival Premadasa has been asking for a friendship treaty to replace the agreement.

1 Dec. India warns Bandaranaike and Premadasa of 'unpredictable consequences' if the agreement is abrogated unilaterally.

19 Dec. Premadasa wins the presidential contest against Bandaranaike.

1989

22 Jan. The Dravida Munnetra Kazhagam (DMK) party of Tamil separatism, known to be friendly to the Sri Lankan Tamil cause, returns to power in Tamil Nadu after thirteen years. It is a defeat for Prime Minister Rajiv Gandhi. The political vacuum in Tamil Nadu, since the demise of Chief Minister M.G. Ramachandran of the AIADMK (a special friend of the LTTE), had been used by New Delhi to get tough with the LTTE. Now the defeat by the DMK of Rajiv Gandhi's Congress Party, which had lost the state in 1967 never to regain it, is a defeat for his Sri Lanka policy.

16 Feb. Elections to Sri Lanka's Parliament after over eleven years. Though the LTTE has called for its boycott, its ally the Eelam Revolutionary Organization of Students (EROS) emerges the largest Tamil group in the new Parliament (of course with the LTTE's tacit support).

Despite the JVP violence aimed at disrupting the elections, the turnout of sixty-five per cent is higher than the fifty per cent at the presidential poll eight weeks earlier. Premadasa's UNP retains office but with a reduced majority.

The season of elections is over but not the season of killings.

5 Mar. The IPKF resumes its offensive against the LTTE. Has New Delhi decided to eliminate it finally? Premadasa is continuing his war against JVP terrorism in the Sinhala areas.

Has the India-Sri Lanka agreement precipitated the very danger it tried to avert? India's military involvement in the island has sharpened the ethnic polarization and united all shades of Sinhala opinion against India.

All that remains of the India-Sri Lanka agreement is its debris because a time-frame for the withdrawal of the IPKF appears a mirage and it looks a long, barren involvement.

2 Apr. Premadasa says the JVP and the LTTE are continuing their struggles because they are victims of social, economic and political injustice. He offers to vacate some of the seats in Parliament held by his party to give them representation if they lay down arms. There is no response from either of the groups.

5 Apr. The JVP calls a successful one-day general strike to mark the anniversary of its 1971 insurrection.

12 Apr. The Sri Lankan government announces a unilateral cessation of operations against the JVP and the LTTE for six days because of the Sinhala/Tamil new year day. Though India says it was consulted about this, the IPKF maintains it is a matter between the Sri Lankan government and the LTTE.

LTTE rejects the cease-fire and says there will be no need for fighting or a cease-fire if the IPKF leaves Sri Lanka and the Tamils are recognized as a nation.

15 Apr. There is a dramatic turn-around in the LTTE's position. It is now willing to talk to Premadasa while the JVP is not.

Is this an LTTE ploy to get the IPKF out of the island? The interests of the LTTE and the Premadasa government appear to be converging on getting the IPKF out (the JVP wants this as well) and in demolishing the Trincomalee-based North-Eastern Provincial Council seen as India's client.

So far as India (and by extension the outside world) is concerned, at stake is India's *locus standi* in Sri Lanka's ethnic conflict because everyone except the North-Eastern Provincial Council wants the IPKF out.

The new reality is that Colombo is talking to the LTTE direct once again after a long break.

Have events come full circle?

1

One Language, Two Nations

Wherever one flies in from, as the plane approaching Colombo begins its gentle descent, the 'Taste of Paradise' promised by Air Lanka's brochures seems imminent and almost tangible. The picture postcard-like perfection of the island continues on the ground: the trees, greens and beaches of this land of fantastic colour and sound all appear to be in the grip of a perpetual spring. Paradise enow.

Of the size of Ireland, Sri Lanka, lies five to nine degrees above the equator and almost midway between the Tropics of Cancer and Capricorn. It is a land of diverse faiths and holy to many. Adam's Peak in eastern Sri Lanka is perhaps the earth's loveliest landfall and the world's most sacred mountain because of the famous foot-print on it that many faiths revere. Muslim belief has it that Adam landed there on his fall from the Paradise. The Chinese connect the mountain with the father of the human race. To the Hindus the country's uplands are linked with the mythology of Vishnu's incarnation. Christian missionaries ascribe the mysterious foot-print to St Thomas, the Apostle. The Buddha is believed to have come to the island many times and left traces of his foot-steps.

Aside from its plethora of faiths, Sri Lanka is also a country of racial diversity revealed in the frequency of eyes coloured from brown to blue, crinkly and smooth hair, flat and hooked noses. Proof enough that no racial stock has escaped mixture with several others.

The tranquillity and apparent racial amity was destroyed in 1983. Anyone arriving in Colombo after the July 1983 anti-Tamil pogrom, would have found it a shattered city in a fractured island. The explosion occasioned little surprise, however, for Sri Lanka, divided over language, race and religion, was close to combustion point in mid-1983. All it needed was a spark, which was provided by the abduction and rape of three Tamil girls and the killing of two secessionist guerrillas of the Liberation Tigers of Tamil Eelam in Jaffna peninsula by Sri Lankan soldiers. In retaliation, the Tamil guerrillas drew a Sri Lankan army patrol out of its fortified camp in Palaly around midnight of 23 July. A false tip-off over the telephone did the trick, though the soldiers had been advised not to venture out at night. The patrol was ambushed and thirteen soldiers were killed.

News of the ambush reached Colombo the next day and set off an anti-Tamil pogrom, the worst in the island's history, in the Sinhala-majority areas.

*

The complexities of the island's ethnic conflict go deep into history.

Buddhist legends and mythology have it that the Sinhala race was founded by Vijaya, grandson of the union between a petty north Indian king and a lioness. Banished by his father for misconduct, Vijaya is believed to have arrived in the island in 500 BC with a band of 700 fair-skinned Aryans. The Sinhalas say the name of the race is derived from the legend of the lioness. (*Sinha* in Sanskrit means lion.)

Mythology also emphasizes the fact that Vijaya's arrival coincided with Gautama Buddha's *nirvana* (the final release from the cycle of reincarnation—attained by the extinction of all desires—and individual existence culminating in absolute blessedness). It is claimed that the Buddha had visited the island thrice and this legend is the basis of the Sinhala claim that, as Aryans from north India, they have inherited a much older culture and civilization than the Tamils who are descendants of Dravidian settlers from peninsular (south) India.

But the Tamils claim they inhabited the island before Vijaya's arrival and that Buddhism came to the island long after the Sinhala king and not with him. A Tamil kingdom was centred in Anuradhapura until the defeat of Eelala or Elara in 101 BC by a Sinhala prince Dutthagamani. Eelam, the name of the homeland the Tamils claim, derives from Elara, the last Tamil king of Anuradhapura which became the seat of a Sinhala dynasty after 101 BC.

In the absence of continuous recorded history, little is known of the Tamils after Elara's defeat. Pali chronicles speak only of the struggles between Sinhala kings and Tamil invaders. But a Tamil kingdom emerged around AD 1215 in Jaffna in the north. Sinhalas say the kingdom was a peripheral one, a result of the national dissension and chaos at the time. To the Tamils however, the period when their northern kingdom flourished was a golden age until western colonialism ended it.

The Portuguese were the first to come from the West, in 1505. The Portuguese found three sovereign kingdoms, one of the Sinhalas based in Kotte near present-day Colombo which ruled the south and the west, another in present-day Kandy ruling the central highlands, and a Tamil kingdom based in Jaffna ruling the Tamil-speaking areas of the north and the east.

The Sinhala and Tamil areas had distinctive social formations, languages and cultures and to all intents and purposes were distinctive nations.

The Portuguese entered into treaties and fought battles. They brought the Kotte kingdom, and later the Jaffna kingdom, under them but ruled them as separate entities. The Kandyan kingdom defied the Portuguese (1505–1658) and the Dutch who followed them (1658–1796). The British who expelled the Dutch in 1796 could annex Kandy only in 1815 though the rest of the island had been a Crown Colony since 1802 when the Tamils had ceased to be ruled as a separate entity.

For the first time the British brought the island under a unified structure and a centralized administration. The history of modern Ceylon begins at this point.

The British ushered in a plantation economy which transformed the island's subsistence agriculture. The plantations dispossessed Kandyan farmers of their land. But, as the farmers refused to work as wage labour in the plantations, the British turned to low-caste, debt-ridden and impoverished labour from the drought-prone Tamil districts of India to provide the sinews of the new economy. The indentured labour from across the channel were little more than serfs, initially in the coffee plantations where the operations were seasonal, and when coffee failed due to plant disease and tea became king, in tea estates which needed labour round the year.

Soon the immigrant Tamil plantation labour outnumbered the indigenous Tamils (who, like the Kandyan farmers, would not work in the tea gardens though segments of the Sinhala and Tamil populations had reluctantly begun participating in the plantation economy).

The island's economy changed remarkably with the plantations. The modern (or export) sector grew larger in relation to the traditional sector and thereby ended the island's self-sufficient economy. Alongside emerged a new class of English-educated professionals and white-collar workers who owed their education mainly to the Christian missionary activity that followed the British.

Soon the British began the time-honoured colonial game of playing one section off against the other to ensure their hegemony. The emergence of new professions and new elites made this possible. The British rulers encouraged the Tamils who belonged to the arid, infertile and underdeveloped tracts of the north and the east, to look to the English systems of education and professions for economic advancement, all the while looking to their own interests of course.

Numerically, the indigenous Tamils were unequal to the Sinhalas. But the recognition of Tamil claims to a share of the professions was a major concession to the Tamils and therefore a counterpoise against the Sinhala majority. Thus the ethnic Tamils, at least the section which had acquired a stake in the system, were won over by the British who all the same had little interest in granting a responsible government to the people of Ceylon. They believed in ensuring their paramountcy through cheap concessions now and then to the educated sections and the intelligentsia.

Representation on the basis of religion and ethnicity was also introduced on the plea it would help democratic institutions in a country with racial and religious differences. In the 1920s, separate and distinctive political demands by various political groups, each designed to safeguard and promote sectarian interests, all under the plea of 'national interest', became the trend.

After universal adult franchise was introduced in 1931, the legislative council was so constituted (in 1933) that its non-official (that is, elected membership) had distinct categories—Burghers (the descendants of Europeans), Sinhalas, Tamils, and Europeans. This began the trend of leaders of social groups assuming distinct postures in politics. When the legislative council was restructured later, the British split the Sinhalas into Kandyans (who thought they were superior) and low-country Sinhalas. The Muslims (who were divided into those of Indian origin and those who spoke Tamil, and those who fell into neither of the first two categories) were to get representation in the council later, separating Tamil-speaking Muslims from other Tamils. Thus the people of Ceylon were divided along ethnic lines and again along lines of religion—for example, as Tamils and Muslims, and as Burghers and Europeans. All this reinforced ethnic and religious divisions and inhibited the growth of political parties cutting across them.

From unfettered Crown rule under a Governor, the island evolved through a limited franchise representative government with limited powers, to a semi-responsible government under an adult franchise system (with both elected and nominated numbers in the legislative council), to responsibility and independence in 1948.

But Ceylon's attaining of independence had none of the excitement of a struggle, violent or non-violent. It lacked drama. In fact it was a by-product of India's freedom struggle (which began with the formation of the Indian National Congress in 1885), and the British decision to quit the South Asian sub-continent after the Second World War.

As the Japanese overran Burma, the British fled the place in 1941. Then they abandoned Malaya, Sarawak and Brunei in 1942, but held on to undivided India and the islands of Ceylon and the Maldives. They ran their South-East Asia Command (SEAC) from Kandy in Ceylon under Lord Louis Mountbatten of Burma. Trincomalee was his main naval base. (David Lean's film, *The Bridge on the River Kwai*, on British prisoners of war on the Thai-Burma border, was shot in the Trincomalee area.) The British returned to Burma and their south-east Asian colonies in 1946, but by then it was evident that most of the colonies in Asia would have to be granted their independence soon.

India and Pakistan obtained their independence in 1947 through an Act of British Parliament. Burma got it through a specially negotiated treaty in 1948.

The freedom movement in Ceylon began as late as 1915 (when the Ceylon National Congress comprising both Sinhalas and Tamils was formed). The British had begun preparing the Crown Colony for freedom, longer than any other former colony. In 1944, they sent the Lord Soulbury commission to replace the 1931 constitution (which introduced universal adult franchise, recommended by the Donoughmore commission). Lord Soulbury (who was to be rewarded with a Governor-Generalship) drafted his constitution on the basis of the following guiding principles: Ceylon was a multi-racial democracy and its commitment should be to the liberal concept of a secular state where the line between state power and religion should be clearly drawn, and the legislature should be barred from laws that discriminated against minorities. The Soulbury constitution survived the uneventful transfer of power until it was replaced by the republican constitution in 1972. Ceylon also became Sri Lanka the same year. It is usual, when a country achieves independence for it to mark the transition by giving itself a constitution even if one existed already. India gave itself an autochthonous constitution in 1950, a couple of years after it became free. But Sri Lanka waited over two decades after independence to work out its own constitution and much of the post-independence conflict in the country can be attributed to this. Said differently, the Soulbury constitution was just not enough. It was close to the Westminster model (based on the unitary system*) that obtains in the United Kingdom. But the constitution was ineffective in safeguarding the pluralistic nature of the island. It did not have a Bill of Rights and lacked effective checks against discrimination towards minorities.

Lord Soulbury was to ruminate in 1963, in the light of later happenings: 'I now think it is a pity that the Soulbury commission did not recommend the entrenchment in the constitution of guarantees of fundamental rights on the lines enacted in the constitutions of India, Pakistan, Malaya, Nigeria and elsewhere.

Don Stephen Senanayake, a Cambridge-educated politician, formed the right-of-centre United National Party (UNP) in 1946. Such a party was needed to work the cabinet system envisaged by the Soulbury reforms. His party won the 1947 elections, and found itself ruling Ceylon, when the British left in 1948 (without negotiating an accord

---

* A unitary system means the state is a single unit, unlike a federal set-up in which several states, while independent on internal affairs, unite for general or national purposes.

between the Sinhala majority and the Tamil minority or without even creating the constitutional mechanism to promote co-operation and compromise between the two races).

. The first major conflict that arose in the newly independent nation was over the residents of Indian origin. The Soulbury constitution did not define citizenship of Ceylon. When the British left, the island had Sinhala, Ceylon Tamil, Burgher, Ceylon Moor (Muslims), Tamil-speaking Muslim and Tamil inhabitants, besides others of Indian origin.

Among the early enactments of the multi-ethnic, but Sinhala-dominated, UNP government was an act to deprive most residents of Indian origin of their right to citizenship (by rendering them 'stateless') and franchise.

The Ceylon Citizenship Act of 1948, together with the Indian and Pakistani Residents (Citizenship) Act of 1949, provided that citizenship would be determined either by descent or by stringent conditions of registration. There was no provision for citizenship by birth or by virtue of the country's membership of the British Commonwealth.

Citizenship by descent was contingent on proof of three generations of paternal ancestry in the island. The registration of births began in Ceylon only in 1985. Therefore it was impossible for an applicant to prove the birth of the paternal grandfather and of the paternal great-grandfather. Most plantation workers did not have their or their parents certificates of birth. Although the laws applied to all those who lived in the island, only the Tamils of Indian origin were called upon to establish their claims to citizenship. Most of the 237,034 applications (that is ninety per cent of them), requesting citizenship from 825,000 persons of Indian origin, were rejected because they were not backed by evidence of date of birth or because they failed to establish that the applicants were residents for the requisite period or did not prove that they had an assured income of a reasonable amount. Many of the applications were rejected on flimsy grounds such as the illegibility of the signature of the Justice of Peace attesting them.

Citizenship by descent was conferred automatically on the ethnic Ceylonese while in contrast only an infinitesimal proportion of the Indians (who constituted twelve per cent of the island's population) could qualify for it. While an unemployed Ceylonese could get his citizenship without questions, even an Indian who met all the conditions had to prove his income or possess property.

Compounding their sins, the Senanayake government disenfranchised the 'stateless' immigrants. An amendment to the electoral law in late 1949 restricted voting rights to citizens. The plantation labour had voted at every election. (100,000 of them had been registered when adult franchise was introduced in 1931 and the number rose to 145,000 in 1936. A 1946 order had provided that every British subject resident in the island for six months or who was otherwise qualified could vote and hold office.) But now non-citizens could not vote.

The plantation workers, the most organized and cohesive section of the island's working class, were sought to be isolated from the political mainstream for two reasons. If they got citizenship rights, they would also get the right to vote and might return Indians to Parliament from the plantation districts. The immigrants were a decisive minority in some other districts. So the Sinhalas would be 'swamped'. Also conjured up was the bogey of Indian 'expansionism' with the immigrant Tamils as its 'fifth column'.

The two measures were overtly racist. The Indians were the immediate target but there was a danger of similar discrimination against other minorities who had been accepted as Ceylonese. The statements made by elected officials at this time did nothing to allay the fears of the minorities. A. Ratanayake, Minister for Food in the then government, and a Kandyan Sinhalese, even alleged that S. Thondaman, leader of the Ceylon Workers Congress*, which represented the plantation Tamils, had a vision of Ceylon 'federated with India, dominated by India, overwhelmed by India', and they had to rationalize the composition of the country's nationals because the 'freedom we have won is already in danger'.

In contrast to the typical Sinhala view, the leftist parties (though led by Sinhalas) saw the racism implicit in the assault on the rights of plantation Tamils. 'I thought racialism of this type ended with Adolf Hitler', said Dr N.M. Perera of the Lanka Sama Samaj Party. Dr Colvin R. de Silva, also of the same Trotskyite party, predicted that 'the moment the government starts applying an anti-racial principle against a particular group' it would lead to discrimination against other minorities 'who are today accepted as Ceylonese'.

The attack on immigrant Tamils was over citizenship and voting rights. The Ceylon Tamils, though unaffected by the overt discrimination against the immigrant community, feared that it would extend to them in some other form. S.J.V. Chelvanayakam, leader of the Tamil Congress (founded in 1944 to represent the ethnic Tamils) said: 'Today justice is being denied to Indian Tamils. Some day in the future, when language becomes the issue, the same would befall the Ceylon Tamils'. His words were prophetic.

Other issues had still to be settled. For a start the newly free country had not come to grips with the language issue yet. English was still the official language though the minority spoke Sinhala. But the assault on the language rights of the Tamil minority was to begin soon.

Some politicians were quick to see the opportunities in the ferment.

* The same as the Ceylon Indian Congress

S.W.R.D. Bandaranaike, the Oxford-educated son of an Anglican Christian knighted by the sovereign, became a Buddhist out of political expediency. He quit the UNP, still led by the Anglicized elite, to form the Sri Lanka Freedom Party (SLFP) in 1951. The new party directed its appeal to the emerging sections aspiring for a share of political power—the rural elite (landlords and rich farmers), school teachers, Buddhist monks and practitioners of *ayurveda*. Its ideology was left-of-centre and its orientation Sinhala-Buddhist nationalist. Radical rhetoric and Sinhala chauvinism were invoked by it to win the support of the sections of the polity which had no links with the plantation economy that had produced the Anglicized elite. The British had ruled the island through this elite which was content to shape policies to advance its own economic interests. But independence had roused new expectations and the power of the vote had acquired a new significance.

The SLFP was too new to be able to make language the issue at the 1952 elections. But there was already a snowballing demand for the replacement of English by *swabasha* (own language). This issue got more complicated when Prime Minister John Kotelawala sparked a controversy by promising parity of Sinhala with Tamil when English was phased out.

The English versus *swabasha* demand, which related to the replacement of a foreign language was more or less acceptable across the board. But the parity of Sinhala and Tamil concerned the relative status of two indigenous languages. The *swabasha* demand epitomized the antagonism of educated and semi-educated Sinhalas who felt the dominance of English left them at a disadvantage in education and employment and was a corollary to their antagonism towards the Anglicized elite who ruled the country through its command of English.

In sum, the Tamil-Sinhala parity issue was substantially more sensitive. At its inception, the SLFP had called for the parity of Sinhala and Tamil. By the end of 1955 it was advocating the primacy of Sinhala, as the sole official language in the place of English. But the UNP was for parity. So were the main left parties, the Lanka Sama Samaj Party (LSSP) and the Communist Party of Ceylon.

The issue began hotting up as the four-year term of the Parliament elected in 1952 was ending. The Tamil Congress which had settled for responsible co-operation with the ruling UNP found it necessary to end the alliance because there was growing Tamil anxiety over the language issue. All the Tamil Congress ministers resigned from the government and all the party's members quit Parliament because the UNP conference would not discuss issues concerning the Tamil minority or the language issue in particular.

The Tamil Congress leaders announced a united front to defend the Tamil language and culture and to carry on the struggle for a Tamil state which would offer to federate with the Sinhala state on terms of complete equality if acceptable to both the nations, failing which it would elect to become independent. This was inchoate Tamil secessionism going beyond the federal concept of S.J.V. Chelvanayakam who had broken off with the moderate Tamil Congress to form his Federal Party in 1949.

The 1956 elections were a watershed both in terms of the country's political development as well as a preparation for the ethnic issues that would have a decisive impact in the future. The UNP and Philip Gunawardene's Viplavakari Lanka Samaj Party (Trotskyite in orientation) campaigned for Sinhala as the sole official language. The Mahajana Eksath Peramuna, a coalition of the Sri Lanka Freedom Party and the Viplavakari Lanka Samaj Party, won fifty-one of the ninety-five seats at the elections. The LSSP and the Communist Party of Ceylon together won seventeen seats. The Federal Party won ten seats.

Among the earliest measures of the new government, headed by Bandaranaike, was the 'Sinhala Only' bill in the year of the Buddha Jayanti, the 2500th anniversary of the Buddha's *nirvana*, an event which was sought to be vested, in Ceylon, with triple significance—the founding of the Buddhist faith, the founding of the Sinhala race and the arrival of Buddhism in the island. The year-long Buddha Jayanti celebrations heightened the tension over language.

The Federal Party thought the proposed law was unconstitutional and challenged it in the courts and reiterated its objective of an 'autonomous Tamil linguistic state' in a federal set-up to protect the cultural freedom and identity of the Tamil-speaking people. It called the Tamils to transact all their business in Tamil or if necessary in English and not to learn Sinhala.

In early 1957, Sinhala mob attacks on Tamils grew frequent and serious. The government added to the tension by insisting on the use of the Sinhala character 'Sri' on the number plates of all motor vehicles. The Tamils defied the order and instead used the Tamil letter 'Sri'.

That the polarization of the different groups in the island had reached a new high is perhaps best shown by the way each of them reacted to 4 February 1957: the Sinhalas celebrated as that was the day Sinhala had triumphed over English, but to the Tamils it was a day of mourning because their language had been denied parity with Sinhala.

Though Bandaranaike had announced in April that Tamil would have a reasonable place in official business, the Federal Party decided to launch a civil disobedience movement in August to press for parity. Bandaranaike began negotiations with Chelvanayakam to forestall it. Their agreement in July provided for Tamil as one of the national languages of the country (along with Sinhala) and as the language of administration in the Tamil-majority northern and eastern provinces with a measure of decentralization of power through provincial councils (i.e. council at the provincial level). Bandaranaike also promised to reconsider the disenfranchisement of Indian Tamils achieved through the 1948–49 laws.

It was now the turn of the Sinhalas to act. The UNP, out of office and reduced to eight seats in a Parliament of ninety-five, set the pace for a movement against the concessions to Tamils declaring that the Bandaranaike-Chelvanayakam accord spelt the disruption of Ceylon's unity. There were dissensions in the cabinet. Several Buddhist organizations threatened a civil disobedience movement if the agreement was not scrapped by 1 October.

The threatened Buddhist agitation did not materialize but the UNP leader J.R. Jayewardene led a Buddhist march to Kandy to invoke the blessings of the gods for his campaign against the agreement. The march was intercepted by the government.

The pact continued to remain alive. The Prime Minister commended it to his party's annual conference as an 'honourable' solution. But the promised legislation to implement the various measures contained in the accord had not yet occurred and there was an agitation in the Tamil areas, led by the Federal Party, over the delay. Sinhala mobs in Colombo and outside, led by the UNP, reacted to the demonstrations by defacing the letterings and signs on Tamil shops and attacking them.

Bandaranaike felt obliged to assure Parliament that he would not allow the Tamil agitation and the counter-agitation by the Sinhalas, despite the embarrassment it caused, to stand in the way of justice to the minorities. But he was to be cowed down within twenty-four hours of his brave statement.

All it needed to unnerve the Prime Minister was a procession of Buddhist monks by one of his ministers, Wimala Wijawardane, a widow, to his residence. The monks squatted in front of the house and refused to leave until the pact was abrogated in writing. Bandaranaike met their demand after hurried consultations with his ministers. That night he went on the air criticizing the 'illegal' act of the Federal Party in defacing the Sinhala lettering on state-owned buses. (Chelvanayakam had been jailed a week earlier because he had violated the motor vehicles law by symbolically using the Tamil letter for 'Sri' on the number plate of his car.) The Prime Minister in his address cited the Federal Party's agitation as the reason he was repudiating his agreement with its leader, Chelvanayakam.

The Tamils had no one to speak for them except the Federal Party which had no option but to continue with its extra-constitutional but peaceful agitation. The Sinhala reaction to it turned extremely violent. This, in turn, set off riots by Tamils in the northern and eastern provinces in response to Sinhala atrocities in Colombo and elsewhere. The ghastly climax to the disturbances came at Panadura near

Colombo, where the official priest of a Tamil Hindu temple was doused with petrol and burnt.

Finally, the government clamped an Emergency on the country in May 1958 at India's instance. Over 10,000 Tamils were shipped from Colombo to the safety of Jaffna up north. Another 12,000 lived huddled in camps.

When Parliament met for an Emergency session in June, the Prime Minister blamed the violence on the Tamil leadership. He saw in the agitation a movement against the government and the state.

'Two torn little bleeding nations may yet arise out of one little state,' Dr Colvin R. de Silva, academic, theoretician and legal luminary of the LSSP, had warned Parliament in 1956 when the 'Sinhala Only' bill was debated. Leslie Goonawardene, his party colleague, was more precise in his prophecy. He said the Tamils might secede if grave injustice was done to them.

And the injustice being done to the Tamils was not minor. Initially the Tamils of Indian origin had been deprived of their rights to citizenship and disenfranchised. Now the Tamils, ethnic and immigrant, were being stripped of their language rights. When the British departed, the Tamils had left too much to trust. Chelvanayakam was to rue later (in 1975) that the Tamils had made a mistake in not demanding independence for themselves when the island got freedom in 1948.

Parity for Sinhala and Tamil might have held the nation together and the Bandaranaike-Chelvanayakam pact might yet have saved the island from a disaster. Jayewardene, who had opposed Tamil in 1956, was to realize thirty-one years later that the decision on an official language was a major mistake. A mistake that would lead to secession.

2

The Tamil Quest for Nationhood

The Tamil demand for secession crystallized in 1976 when their leaders called a convention at Vadukkodai and set themselves the goal of a sovereign Tamil Eelam. Tamil classics refer to the whole of Sri Lanka as Eelam. But the newly formed Tamil United Liberation Front (TULF) was asking for a sovereign state comprising the Tamil homeland in Sri Lanka—hence Tamil Eelam.

The demand was in response to the Sinhala-Buddhist drive for hegemony which culminated in the 1972 constitution marking pluralistic Ceylon's transition to an ethnocentric Sri Lanka. The republican constitution entrenched Sinhala as the sole official language and Buddhism as the only religion meriting state support. And it was based on the unitary principle, forestalling federal accommodation of Tamil demands.

Tamil politics has gone through four distinct phases since Ceylon's independence. The first, until 1956, was one of responsive co-operation. The Tamil Congress had participated in the government since 1947 (before independence). The citizenship and disenfranchisement laws of 1948–49, which made an overwhelming proportion of the Tamils of Indian origin stateless and deprived them of their voting rights, split the Tamil Congress, the breakaway section forming the Federal Party.

The second phase, of Tamil non-violent non-cooperation, alternating with participation in the government in the hope of securing their demands, began in 1956 after the Sri Lanka Freedom Party (SLFP) won the elections riding a wave of Sinhala-Buddhist nationalism. At this time, the Federal Party, through a pact between its leader S.J.V. Chelvanayakam and Prime Minister S.W.R.D. Bandaranaike in 1957, tried to win some of its demands. But Bandaranaike reneged on it in 1958 under Sinhala pressure.

The anti-Tamil riots, in response to the opposition to Sinhala as the sole official language, polarized the country into Sinhala and Tamil groups. The Federal Party launched a peaceful agitation over the language issue in the Tamil-majority northern and eastern provinces. It was a mass civil disobedience movement that abjured violence in word and deed but openly defied authority by court imprisonment. The Federal Party even launched its own postal service in 1961 and was rumoured to be planning its own police force and a take-over of Crown lands for distribution to the poor when the government proclaimed an Emergency and troops moved into Jaffna to crack down on the non-violent agitators.

After a lull (during the two-year Emergency), the Federal Party announced plans for a new movement if the imposition of Sinhala was not ended. But the movement, planned to begin on 10 October 1963, did not take off.

Ceylon had elections in March 1965 after Sirimavo Bandaranaike, Prime Minister since 1960, following her husband, S.W.R.D. Bandaranaike's assassination a year earlier, completed her term. The alliance of her SLFP and its coalition partner the Lanka Sama Samaj Party (LSSP) was trounced but it was a hung parliament, neither the United National Party (UNP) with sixty-six seats nor the outgoing alliance with fifty-one commanding a house majority (that is seventy-six). The Federal Party with fourteen held the balance and announced its support to the UNP which formed a government.

A pact, then unpublicized, between the Federal Party leader, S.J.V. Chelvanayakam, and Prime Minister Dudley Senanayake provided the following:

- Tamil would be made the language of administration and of record in the northern and eastern provinces
- Court proceedings in these provinces would be conducted and recorded in Tamil
- Administration throughout the entire country would be decentralized through district councils
- There would be a reasonable restriction on the colonization of the Tamil provinces by the Sinhalas

The Chelvanayakam-Senanayake pact did not end the conflict.

When the government moved bills in Parliament in early 1966 to implement concessions to the Tamils over the official language issue, there was bloodshed. Outside Parliament, 3,000 demonstrators, led by Buddhist monks, agitated against the proposed reforms and in the ensuing police firing one demonstrator was killed. Another State of Emergency was declared, the third since 1958. The Tamils had won limited concessions in the 1965 pact but the promises were not fully honoured. In no small measure, the government's timidity was because of the pressure tactics of the Sinhala-led youth who, led by the ultra-left JVP, even attempted an abortive insurrection in 1971. Came the next elections in 1970, and Sirimavo Bandaranaike was back in power, this time in alliance with the LSSP (which is Trotskyite) and the Communist Party of Ceylon, to usher in an era of populist left-of-centre politics that roused the expectations of the people.* For the first time, Ceylon had a government that could command a two-thirds majority in Parliament and think of giving the country a new constitution. Besides, all the parties supported the SLFP's proposal for a constituent assembly. Of the Tamil groups, the Federal Party and the smaller Tamil Congress even participated in steering and subjects committees of the assembly. But the government's constitution-making efforts ran into difficulty over crucial issues affecting the Tamils.

The Tamil parties demanded that Tamil should have constitutional recognition as an official language, which meant parity with Sinhala. They were opposed to the demand already voiced for Buddhism as the sole state religion. In addition they demanded a ban on caste discrimination and an end to the distinction between Ceylon Tamils and plantation Tamils of Indian origin.

But the constitution that eventually found passage did not represent a consensus. The plantation Tamils of Indian origin were not represented in the constituent assembly. The Federal Party, the main representative of the Ceylon Tamils, dissociated itself from the whole process after initial participation and the UNP voted against it. However, the SLFP and its allies took the massive majority they held in Parliament as proof enough that they were   trusted by the people to make their laws (and constitution) for them.

The 1972 constitution made Ceylon (or Sri Lanka as it now was) a republic, perhaps the only aspect of the document that was the declared intention of all the parties. But it also entrenched the unitary state structure ignoring the Federal Party's demand for Tamil autonomy through a federal set-up. It gave constitutional status to Sinhala as the sole official language, as enacted in 1956. Though the Tamil Language (Special Provisions) Act of 1958 (further refined in 1966) qualified the 1956 enactment to permit the limited use of Tamil in the northern and eastern provinces, the new constitution institutionalized the disadvantageous position of the Tamils in the rest of the country. All laws were to be made or enacted in Sinhala (with Tamil translations), and Sinhala was to be the language of the courts and tribunals throughout the island.

The constitution stopped short of proclaiming Buddhism the state religion or declaring Sri Lanka a theocratic state. But it conferred special status on Buddhism and made it the state's duty to 'protect and foster' this religion while other faiths had to be content with rights guaranteed to all.

Such a distinction favouring Buddhism would have been impossible under the constitution the British had bequeathed to the island; the

* The three parties—the SLFP, the LSSP, and the Communist Party—formed the United Front.

'British constitution' had safeguarded the rights of the minorities by barring discrimination and indeed this had been the only bulwark the minorities had had against any onslaught on their rights. The Tamil leadership had agreed to the transfer of power arrangements by the British because of this built-in safeguard in the form of Section 29 (which the Privy Council had held to be 'entrenched, unalterable and immutable') but now this safeguard went overboard. The 1972 constitution in sum was nothing short of a blatant expression of the Sinhala-Buddhist nationalism that had dominated the island's politics since the 1950s.

It is a given that pluralism does not permit the dominance of any group over the rest. But where accommodation was called for the Sinhalas opted for the perceptions of the majority, that is themselves, in terms of language and religion.

Unsurprisingly this intransigence on the part of the Sinhalas gave rise to the third phase in Tamil politics. It was obvious to the Tamils that, with the new constitution setting the seal on their marginalization by the Sinhalas, the era of cosy power adjustments and gentlemanly agreements—the Chelvanayakam-Bandaranaike pact (1957) and the Chelvanayakam-Senanayake pact (1965)—was over. Now it was a self-sealing system. Even if the Federal Party won every seat in Parliament from the two Tamil provinces, it would be nowhere near political power which could alternate only between the two mainstream Sinhala parties or alliances dominated by them. 'The consolidation of political forces of the Sinhala nation for confrontation rather than co-existence with the Tamil nation forced the Tamil-speaking masses to the inevitable position of deciding their own political destiny', says a latter-day document of the Liberation Tigers of Tamil Eelam.

If there had been some concessions by the Sinhalas that could in turn have given a certain legitimacy to the old Tamil leadership, which still had illusions of a negotiated solution to the problem through non-violent forms of protest, there might still have been some hope of staving off the crisis that obtains in Sri Lanka today. But the Sinhalas were obdurate and a new youthful generation of Tamils saw little use in the methods of the old guard. The rebellious, militant and impatient Tamil youth, who traced their economic and other kinds of deprivation to ethnic discrimination was to make a decisive impact on the situation, disfiguring the once placid face of Sri Lanka forever.

*

The Tamil-dominated northern and eastern provinces in Sri Lanka have always been poor in resources, affording little scope for economic development. The Tamils of the densely populated Jaffna peninsula have therefore looked to education as *the* means of economic advancement. Entry into the professions was a means of social mobility and the British encouraged them because of their policy of playing them off against the Sinhala majority. Christian missionary activity faced little opposition from the Hindu priests and missionary schools brought education to the Tamil areas. In contrast the Buddhist priests, who were traditional educators and communicators in pre-colonial days, were against Christian educational activity in the Sinhala areas.

To the diligent Jaffna Tamil, upward mobility also meant outward mobility. Jaffna exported manpower for white-collar jobs and the professions in the rest of the island and beyond to other British colonies. When independence came the Jaffna peninsula had an educational infrastructure the rest of the island, with exception of the Colombo region, lacked. And the promoting of free education, in the wake of independence, helped a phenomenal expansion of primary and secondary school enrolment among the Tamils. However, the expansion in all-round education, and the nascent presence of discrimination in favour of the Sinhalas, added to the pressures of competition at the higher level. The Tamils needed to look to higher and more specialized professional education (engineering, medicine and science) to stay ahead in the competition, all the more so because the white-collar job market was shrinking for them. With Sinhala as the sole official language since 1956, those who did not know it were at a disadvantage. Despite an expansion of the administrative services, the Tamils suffered because the lower and middle rung administrative jobs in the Sinhala areas were lost to them. A similar expansion of services in the Tamil areas did not help much because the proportion of Tamil school-leavers were more than could be absorbed there. So the Tamils tried to meet the new situation by turning out a disproportionately large number of science graduates aspiring to enter the specialized professions. This attempt to solve the problem only brought new problems in its stead. For instance, unemployed science graduates settled for teaching in schools, and swelled the stream of Tamil school-leavers majoring in science.

Despite all this, those who studied in the Tamil language formed the major proportion of those admitted to coveted disciplines. The Sinhalas, taught through their mother-tongue, began feeling they were denied equity and criticized the advantage the Tamils enjoyed because of the higher marks they scored in qualifying examinations with the collusion of Tamil examiners. This imbalance was sought to be corrected through a new system of selection called 'standardization' introduced in 1971. It weighted the marks of the Tamil applicants downwards which meant they had to score more marks than the Sinhalas to compete with them for access to higher education. The Tamils quite naturally thought this was blatant discrimination.

In 1969, the Tamils secured 50 per cent of the admissions to the medical faculty and 48.3 per cent to engineering. After the 1971 standardizaiion formula, their share dropped to twenty-eight per cent and nineteen per cent respectively in 1977. The formula was scrapped in 1978 but was reintroduced in a modified form to placate Sinhala opinion and the discrimination against the Tamils continued.

The disadvantage in the matter of access to higher education extended to employment opportunities. The Tamils had dominated the civil service and the professions in the past but their share began declining. In 1980, Sinhalas who were about seventy per cent of the population held eighty-five per cent of all the jobs in the state sector, eighty-two per cent in the professional and technical categories, and eighty-three per cent in the administrative and managerial services. The Tamils (Sri Lankan and those of Indian origin who together constituted eighteen per cent of the population) had only eleven per cent of the public sector jobs, thirteen per cent of the professional and technical posts, and fourteen per cent of the administrative and managerial positions. The Tamils constituted five per cent of the civil service in 1970. In 1977 no Tamil gained entry to it.

Though the Tamils have a low unemployment rate (10.9 per cent against 13.9 per cent for Kandyan Sinhalas and 18.5 per cent for low country Sinhalas), the high incidence of unemployment among educated Tamils is significant. In 1983, the unemployment rate among young Tamil males who had passed the A level examination was forty-one per cent while among the Sinhalas it was twenty-nine per cent. As the Liberation Tigers of Tamil Eelam said in 1984: Angered by the imposition of an alien language; frustrated without the possibility of higher education, plunged into the despair of unemployed existence, the Tamil youth grew militant with an iron determination to fight back the national oppression.'

The conservative Tamil political leadership, dominated by the Colombo-based Jaffna elite could not articulate the aspirations of the restive youth. The Federal Party, the Tamil Congress, and the Ceylon Workers Congress, representing the plantation Tamils of Indian origin, had formed the Tamil United Front in 1972 but, according to the LTTE, the party was founded on 'bourgeois ideology'. It was evident that there had to be some more dynamic and forceful group to appeal to the youth and this is where the LTTE scored. The youth had no use for the parliamentary system which had brought them no gains whatsoever (but which the old leadership still hugged). Velupillai Prabhakaran, then 18, formed the Tamil New Tigers in 1972. The organization became the Liberation Tigers of Tamil Eelam four years later. The tiger emblem has deep roots in Tamil political history, and symbolizes patriotic resurgence. It also symbolizes the group's mode of struggle—guerrilla warfare.

All too soon it was clear that, so far as the Tamils were concerned, secession was the only answer to their problems. Although a Tamil leader, C. Suntheralingam, had been campaigning for it since 1956, it had evoked little response until 1975.

Chelvanayakam had quit his Kankesanthurai seat in Parliament to protest against the 1972 constitution. The government stalled elections to the seat for three years but when elections were finally held Chelvanayakam won back his seat by a bigger margin. The first demand for secession came from the audiences during his campaign.

The advent of the LTTE, pressures from the militant youth and the growing call for secessionism by the Tamils in general galvanized the Tamil United Front to call a convention at Vadukkodai in 1976. The Tamil United Liberation Front (as it called itself now) denounced the 1972 constitution saying it had reduced the Tamils to a 'slave nation' by the Sinhalas. It called for the 'restoration and reconstitution of the free, sovereign, secular, socialist state of Tamil Eelam based on the right to self-determination inherent to every nation'.

The fourth phase of Tamil politics was marked by the Vadukkodai resolution, which gave specific expression to the Tamil leadership's strategy. The Tamil demand had grown from one for equal rights for Tamils to federalism because the Tamil leadership saw the advantages of concentrating their strategies on the northern and eastern provinces. Now the demand had evolved into one for secession which simply meant that the Tamil question was being narrowed down spatially to what the Tamils regarded as their traditional homeland. The Tamils outside the homeland were welcome to Tamil Eelam and those who chose to live outside (in the plantations or outside them which covered the Tamils of Indian origin as well as smaller groups of ethnic Tamils) were to be a residual problem.

*

The Tamils resent description of their demand for a sovereign state as secessionist. They insist that they were a nation in the past and that the kingdom of Jaffna was an independent state until the Portuguese conquered it in 1619. In other words they say they are only demanding the 'restoration and reconstitution' of their homeland.

The Tamil Eelam demand assumes that Sri Lanka is an island with two nations within one geographic entity and state. It also assumes that the Tamils are not a minority but part of an integral whole. The Tamils, proud of their distinctive culture and language, also say that they cannot be classified as a cultural sub-group living outside the country of their origin. In this they are different from the Tamils— both of Indian as well as of Sri Lankan origin—in Malaysia, for example, who are a minority immigrant group. Again, unlike the Tamils in Malaysia, who are spatially dispersed, Sri Lanka's Tamils inhabit a contiguous area (the northern and eastern provinces) and therefore have a territorial enclave which is the most crucial element in a national identity. Outside India, Tamils have no such enclave except in Sri Lanka.

Most quoted in the context of the Tamil demand for a separate state (in terms of the discrete area they inhabit) is the report of Sir Hugh Cleghorn, a British administrator to the Colonial Office in 1799: 'Two different nations, from the very ancient period, have divided the island, first the Sinhalese, with the southern and western parts from the river Wallouve to that of Chilaow; and secondly, the Malabars, in the northern and eastern districts which extended from the west coast of the island, from Puttalam to Mannar in the east, southwards upto the limits of Kumana, or the river Kukbukkan Oya, that separated Batticaloa from the southern Sinhala district of Matara'. (The Malabars referred to are the Tamils and the northern and eastern districts referred to are the present-day northern and eastern provinces and parts of the present-day north-central and Uva provinces.) Aside from the compulsions of geography the Tamil national identity, as we've noted earlier, is unique unto itself in terms of language and culture. The Tamils speak a common language and have common cultural traits though they profess different faiths. The majority of the Sri Lankan Tamils are Hindu though there are Tamil-speaking Muslims and Christians. And all of them have certain cultural traits that cut across religion.

The TULF fought the 1977 elections with a manifesto that sought a Tamil Eelam state. It was to comprise all the contiguous areas that the Tamils regarded as their traditional homeland. The party's manifesto pledged that those elected on the Front's nomination, while being members of Sri Lanka's Parliament, would also constitute themselves into a 'national assembly' of Eelam to draft a constitution for the new state to be achieved 'by peaceful means or by direct action or struggle'.

Though the boundaries of Tamil Eelam were not defined either in the Vadukkodai resolution or the election manifesto, a clue to it was available from the Front's decision to contest every one of the fourteen electorates in the northern province and eight of the ten in the adjoining eastern province. (It ran a lone candidate outside the two provinces, at Puttalam, where only seven per cent of the people speak Tamil.)

The TULF won all the fourteen contests in the northern provinces polling 71.81 per cent of the vote in Jaffna district, 71.44 in Mannar district, 58.82 per cent in Vavuniya district and 52.16 per cent in Mullaitivu.

The performance was less impressive in the eastern province where it could win only four of the ten contests, the United National Party (UNP) winning the rest. In this province, the Tamil showing was best in Batticaloa where it got 32.14 per cent of the vote. For the rest, it obtained 27.18 per cent in Trincomalee and 20.25 per cent in Amparai which is a Sinhala-majority district.

While the Front claimed it had got a mandate for Eelam, an official Sri Lankan assessment stated that only forty-eight per cent of the voters in the northern and eastern provinces favoured the TULF, and by extension its demands. (The two provinces together returned a population of 2.09 million in the 1981 census.)

There was no way of gauging the mind of the Tamils outside the two provinces—0.51 million Sri Lankan Tamils, 0.69 million Tamil-speaking Muslims, and 0.74 million Tamils of Indian origin.

The 1977 elections were significant for yet another reason. The UNP, routed in 1970, had been voted back into power with 139 of the 168 seats—a five-sixths majority—and a regional ethnic party (the TULF) with eighteen seats emerged the main opposition. And, most tellingly, the Sri Lanka Freedom Party (SLFP) which had won over two-thirds of the seats in 1970 was now a distant third runner with eight seats.

Yet the second largest group in Parliament was not the real alternative to the ruling party. Since 1970, Sri Lanka had been going through a political polarization at two levels. At the centre this had occurred between the SLFP and the UNP, the irony being that the cause for the polarization was the effort each party made to be more pro-Sinhala than the other in its attitude to Tamil demands.

As a result of this, there was polarization at another level—between the Tamil majority provinces and the rest of the country. The pattern for the future was nearly formed.

Until 1970, the governments were by and large coalitional (the UNP depending on the Tamils represented by the Tamil Congress, and later, the Federal Party, and the SLFP looking to the leftist parties). Neither of the core parties was strong enough to be able to do without the smaller parties. But the leverage of the smaller parties ended when the SLFP won over two-thirds of the seats in 1970 and the UNP over five-sixths in 1977.

By 1977 the Sri Lankan political system had thus achieved a high degree of ethnic centralization in favour of the Sinhala-Buddhist majority. Any accommodation of Tamil ethnic interests was seen as at the cost of the majority. As a result the Tamils were politically marginalized, and worse, were shown to be irrelevant to the system. There would be, it appeared, no chance of a return to pluralism and the fine ethnic balance that had kept violence and anarchy in check.

Whatever illusions the TULF leaders entertained were destroyed when the Tamil youth decided to take the fight to the Sinhalas.

Sri Lanka was rocked by violence in the wake of the 1977 elections. Initially directed against the main loser—the SLFP and its allies—by the winner, the UNP, it took an anti-Tamil turn with widespread killings, assault, rape and damage to Hindu temples during August-September 1977. A presidential commission which inquired into the violence attributed the anti-Tamil flare-up to the killing of two policemen by Tamil youth in the northern province, inflammatory speeches by Tamil leaders, and the vote for Eelam at the elections.

But the Tamil contention was that the violence by youth in the north, where tension between the militant youth and the predominantly Sinhala police forces had been building up since 1977, was the result of growing discrimination against the Tamils. The presidential commission's finding that the violence against Tamils was partly in reaction to their secessionist sentiment, had ominous overtones: if the Tamils persisted in their Eelam demand they could expect a violent Sinhala backlash.

By 1981, even the neutrality of the armed forces, which had been severely strained by the ethnic conflict, was fast eroding. The initial flare-up in 1981, unlike in 1977, was not in the Sinhala majority areas, but in the Jaffna peninsula in the northern province. Here the LTTE had killed a candidate of the UNP at the district council elections and also a policeman. Men in khaki (it was difficult to identify their provenance—whether police, paramilitary or military) ran amok in retaliation burning the famous Jaffna Public Library with its collection of 95,000 rare books and manuscripts, relating mainly to Tamil history, the office of the *Eelanadu* Tamil daily, and the residence of a TULF Member of Parliament, V. Yogeswaran, believed to be a sympathizer of the LTTE.

This was the third anti-Tamil riot since 1958. The second and third were different from the first in two respects. They were not directed merely against the ethnic Tamils (12.5 per cent of the population) or limited to the areas inhabited by them. They extended to the Tamils of Indian origin living mostly in the plantation districts and accounting for 5.5 per cent of the population. The reason for the spreading of the violence to cover all segments of the country's Tamil population was that the plantation Tamils, though they did not support the secession demand, had begun making common cause with the ethnic Tamils over other issues. This was disturbing to the Sinhalas because these Tamils were a crucial minority in several Sinhala majority electoral districts.

The 1977 and 1981 riots were different from those in 1958 in another respect, in that they were not limited to Sinhala-Buddhist areas. For the first time Sinhala-Christians joined the attacks on Tamils, which meant the country was seeing a racial polarization across the barriers of religion (a good proportion of the Tamils are Christian). Interestingly enough the first recorded riot, in Colombo in 1883, was directed by the Sinhala-Buddhists against the Sinhala-Christians.

*

The 1981 riots seemed to be planned, not spontaneous, because posters on Colombo walls proclaimed: 'Aliens, you have danced too much; your destruction is at hand. This is the country of us, Sinhalas'.

But it took two years more before the dire prophecy finally became a tragic reality. Meanwhile Tamil guerrilla activity, which had quietened in the wake of the riots, resumed to become dramatic in 1983—an ambush of a military convoy in March and a bomb explosion an hour before a high-level conference on security to be attended by military officers, and significantly the Tamil United Liberation Front (TULF) leaders in April. Alongside, the Liberation Tigers of Tamil Eelam (LTTE) mounted a political campaign for the boycott of the local government elections in May. The election campaign was marked by the assassination of United National Party (UNP) candidates as a warning to 'Tamil traitors' who supported the system. While most UNP candidates from the Tamil areas pulled out of the contest, and many of its Tamil members quit the party, the TULF which defied the call made little impact at the poll which meant it had squandered away its 1977 mandate.

Meanwhile, the government forces pushed their campaign against the guerrillas in the northern province. Alongside there was an orchestrated campaign of terror in the eastern province to drive the Tamils out and tilt the demographic balance in favour of the Sinhalas.

The turning point came on 23 July 1983. A Tamil guerrilla assault unit had mined the Palaly-Jaffna road and was waiting to ambush the 'Four Four Bravo' patrol of the Sri Lankan army. The jeep leading the army convoy blew up. Soldiers jumped out of the trucks that followed it and ran into a hail of machine-gun fire and grenades. The ambush left thirteen soldiers dead.

The anti-Tamil pogrom which began in Colombo the next day was to be a watershed in the ethnic conflict. But the 23 July ambush was certainly not the only cause of the holocaust for there were violent flare-ups long before it. These had occurred even when the Tamil movement was peaceful and there had been no demands for secession. Therefore, despite claims to the contrary, the phenomenon of anti-Tamil racial violence cannot be traced to any single event.

Enough evidence points to the fact that there was a well-drawn-up plan behind the post-ambush riots which began in faraway Colombo and extended to other areas where Tamils were in minority. The violence was vicious and bloody, rampaging mobs singling out specific business premises while Sri Lankan troops and the police were passive spectators. In some cases they even joined the rioters.

Also President J.R. Jayewardene either failed intentionally to crack down on the rioters or found he could not assert his authority over the government forces. He was to admit that the riots showed a serious lack of discipline and a strong anti-Tamil feeling among the armed forces. In two instances, one in Jaffna and the other in Trincomalee the army and the navy had gone about burning houses and attacking Tamils.

The week-long orgy of arson, looting and killing took place only in Colombo and other towns where Tamils were in the minority. In contrast, there was no Tamil reprisal against the Sinhalas in the northern or eastern provinces. The gory climax to the vengeful killing of Tamils came in Walikede prison near Colombo where fifty-two political detenus were massacred in what was to be described by the government as a riot. Island-wide the pogrom destroyed at least 18,000 Tamil homes and 5,000 of their business premises and establishments and drove 150,000 into refugee camps. Three thousand Tamils died. President Jayewardene, when he spoke for a precious four minutes and thirty seconds after the third day, had no word of condemnation for the riots or of sympathy for the Tamil victims. Instead he sought to placate the Sinhala sentiments: 'The time has come to accede to the clamour and the natural respect of the Sinhalese people', he said, thereby indirectly endorsing the carnage and encouraging a more frenzied attack on the Tamils. And the hostility of the state towards the Tamils did not stop there. Jayewardene declared that any organization advocating the division of Sri Lanka would be proscribed and anyone subscribing to such a cause would lose his voting and civil rights, would be barred from holding office or practising a profession, and would not be able to join any movement or organization.

A special session of Parliament in early August 1983 amended the constitution to ban political parties advocating secession. Not only was the TULF, the premier opposition group in Jayewardene's Parliament, banned, but it was stripped of its representation in Parliament because it refused to take the anti-secession oath obligatory in the wake of the ban. Three Tamil newspapers were muzzled. All riot-affected property was brought under state control, adding to the deprivation of the victims of the holocaust.

All this amounted to a *de facto* division of the country along ethnic lines. The *Guardian* wrote on 7 August: 'The President has, at one stroke, disenfranchised the great mass of the Tamil population and turned them into a race of *Untermenschen* or institutionalized second-class semi-citizens'.

With the Tamils as a race denounced as secessionist and untrustworthy, it was natural and logical that they be driven out of their homes and their occupations and business, just as the government's new edict had driven them out of public life and the professions.

At the end of it all, the alienation of the Tamil region from Colombo was near complete. But it appeared that Jayewardene wasn't particularly concerned about regaining popular support for his government in the Tamil areas, especially the northern region where the secessionist guerrillas were strong, through policies and measures. Wiping the terrorists out was the objective. 'You cannot cure an appendix patient until you remove the appendix', he said.

*

Although Jayewardene managed to muzzle the Tamil United Liberation Front (TULF) with the newly enacted laws, it soon became apparent that the true secessionist challenge would be from the Liberation Tigers of Tamil Eelam (LTTE) who wouldn't be put down as easily as the parliamentary party. The Liberation Tigers had taken more than a decade to build up their challenge, but in 1983 there was no question that they would pose a serious threat to Jayewardene's policies. The early campaign of the LTTE was against the state's police-intelligence network in the north comprising Tamil police officers and civil informants. Among their first targets was Alfred Duriappah, Mayor of Jaffna, who was killed in July 1975. Armed campaigns to paralyze the police apparatus was the second stage. In 1978, the LTTE claimed responsibility for annihilating a police party which had attempted a raid on one of its camps, and the earlier liquidation of police informants and 'traitors'. These were their first attempts to tell the world that theirs was a movement for a Tamil homeland through armed struggle.

The state responded with a law in May 1978 to proscribe the LTTE and 'other similar organizations' and to invest security forces with extraordinary powers. A few months later Sri Lanka replaced its 1972 constitution with a new one that gave the Sinhala language and the Buddhist religion special national status. The TULF acquiesced in the provisions of the constitution, but the LTTE dramatized its protest against the assault of Tamil rights by blowing up the lone aircraft Sri Lanka's flag carrier Air Lanka owned. Minutes after the bomb went off in the Avro aircraft (all the passengers had deplaned) at Colombo's Ratmalana airport, the LTTE claimed responsibility for the explosion and made a statement saying that the Tamil nation had been betrayed by the new constitution which was a 'whimsically changeable, whitewashed charter of slavery'.

Tamil guerrilla activity expanded over the year and in mid-July 1979 a new law to check terrorism replaced the earlier one proscribing the LTTE. President Jayewardene set 31 December 1979 as the deadline for eliminating all 'terrorism' in the island, placing 'all the resources of the state' at the disposal of the army. Troops were moved into Jaffna.

There was low intensity skirmishing between the guerrillas and the army and the President's deadline came and went with no cessation in hostilities. Meanwhile, state terror against the Tamils peaked in May 1981 to be followed by another anti-Tamil riot. The flare-up this time was in Jaffna, unlike in 1977 when it was in the Sinhala area.

'The cumulative effect of this multi-dimensional oppression threatened the very existence of the Tamils', a document of the LTTE said in the wake of the 1983 holocaust. 'It aggravated the national conflict and made co-existence between the two nations intolerable. It has shattered all hopes of a peaceful negotiated resolution of the Tamil national question'.

By 1983, the TULF, though deprived of its representation in Parliament was still the only political party of the Tamils, while the guerrilla movement had grown and fragmented into numerous groups.

Foremost among them was the LTTE, structured as an urban guerrilla organization. The group's propaganda machine claimed that its total strategy integrated both the national struggle and class struggle to achieve national liberation and a socialist revolution. Its main influence was in the Jaffna peninsula.

The second largest, but militarily not as significant, guerrilla group was the People's Liberation Organization of Tamil Eelam (PLOTE)[*] set up in 1980 by Uma Maheswaran who was the Secretary-General of the LTTE before he founded his own organization. Though the PLOTE claimed to have several hundred trained guerrillas, it laid a premium on mass political action and disapproved of the 'hit-and-run' tactics of the LTTE.

The Eelam Revolutionary Organization of Students (EROS), a small well-knit group, was founded by E. Ratnasabapathy in London in 1975 and was Marxist-Leninist in orientation. Its initial cadre was the first outside group to be trained by the Palestine Liberation Organization (PLO) led by Yasser Arafat. Unlike the other groups it claimed links with the plantation Tamils (which it refused to call Indian Tamils) and viewed them as part of the island's Tamil people is search of a nation.

The Eelam People's Revolutionary Liberation Front (EPRLF), another Marxist group, was the result of a split in the EROS in 1981. It concentrated its activities in the eastern province.

The Tamil Eelam Liberation Organisation (TELO) founded in 1979 was decimated by the LTTE in May 1986 and those killed included its leader Sri Sabaratnam.

*

After the 23 July, 1983 holocaust, the war between the state and the Tamils was joined in right earnest. The hardened Sinhala attitude was reflected in Jayewardene's resolve: 'I am not worried about the opinion of the Jaffna people now. We cannot think of them. Nothing will happen in our favour until the terrorists are wiped out.'

There was no room for a political dialogue. Early in July 1983

* Also known as PLOTE—People's Liberation Organization of Tamil Eelam.

Jayewardene had called a round table conference to discuss the devolution of power at the district level and the Tamil United Liberation Front (TULF) had participated in the inconclusive deliberations. But the holocaust put paid to the proposals. And the rift between the TULF and the militant groups (except the PLOTE) widened as the guerrillas stepped up operations. Soon the TULF was rendered totally inoperative, and its Members of Parliament dared not visit their constituencies in the Tamil provinces for fear of the guerrillas (the militants killed two of them and two others bought peace with them to be able to visit their homes). Shortly after this, the TULF went into self-exile in Madras and looked haplessly to New Delhi for political guidance while the guerrilla groups, directed by their leaders from their headquarters in exile in Madras, did the fighting.

It took time and not a little pressure for Jayewardene to accept India's proffered good offices to explore a political settlement. Prime Minister Indira Gandhi named the suave Oxford-educated journalist-turned-diplomat G. Parthasarathi as her special envoy. Himself a Tamil, Parthasarathi talked to the Sri Lankan leaders and the TULF and then, along with President Jayewardene, drafted a set of proposals for devolution of power. The proposals known as Annexure C, centred on the creation of separate regional councils for the northern and eastern provinces. These councils were to be granted substantial powers including the subjects of law and order, land policy, education, etc. The councils were also to have powers of taxation and so on.

India regarded these proposals adequate to meet the Tamil aspirations because of the degree of autonomy they promised. Initially Jayewardene agreed that the Annexure C would be the basis of negotiations, but when he called an All Party Conference in January 1984 to get a consensus on the proposals the deliberations did not focus on Annexure C but considered a diluted set of proposals. Committees were set up to study individual aspects of this limited devolution but even this process was lengthened unnecessarily. As discussions dragged on through 1984 the cycle of militant violence and reprisals by the state spiralled.

The reasons for Jayewardene's volte-face were clear: he was unnerved by the Sinhala opposition to the proposals (the Sri Lanka Freedom Party denounced them as an Indian product). So he put across a new set of proposals (known as Annexure B) which did not aim at any meaningful devolution of power but merely extended the scheme of decentralization at the district level to the provincial level.

Jayewardene was to formally table the diluted proposals when the Conference reconvened on 21 December 1984. Before the Conference was to meet, the TULF expressed its dissatisfaction with the proposals and Jayewardene made this the pretext to promptly call off negotiations. He announced the termination of the Conference as soon as it met, saying the deliberations would serve no purpose because of the TULF's reservations. He then went back to talking of tackling 'terrorism' before a political solution. Military operations against the guerrillas were stepped up but made little headway; indeed, the guerrillas seemed to have the upper hand and when 150 Sinhalas were massacred at Anuradhapura in May 1985, Jayewardene responded to India's offer of help to implement the new proposals, i.e. Annexure C. After his visit to New Delhi in June 1985 it was agreed that India would help bring about a cease-fire and arrange direct negotiations between the Tamil groups (the TULF and the five main guerrilla groups—the LTTE, the PLOTE, the EROS, the EPRLF, and the TELO).

After a hurriedly arranged cease-fire (each side charged the other with violations) direct negotiations between a Sri Lankan government delegation and the six Tamil groups were held in Thimphu, capital of the landlocked Himalayan kingdom of Bhutan, early in July 1985. The secret talks were on 'substantive issues' and aimed at a political settlement. Four of the militant groups (LTTE, EROS, EPRLF and TELO) displayed rare unity in forming the umbrella Eelam National Liberation Front, despite having earlier opposed participation in the Thimphu talks (in actual fact they attended the talks under pressure from India).

The militants gained the most out of the talks, primarily because of the legitimacy they got from the fact that the government was talking to them for the first time.

At the Thimphu talks, the four groups and the PLOTE together authorized the TULF to speak for them because it had experience of negotiations which they lacked. The long-divided Tamil movement was able to express itself unitedly at last.

The Thimphu talks broke down after two rounds of meetings in July and August. The proposals seemed inadequate to the Tamil groups, who enunciated four cardinal principles on which any set of proposals should be based:

1. The recognition of the Tamil national identity
2. Respect for the integrity of the Tamil homeland
3. Recognition of their right to self-determination
4. Citizenship rights for all Tamils who had made Sri Lanka their homeland

The four principles flowed from the basic Tamil position that the Tamils were a nation with a common language and culture, inhabiting a geographically distinct and contiguous territory, and with a united will expressed through electoral and other political processes. For all these reasons, they said they constituted a nation with the right to self-determination within the meaning of the expression in article (1) of the International Covenant of Civil and Political Rights, which says: 'All people have the right to self-determination. By virtue of their right they freely determine their political status and freely pursue their economic, social and cultural development'.

Implicit in this set of principles was the demand for the merger of the northern and eastern provinces, prompted by Tamil apprehensions that they would be swamped by Sinhala colonization. (In addition to normal internal migration, the Tamils are especially wary of state-aided colonization schemes that accompany major irrigation projects which favour the Sinhalas.) The Tamil fear about the changing demographic composition of the Tamil provinces, was based on the following statistics. The Tamils claim they form sixty-eight per cent of the population of the eastern province (however, this includes Tamil-speaking Muslims who have begun asserting their identity and have been ambivalent about the Tamil Eelam demand; non-Muslim Tamils are only forty-two per cent) and that their majority is being whittled away with each passing year. Nowhere is the changing face of the Tamil area as marked as in Trincomalee, the erstwhile capital of the eastern province and now the seat of the combined northern and eastern provincial council. In Trincomalee, Tamils (33.8 per cent) and Tamil-speaking Muslims (29 per cent) accounted for 62 per cent in 1981 against 93.3 per cent in 1921. A planned increase in the Sinhala population (from 33.6 per cent in 1980) here could not only destroy the crucial geographical link between the northern and eastern province but it could also threaten the Tamil claim to a contiguous homeland. In other parts of the eastern province the Tamils fears are even more justified. They are very vulnerable in Amparai where they form only 20.1 per cent of the population with Tamil-speaking Muslims composing 41.5 per cent and Sinhalas 37.7 per cent. They are not as beleaguered in Batticaloa where Sinhalas constitute a meagre 3.2 per cent and Tamil-speaking Muslims 24 per cent against their 70.8 per cent. The problem is overall the Tamils cannot be sure of controlling the provincial council of the eastern province and therefore would not be able to check their demographic erosion if land development was a provincial subject under a devolution package. This is why they are so keen on a united Tamil province which, with the 92 per cent majority the Tamils hold in the northern province, would ensure Tamil dominance. For this very reason Muslim Tamils might not wish to ratify the proposed merger of the two provinces preferring to be a minority in a Sinhala majority Sri Lanka than be part of a Tamil minority's homeland in a Sinhala majority Sri Lanka.

*

While the first three Tamil principles enunciated at Thimphu were inter-related and asserted the Tamil national identity culturally, spatially and politically, the fourth assumed that the groups at Thimphu could speak for all Tamils in the island including plantation Tamils of Indian origin.

The Sinhalas refused to accept this, but this was a relatively minor issue for there was no common ground at all at Thimphu, Sri Lanka rejecting every one of the four principles. In any case, the militant groups did not seriously believe in a negotiated settlement. But India continued its efforts, talking to both the sides separately, to narrow the differences down. A draft framework of 'accord and understanding', contained in a Sri Lankan working paper, was proposed by India as the basis for further negotiations. But the militant groups vetoed it. Exasperated, Prime Minister Rajiv Gandhi said in November 1985, 'the ball (is) in the Tamils' court'. With the militants showing no signs of accommodation the Tamil United Liberation Front (TULF) attempted to take charge of negotiating on behalf of the Tamils. It drew up an alternative set of proposals in December 1985: a federal structure in which the northern and eastern provinces would be combined into a single Tamil language state. But Sri Lanka rejected the demand because it would not countenance any proposal which altered the unitary character of the Sri Lankan constitution. This was unfortunate for bilingualism or federalism could have been a solution to the problems of a plural society that Sri Lanka is. But the 1972 republican constitution, which retained the Westminster parliamentary model, entrenched Sinhala as the sole official language as well as the unitary state structure (which rules out federal accommodation); and the 1978 constitution which brought in a Gaullist presidential model left the unitary structure untouched because it made no concessions to the federal demand.

It was soon evident that there was little maneouvrability in the situation because the government would not agree to the merger of the two Tamil provinces or even a federal set-up which would include the two provinces.

Indian mediation was revived in April 1986 and a new set of proposals offered by Colombo was handed over to the TULF and the five militant groups. These did not propose any changes in the unitary character of the constitution but made provision for provincial councils as the unit of devolution. To meet the Tamil demand for a 'linkage' between the northern and eastern provinces the new package offered institutional arrangements for a measure of co-ordination on certain matters. Other concessions included the bifurcation of the police force into a national division and separate provincial divisions.

The TULF re-opened negotiations with the Sri Lankan government which now prepared the draft legislative proposals. The TULF discussed them with Indian constitutional experts. Alongside they were also discussed with the Tamil Nadu government and the Tamil militant groups in late 1986. For the first time the Tamil Nadu government played a role in the negotiations, obviously at New Delhi's instance, and thus became a direct link between the Indian government and the militant groups. This made sense for it was clear that no political settlement was possible without the militant groups, the Liberation Tigers of Tamil Eelam (LTTE) in particular, which had a special equation with the Tamil Nadu Chief Minister M.G. Ramachandran.

The militant groups presented a detailed critique of the proposals, suggesting that the powers granted to the provincial councils in respect of law and order, land settlement, etc. were still inadequate, and that the proposals did not specify the identified Tamil homeland (that is, they did not mention the merger of the two Tamil provinces).

The negotiations bogged down, with the unit of devolution being the sticking point. This, because the Tamil militants were united in their demand for the merger of the two provinces which in turn meant recognition by the government of the concept of a Tamil homeland— something unacceptable to Sinhala opinion which saw dangerous implications in the merger. So far as the the Sinhalas were concerned this amounted to conceding the Tamil Eelam demand in principle and they were vehemently opposed to it in any form. However, the LTTE was the most intransigent group of the lot, vetoing one set of proposals after another and even M.G. Ramachandran could not persuade it to think of a political solution.

Despite the despair in New Delhi at the failure of the talks, Rajiv Gandhi tried to mediate again in December 1986 after he and President Jayewardene met in Bangalore. Indian officials tried to persuade the LTTE leader Velupillai Prabhakaran to agree to a political settlement. The 'December 19 proposals', that resulted from talks Indian ministers had in Colombo, essentially involved the formation of a new eastern province by excising the Sinhala-majority areas (the Amparai electoral district) so that the Tamils need not fear their inability to control the set-up because they were not in the majority. The smaller province was meant to ensure Tamil dominance by improving the demographic composition to their advantage. The two councils would have institutional linkages for co-ordination between them. Sri Lanka also agreed to consider a proposal for a second stage of constitutional development providing for the merger of the two provinces, subject to the wishes of the people, to be ascertained separately after a period of time.

India thought the 19 December package was the best that could have happened to the Tamils, but President Jayewardene resiled from this position and tried to negotiate directly with the LTTE without informing India. Nothing came of this, except that India was growing tired of three years of mediation efforts that had produced nothing.

The new year saw a turning point. The LTTE, which had owed its presence in India to Tamil Nadu Chief Minister M.G. Ramachandran's sympathy for the aspirations of the Sri Lankan Tamils and Indian government's hopes that it would be an instrument of its diplomacy, was now hounded out of its havens in Madras. On New Delhi's orders the Tamil Nadu police disarmed the militant groups, seized their communication equipment and indirectly served notice on the LTTE that it would have to leave India immediately if it did not agree to a political settlement. M.G. Ramachandran endorsed this by telling Prabhakaran to decide whether he wanted a negotiated settlement or not, and if it was the latter to continue the war from Jaffna.

Prabhakaran refused to bow to India's strong-arm tactics and shifted his guerrillas and *matériel* to Jaffna leaving only a skeleton set-up behind in Madras. Soon after, the LTTE announced its decision to take over the civil administration in the Jaffna peninsula from New Year's Day to fill the vacuum left there, only confirming the government view that the Tigers were running a state within a state in the peninsula.

The announcement amounted to a unilateral declaration of independence through a parallel government and forced an awkward choice on India—it would either have to be recognized or disowned. Under ill-concealed Indian pressure, the LTTE backtracked clarifying that what it meant was not the setting up of a parallel government but the forming of a secretariat to co-ordinate routine civil administration. This, however, was the opportunity Sri Lanka had been waiting for and using the unimplemented threat of a parallel government as an excuse it mounted a major military offensive against the guerrillas. A virtual economic blockade of the Jaffna peninsula, denying it food and fuel and isolating it from the rest of the island, accompanied the operations. In the face of this all-out assault, the LTTE who had been militarily on top in November of the previous year was on the defensive by April 1987. But it was not vanquished. It pulled out its cadres from the rest of the Tamil areas to hold the Jaffna peninsula against a five-pronged Sri Lankan offensive. And throughout it maintained that it would not negotiate at the point of a gun.

After an abortive cease-fire in April, unilaterally offered by Sri Lanka to help a new 'peace process' initiated by India, Sri Lanka launched the final assault on Jaffna. Anxious to prevent the total rout of the guerrillas (which would mean a tremendous loss of its leverage with Colombo), New Delhi acted. Five Indian Air Force transport planes and two fighters flew over Jaffna, ostensibly on a relief mission, but in actuality intended to show Sri Lanka that India could bomb it into submission with impunity. Sri Lanka buckled and the result was the India-Sri Lanka agreement on 29 July. (See Appendix I.)

The agreement aimed basically at meeting the Tamil demands. However, although the TULF was involved in the negotiations leading to it, the militant groups were not consulted about the proposed devolution package or the mechanics of its implementation. They were only told about the agreement after India had decided to sign it. Unsurprisingly, while the TULF welcomed the settlement, the LTTE rejected it. The other militant groups supported it tacitly.

The new package was described as a breakthrough, conceptually and substantively. The political solution it sought was based on the recognition of Sri Lanka's unity, sovereignty and territorial integrity. In return Sri Lanka acknowledged the multi-ethnic, multi-lingual and multi-religious aspects of its plural society, consisting *inter alia* of Sinhalas, Tamils, Muslims (Moors) and Burghers, and their right to security, democracy and equality (a major concession in this context was that it accepted parity for Tamil and English with Sinhala).

The agreement also recognized the concept of a Tamil homeland: 'The northern and the eastern provinces have been areas of historical habitation of Sri Lankan Tamil speaking peoples, who have at all times lived together in this territory with other ethnic groups'.

The formula for devolution of power was seen as an advance on the 19 December 1986 proposals which had offered separate councils for the Tamil provinces while excising the Sinhala areas of the Amparai district in the eastern province. Under the new agreement the two provinces were to be merged into one though the merger would be ratified by the eastern province through a referendum at a later date.

The proposals under the agreement were conditional to the acceptance, by the various groups, of the proposals negotiated since May 1986 culminating in the 19 December 1986 package. Residual matters not finalized during the negotiations were to be resolved between India and Sri Lanka within six weeks of the agreement.

Despite its advances over previous packages, the agreement did not meet the minimum demands enunciated by the six Tamil groups at Thimphu in August 1985: recognition of the Tamil national identity; respect for the integrity of the Tamil homeland; recognition of the right to self-determination; and citizenship rights to all Tamils who had made Sri Lanka their homeland.

These demands for the recognition of the Tamil national identity could be the only basis for a long lasting solution to the Tamil problem and it was in not ceding them that the agreement erred. At best it viewed the Tamils as one of the minority ethnic groups and drew a clear line between them and the Tamil speaking Muslims. And since the Tamils were not a nationality, there was no question of their right to self-determination.

Though implicitly acknowledging the concept of a Tamil homeland, the lasting merger of the two Tamil provinces was left to the mercy of all the inhabitants of the eastern province. The ethnic composition of the eastern province made this a very uncertain gain for now the onus of making sure the merger was ratified would be on the Tamils, the Muslim inhabitants of the province having been incited into opposing the merger. Failing ratification, the merger of the two provinces would have to be undone which would mean a truncated Tamil homeland, limited to the northern province.

Also upsetting to the Tamils, including groups like the TULF which had initially welcomed the agreement, was the fact that the devolution of power would be within the unitary framework; a federal set-up would have ensured a more satisfactory deal.

As government legislated on the provisions of the agreement after it was signed, it was clear to the Tamils that they would be getting far less than they had bargained for. Some of the provisions the Tamils objected to were:

- Undefined discretionary powers to the Governor of the Tamil province, to be exercised on the directions of the President, contrary to the understanding that the Governor would be a ceremonial head. This would render the Council of Ministers ineffective and meaningless.
- Unacceptable grounds for the declaration of Emergency in the province. In addition to war, external aggression and armed rebellion which had been agreed to, the government's legislation provided for an additional ground: the breakdown of essential services and supplies. This, the Tamils claimed, would seriously detract from the substance of the devolution exercise because the provincial government could be suspended on flimsy pretexts.
- Again, contrary to the spirit of the agreement, a wide area of subjects which should have belonged to the provincial list were dropped or incorporated into the concurrent list.
- On the sensitive issue of state land, the government legislation vested the powers of control in the President and not with the provincial council which was contrary to the understanding. The Tamil fear was this would keep the door open for continued demographic changes especially in the eastern province where the Sinhala presence has increased 883 per cent between 1947 and 1981 against a national increase in the Sinhala population of only 238 per cent.

The gap between promise and the reality of the devolution exercises raised doubts in the minds of the Tamils about President Jayewardene's ability to deliver even the diluted concessions that had been been legislated on. But Jayewardene had a convenient loophole to exploit and this was the fact that India was committed to underwriting the implementation of the agreement. In other words this meant India would have to ensure the militants laid down arms to enable the resumption of political processes in the Tamil areas before devolution could take place.

*

An Indian Peace-Keeping Force (IPKF) was assembled and despatched to Sri Lanka the day after the agreement was signed to deliver the military component of the agreement. A rigid time frame for the implementation of the agreement was set up: cessation of hostilities within forty-eight hours of the signing of the agreement, to be followed by the surrender of arms by the militant groups and the confining of the Sri Lankan forces to the barracks within seventy-two hours.

But the problem of entering the guerrillas into the equation remained. The Liberation Tigers of Tamil Eelam (LTTE) had rejected the accord because it thought there was no solution to the Tamil problem short of a sovereign state. Its leader Prabhakaran, flown from his operational headquarters in Jaffna to New Delhi to meet Prime Minister Rajiv Gandhi, made his reservations known. But India was determined to go ahead with the agreement and Indian officials put across the message that the militant groups would be disarmed if they did not surrender. Prabhakaran in turn told them the LTTE did not want to fight India but would do so if necessary.

Rajiv Gandhi offered Prabhakaran assurances on the protection of Tamils. India was taking the entire responsibility from the disarmed guerrillas, he said. Secondly, the LTTE would have its due place in the Interim Administrative Council to be set up for the political transition in the Tamil provinces.

Prabhakaran realized that an outright refusal to lay down arms would mean taking on the Indian army. So the fight for Tamil Eelam would have to continue in some other form. He was flown back to Jaffna because the Tamils there had become restive after receiving reports that he was held incommunicado in New Delhi.

Prabhakaran appeared at a public meeting on 4 August 1987 to set out the LTTE position on the agreement[*], and said his group was prepared to give India a chance. But the struggle for Tamil Eelam would continue, he said, rounding off his speech with, 'the Liberation Tigers of Tamil Eelam long for the motherland of Tamil Eelam.'

Meanwhile the IPKF had arrived to the welcome of a war-weary people. All the militant groups claimed to have turned in their weapons, with the exception of the LTTE who surrendered their arms on 5 August, a day after Prabhakaran's return. They rejected the idea of a public ceremony (as suggested by the IPKF) and instead laid down arms at a brief ceremony at the Palaly air base. For all the ceremony, it

---

[*] See Appendix II

transpired later that no group had really parted with all its arms. The operation supervised by the Indian troops proved to be a farce and soon, much to Sri Lanka's satisfaction, India and the LTTE were fighting a vicious little war.

Sequentially, the deterioration in India's relations with the main guerrilla group began when groups armed by India arrived from Tamil Nadu and began setting up bases in the northern and eastern provinces amidst an inordinate delay in setting up the promised Interim Administrative Council. The groups, belonging to militant organizations patronized by India, began clashing with the dominant group which still controlled large Tamil areas.

This pattern of hostilities is not surprising to those who are aware of pattern of events during the 1971 Bangladesh war. India trained and backed the Mukti Bahini, the liberation force of Bangladesh, which comprised irregular guerrillas and later Bengali deserters of the Pakistani armed forces. When the war to break up Pakistan was joined, India simultaneously recognized what it called the Bangladesh government and announced a joint command with the Mukti Bahini. It was all so much legal fiction and the Indian army, under the guise of a joint command, overran Pakistan's eastern wing (a geographical absurdity because it was separated from the western wing by 2,000 miles of Indian mainland). The result was of all this was Bangladesh. But India unsure that it would have its way in Dacca (now Dhaka) when Bangladesh finally became a reality, wanted to ensure that a regime friendly to it would be in power. So *émigré* leaders, often seen in Calcutta's bars and brothels, virtually rode back to Dacca on Indian tanks to provide the government when Sheikh Mujibur Rehman, the 'father of Bangladesh', was still a prisoner in Pakistan. India's contingency plan, in the event the protégé leadership did not make it in Dacca and the Mukti Bahini staked its claim to power, was a surrogate guerrilla force called the Mujib Bahini, armed and trained by it. Since the *émigré* leadership *was* installed in Dacca there was no need to use the shadowy Mujib Bahini for a proxy war.

The redundant force of 20,000 Mujib Bahini men was dropped and left to fend for itself: its remnants now live in Meghalaya in India, with no future and with no legitimacy like the Kuomintang army remnants stranded in northern Burma when the Communists grasped power in China in 1949.

Likewise, in Sri Lanka, India practised dissimulation. Its ostensible aim was the disarming of the LTTE. But at the same time its Research and Analysis Wing (RAW), which despite its academic sounding name is India's equivalent of the United States CIA (Central Intelligence Agency) with a covert and overt role, was trying to play off groups chosen by it against the main group. The groups armed and inducted into Sri Lanka by India, to go by the LTTE's insinuations, were part of a diabolical plan to take control of the situation.

The promised Interim Administrative Council did not take off. And India did not heed complaints by the LTTE that Sri Lanka was violating the agreement. The LTTE in a masterful display of irony (and strategy) decided to tackle India non-violently. One of its leaders, Amirthalingam Thileepan, went on a fast unto death to press a charter of demands. Around the fast built up a Tamil political upsurge which made India's role in the Tamil areas tenuous.

It was not until Thileepan died that India made a commitment to the LTTE that it would have eight places in the Interim Administrative Council of twelve.

But the matter did not end there. An even more tragic episode was to follow, permanently embittering relations between the LTTE and the Indian forces. The 5 August laying down of arms was in return for the promise of a general amnesty to the group. However, in a flagrant contravention of the truce, a Sri Lankan naval patrol intercepted a boat and took two regional commanders and ten senior members of the LTTE prisoner. They were shifted to Indian custody but were to be taken to Colombo for interrogation.

The twelve guerrillas in custody warned India that they would end their lives if taken to Colombo. (Each guerrilla of the LTTE has a four-inch cyanide capsule slung around the neck—a symbol of the Liberation Tiger's dedication and determination never to be taken alive. This explains the virtual absence of Liberation Tiger prisoners with the enemy.) When India did not act, the twelve ingested their suicide capsules and died.

Even though India stated that it was helpless in the matter (because Jayewardene was adamant that the captives be brought to Colombo) the LTTE charges that India had tried to bargain with it: the captives would be freed if they accepted the India-Sri Lanka agreement and the Interim Council. Further, the LTTE says that it made a sincere effort to abide by its commitment. It claims that it sent a list of its nominees to the Interim Administrative Council only to have two of its people dropped when the Council was formed, one because Jayewardene did not approve and another because he was unacceptable to India (for having made anti-India speeches). Even as the fragile trust between the LTTE and India broke, there was violence against Sinhala civilians because of the LTTE suicides. The LTTE executed Sinhala policemen who were their prisoners. Sri Lanka blamed everything that had gone wrong on the Liberation Tigers and India endorsed the charge.

If the LTTE and India had had some faith in each other something might still have been worked out. But India was convinced that the LTTE was primarily a guerrilla force without political or ideological direction, and would therefore be unable to adjust to the political process. Because it was unsuited to politics, it was determined to destroy the basis of the agreement, or so the thinking in New Delhi went.

For its part, the LTTE thought that India was imposing an unfair agreement on it to make sure its own strategic interests in Sri Lanka were protected and had decided that the Tamils were now an expendable quantity. Whatever the misconceptions on both sides, the stage was being readied for an all-out war.

*

The first plans for the war, that continues even today, were laid at a high level conference in Colombo early in October 1987 after the Liberation Tigers of Tamil Eelam (LTTE) had resumed fighting the Indian forces. The plans called for the world's fourth largest army (which began its presence in Sri Lanka in July 1987 with 6,000 men) to wage a full-scale war against a rag-tag guerrilla force of about 2,000 which controlled Jaffna city, the symbol of Tamil secessionist resistance. The LTTE guerrillas were the only ones arrayed against the Indians, for in the brief respite they had gained during the talks the LTTE had systematically wiped out virtually all the other guerrilla groups and prepared for a renewed war.

Ironically, the Sri Lankan forces had not been able to take Jaffna city, because India was opposed to a military solution of the ethnic conflict. Now India had decided to take Jaffna for Sri Lanka. The Indians advanced along five axes with heavy troop concentrations which included crack commandos. The land mines and booby traps of the guerrillas and the advantage they had fighting from densely populated areas where they could just merge with the background presented a major challenge to the Indian forces but they took the city on 25 October by force of their superior manpower and firepower but not without inflicting heavy civilian casualties and doing considerable damage to property. When the Indian forces established control of its nodal points Jaffna was a much battered city. Its main thoroughfares wore a deserted look while skirmishing went on in side-streets and by-lanes.

The pattern for the next two years was set with the fall of Jaffna. From now on there would be no organized resistance by the guerrillas, but they would carry on a ghostly little war—a war of midnight ambushes, mine explosions and sniper fire—fought in the classic guerrilla pattern as codified by Mao Ze-dong: a guerrilla takes like a fish to water, becomes part of the people. The people supported the LTTE and this made the IPKF's job even more difficult as they tried to winkle the guerrillas out of their hideouts or, to take the Mao metaphor further, drain the water to kill the fish or better still to poison the water.

There were plenty of macabre ironies in the war. Once, for instance, an Indian army officer was questioning a group of young Tamils, suspected of being guerrillas. One of the young men looked familiar. Seconds later the officer realized that the young man was one of the LTTE cadres he had trained in an Indian military camp a couple of years earlier. There are many instances of such irony in the history of guerrilla movements—where those who armed and trained guerrillas would have to fight them later. But the war between India and the Tigers is a war that has followed few predictable patterns.

*

He who rides a tiger cannot dismount, says the *Rig Veda*, the Hindu religious text. Over the last couple of years the Indian Army (and its Sri Lankan counterpart) has learned this truth the hard way, for the Tigers have proved a hard and tenacious foe.

Before the advent of the IPKF, to get to Tiger country you had to first reach the 280-year-old Dutch fort in Jaffna where there was a garrison. From there you had to take a frighteningly silent, deserted road to the city, across the no-man's land. It was a lonely, eerie mile for once you had crossed the no-man's land you were in Tiger territory. The reporter looking for an encounter with the guerrillas power was well-advised to walk waving a white handkerchief, to proclaim his neutral status, for the Tigers shot strangers on sight. The initial contact was usually with a boy who looked fifteen (but insisted he was eighteen), with the familiar cyanide capsule down his sweaty neck, and cradling an AK-47 assault rifle. He kept a watchful eye on the fort as he directed the visitor to the nearest Tiger hideout.

Over the decade and more they have been fighting, the LTTE guerrillas (or boys as they are affectionately called by the people of Jaffna) have earned the gratitude of the local Tamils for having saved them from the excesses of the Sri Lankan forces. The LTTE has also become a formidable and self-sufficient fighting force. It makes some of its arms and almost all its own ammunitions. With the exception of some of its cadres, who were trained in India, almost all its recruits are trained in secret camps located in the northern and eastern provinces.

Its efficacy as a fighting force was best demonstrated in the battle for Jaffna. To be sure Operation Pawan, as the Indian army christened its offensive, was launched in unfamiliar terrain against an urban guerrilla force that had the support of the people. But still the fight by the guerrillas against vastly superior firepower and forces (military doctrine recommends a 10:1 numerical superiority for regular armies fighting guerrillas) was commendable. Operation Pawan began as a five-axes thrust on Jaffna city from across the lush green lagoon-laced peninsula on 9–10 October 1987. By mid-October, the IPKF strength had been raised from 3,000 to 24,000 in the peninsula. By 24 October, the

LTTE had been hemmed in, and the axes closed in the next day. And though militarily it was a success for the Indian army, the entire exercise will be remembered more for the resistance the guerrillas put up. The battle is worth recounting in some detail.

Early in April, apprehending a Sri Lankan army push on Jaffna, the LTTE had laid a maze of mines and booby traps along the approaches to the city. It had also built a three-tier defence perimeter with strong bunkers and trenches.

The mines and booby traps were simple but effective, and were, in the main, local improvisations. Plastic explosives, for instance, were moulded into the shape and size needed and put into non-metallic containers which ranged from cans and buckets to the hollows of coconut-tree-trunks. The wires from the explosive would lead to a concealed position fifty to hundred metres away (the trigger was usually a radio receiver set in a home) and the mine would be activated almost literally by the switching on of a radio set. The Indian army was unprepared for this sort of kitchen-sink-and-living-room warfare and suffered massive casualties especially in regard to its wheeled vehicles which were very susceptible to mines. The trucks were then supplanted by tanks which, it was hoped, would crush the mines. But even the 45-ton T-72 tanks (these machines of Soviet provenance are deployed in front-line defences by Warsaw Pact nations) were blown to bits by the mines. As an IPKF officer observed ruefully: 'We have heard of explosives used in ounces to immobilize the enemy. But the LTTE used nothing less than five to fifty kilograms of explosives'. The LTTE also used, to deadly effect, non-traditional weaponry such as burning jerry cans of petrol against tanks and armoured personnel carriers. More conventional weapons included Chinese-made rocket-propelled grenades and mortars. The LTTE snipers were particularly effective.

To combat the deadly combination of arms and sheer guts of the LTTE, the Indian army launched, for the first time in its history, a joint army-navy-air-force operation against an irregular force. Helicopter gunshops strafed densely populated areas where guerrillas were believed to be sheltering and naval ships pounded the city in support of the heavy armour and infantry engaged in operations on the ground.

The result was heavy civilian casualties and damaged civilian targets including the Jaffna hospital. The IPKF destroyed, through shelling, the offices and printing equipment of two Tamil newspapers under LTTE control—*Eelamurasu* and *Murasoli*—and its TV station Nidarsanam. Where it had once been seen as a force that would end the war, the IPKF was now reviled and denounced by the people of Jaffna. The LTTE finally caved in on 25 October. Of its 2,500 guerrillas, 700 had been killed. But it was by no mean a spent force for its leadership as well as hundreds of its cadres had slipped away through the IPKF net and melted into the people, to regroup. And even though Jaffna city had fallen, it was a hollow victory for the IPKF. As an IPKF officer described the war for Jaffna in private '(it was a) dirty little war, that too by proxy'.

Two days after the fall of Jaffna, Ajit Mahatiya, the number two military leader of the LTTE, said the militants were ready for a cease-fire if the Indian army stopped its operations and returned to its pre-10 October positions. Lt. Gen. Depinder Singh, the IPKF commander, was to say, after his retirement, that India should have taken this opportunity and called off the military campaign after taking Jaffna.

The Tigers regrouped in the eastern province where the demographic composition is complex though the Tamils are in the majority. The Tigers controlled only small pockets in the eastern province unlike in the Jaffna peninsula. So it had to be a hit-and-run war, for military survival, unlike in the battle for Jaffna where they had thrown everything in having to fight for political survival.

The cease-fire failed and between mid-February and late March 1988, the IPKF smashed LTTE bases in Batticaloa in the eastern province and carried out search-and-destroy operations picturesquely code-named Rolling Trumpets, Blooming Tulips, Red Rose, Lilac and Goldfish. The operation in Batticaloa seemed simpler than the one in Jaffna where the IPKF did not have to attack fortified positions (which called for artillery shelling and helicopter gun-ship strafing). The IPKF was also more sensitive to Tamil susceptibilities here, especially because the people of Batticaloa had already suffered at the hands of Sri Lanka's Special Task Force which had killed 5,000 civilians from 1984–87. The IPKF's relentless pressure soon had the guerrillas on the run as the LTTE bases were smashed, its cadres killed or captured, and its sources of arms from outside the country blocked by Indian naval ships cordoning the Tamil provinces.

Amidst all this, India kept up informal contact with the LTTE because the guerrillas still commanded popular support. It still remained a guerrilla force to contend with, and was getting new recruits to be able to pin down the IPKF. 'We are prepared for peace but we are also prepared for a Vietnam-type situation if we fail to reach an agreement with India', the LTTE leadership said.

However, there was no question of a compromise at this time for unconditional surrender was what India wanted out of the LTTE in order to keep the India-Sri Lanka agreement afloat. But it was clear that the 'accord of the century' was not working, especially as Tamil opinion was almost entirely in favour of the still-defiant guerrillas. An Indian reporter who visited the Tamil areas at this time said that though most of the Tamils tolerated the IPKF presence for the security it gave them, the thought that they had been reduced to second-class citizens in their homeland rankled. 'The IPKF will always be seen as an outside agency', a retired government employee told the reporter. 'The British did a lot for us but that did not prevent us from asking them to go.'

In the last week of May that year there were 70,000 Indian troops pitted against the LTTE remnants, a ratio of almost 70 to 1. And although the IPKF claimed to have smashed the command structure of the LTTE and trapped its supreme commander, Velupillai Prabhakaran, in a triangular forest tract with its points at Kilinochchi, Mullaitivu and Vavuniya (with the Indian navy cordoning off the coast to prevent his escape by sea), Prabhakaran escaped and an IPKF victory seemed as elusive as ever.

As the first anniversary of the India-Sri Lanka agreement drew near, New Delhi was claiming a breakthrough in the talks its Research and Analysis Wing was having with the LTTE's political representative in Madras, Sadasivam Krishna Kumar, alias Kittu. However the participants diverged on a fundamental issue: India insisted on a peace formula within the framework of the July 1987 agreement while the LTTE opposed the provision for a referendum in the eastern province to ratify the promised merger of the two Tamil majority provinces. (This because, unlike in the northern province, the Tamil majority in the east is not absolute.) The LTTE also held that elections to provincial councils (already completed in the Sinhala majority provinces) were meaningless in the Tamil areas where rehabilitation and reconstruction demanded the top priority. It wanted a dominant role for itself in the reconstruction programme which would use Indian aid channeled through Colombo.

There were other issues too. The IPKF and the Sri Lankan army wanted the LTTE to surrender arms but the Tigers wanted a cease-fire first because they wanted to keep some of their arms (estimated at 1,500 by the Sri Lankan army, and 700 by the IPKF; the LTTE maintained it was just 300) after the elections were over. This the IPKF opposed because it wanted to deny the LTTE the chance to use the interregnum to regroup, rearm, and embark on another campaign. By July 1988, the LTTE's attitude had hardened to everyone's surprise. It threatened to call off the 'farcical' talks and engage in a protracted struggle against 'alien occupation'. This was probably because the LTTE strategists thought New Delhi was desperately seeking a settlement with it before it called elections in Tamil Nadu where the stakes for Prime Minister Rajiv Gandhi and his Congress Party (denied power in the state since 1967) were high.

By the end of the first year of the India-Sri Lanka agreement, its political component had not been fully delivered. President J.R. Jayewardene had enacted the legislation to create provincial councils through which power was to devolve to the Tamils, and alongside to the Sinhalese. But the IPKF had not succeeded in demilitarizing the situation in the Tamil areas to enable elections to be held there. As many as eight operations against the LTTE were on, with crack jungle warfare units and counter-insurgency forces thrown in. But the guerrilla remnants managed to keep an estimated 70,000 Indian troops at bay. India had obviously miscalculated the situation. Adding to India's discomfort were the rumblings of displeasure in the Indian army command over the unacceptably high casualties the IPKF was sustaining (511 killed and 1,526 wounded in one year). The Indian army leadership had no reservations about the political decision to get the LTTE around to talks through military pressure. But when the two track strategy—simultaneous military pressure and political talks—seemed to be increasingly one track, with no movement at all on the political side, the military felt they were being forced to do all the dirty work with no end in sight to their onerous duties. The military made clear that the LTTE should be put on notice to co-operate with the 1987 agreement, inside a clearly charted out period; failing this the IPKF should be given permission to engage in a large-scale war that would liquidate the LTTE entirely. Interestingly, in India the feeling was that it was an unjust war and that India should order a unilateral cease-fire and begin talks with the LTTE. India had reached an impasse. After weighing his options, Rajiv Gandhi acted.

First, he postponed the elections in Tamil Nadu by six months. Alongside, he yielded to the demand of the Indian army leadership that the dichotomous approach, of political negotiations while the operations were on, should end. He rejected the suggestion of the LTTE's representative, Kittu, in Madras that a five-day cease-fire be arranged in a specified area anywhere in the northern or eastern province to enable him to meet Prabhakaran and discuss an agreement under which the LTTE would guarantee to lay down arms and participate in elections if a fair settlement that fulfilled Tamil aspirations was arrived at.

On 31 July 1988, India announced that elections would be held in the Tamil provinces with or without the LTTE participation. The IPKF's Operation Checkmate was stepped up in the northern province: this offensive's mission was to storm all the Tiger strongholds and kill or capture every last Tamil guerrilla. Simultaneously the police in Tamil Nadu, directly ruled by New Delhi since January 1988 after the constitutional breakdown in that state, cracked down on the LTTE cadres, detaining them under India's National Security Act after confiscating their arms. Kittu was placed under house arrest.

The dual approach of talks alongside military pressure was now giving way to a coercive policy which was not surprising for India's options were not many: it could either withdraw the IPKF pleading that it could not implement the July 1987 accord or it could go all out to destroy the LTTE and enforce the accord by force. The first option would have meant the loss of India's credibility internationally and so the second option was chosen. However, even now India proceeded cautiously for there was always the possibility that Jayewardene could renege on his promised concessions to the Tamils once the LTTE was completely destroyed. This caution took the form of a few new concessions to the Tamils (in the hope it would build confidence among them) even as the IPKF stepped up its offensive to overrun the LTTE's 'mother camp' in Vavuniya.

On his part President Jayewardene sprang a surprise by the announcing (on 10 September 1988) the merger of the two Tamil provinces and following it up with an announcement (on 12 September) of elections to the merged North-Eastern Provincial Council in November. (The July 1987 agreement had provided for the merger of the two Tamil provinces *after* they had elected their councils.) Jayewardene also ordered the release of Tamil political detenus. Then, the IPKF announced a five-day unilateral cease-fire from 15 September even as Kittu was arrested along with some others in Madras. The cease-fire, extended by five days to 23 September and the latest round of arrests in Madras, amounted to offering the LTTE their last chance to enter the election by laying down arms. But there was not a single surrender. The LTTE, on the other hand, used the ten-day cease-fire to regroup and build up its supplies. It appeared determined to fight until its 'revolutionary goal of freedom' was achieved.

Kittu, who threatened a fast unto death if he was not freed and returned to Sri Lanka, was flown out along with other LTTE prisoners to Jaffna before he could carry out his threat.

India's last offers of talks having been rejected, preparations for the elections to the North-Eastern Provincial Council were begun. It would be an election without the participation of one of the most significant groups in the region—but India had had enough. Now all that mattered in terms of its own image was the holding of peaceful and orderly elections.

By definition any normal electoral process must have few unvarying aspects: the participation of contenders who matter, an open campaign, and a decent voter turn-out. None of these parameters obtained in the IPKF-controlled elections to the North-Eastern Provincial Council. The contenders were limited to just two of the Tamil groups, one of them an unwilling participant. The two groups were the Eelam People's Revolutionary Liberation Front (EPRLF), which the IPKF had used to spot and hunt the Tigers out. The EPRLF had initially declined to participate for fear of LTTE reprisals once the IPKF left the island. It was persuaded to change its mind with an assurance of prolonged IPKF presence in the north-eastern province, in addition to large infusions of arms, ammunition and funds. The Eelam National Democratic Liberation Front (ENDLF), an amalgam of splinters from several Tamil groups, and known to be a protégé of India like the EPRLF, was the only other formation to enter the election battle. Even the non-militant TULF and the Tamil Congress would not participate in the elections.

The filing of nomination papers was to begin on 2 October, but there was no one to receive them because the electoral offices were closed. Not a single paper was filed until 6 October. Between 7 and 10 October election staff was flown in from outside the area by the IPKF to accept papers from EPRLF candidates in Jaffna and Mannar districts and from ENDLF candidates in the Kilinochchi, Mullaitivu and Vavuniya districts of the northern region. All the thirty-six seats from these five districts (in a seventy-one member house) were filled uncontested.

In the eastern province, the EPRLF, the Muslim Congress and the UNP (the ruling party) filed papers in all the three districts—Trincomalee, Batticaloa, and Amparai after election staff and party representatives had been flown in or transported by the IPKF. But oddly, while contests were announced for all the thirty-five seats (triangular in most of them) the names of candidates were kept secret—unusual for Sri Lanka but then it was an election supervised by the IPKF. Meanwhile the IPKF launched its Operation Mahaan Kartavya (the holy task) to maintain pressure on the LTTE in the north and to eliminate it in the east where all the seats were being contested. Protected by the IPKF, the armed cadres of the EPRLF went about killing the non-combatant LTTE sympathizers. There was little electioneering and the few election meetings held under IPKF protection were poorly attended.

With the LTTE having called for a boycott, the election proved farcical—and was held virtually at gun-point. Of the 576 polling stations proposed for some 600,000 eligible voters, only 324 functioned. Instead of five to six officials deployed in each station there was just one. Anyone could walk in and vote. The same voter turned up again and again. The sixty-three per cent voter turn-out that was claimed was still low by Sri Lanka's norms. The Muslims voted in strength. Most of the Sinhalas and some Tamils did not vote. The EPRLF with forty-one seats and its ally the ENDLF with twelve, had a huge majority in the seventy-one member house; the Muslim Congress totted up seventeen seats and the UNP had to be content with one.

The ritual had been gone through. But in question was the legitimacy of the EPRLF-ENDLF dominated council, elected without the participation of the LTTE, and with the voting confined to the eastern region and over half the seats filled without contest.

The shotgun elections might have helped India proclaim to the world that its peace-keeping role had helped restore the democratic processes in the Tamil areas and that the LTTE had been contained. But the charade would soon be shown for what it was, for the LTTE was far from being eliminated and would sorely harass the new council in the months to come.

India's dissimulation was carried further. Foreign Minister P.V. Narasimha Rao told the Indian Parliament that the elections were a step towards autonomy for Sri Lanka's Tamils and said the IPKF would stay on until all the other steps envisaged in the devolution package had been taken. (These included the enactment of laws to give Tamil parity with Sinhala—with English providing the link—as the official language, and the raising of a provincial police force to take over law and order in the Tamil province.) He also announced that as the IPKF was there under a bilateral arrangement, neither India nor Sri Lanka could decide unilaterally on its withdrawal. India had shifted ground because in August 1987 Prime Minister Rajiv Gandhi had said that the IPKF was in Sri Lanka at the invitation of President J.R. Jayewardene and would leave at his request.

Clearly the new Indian stand was in response to the snowballing Sinhala resentment of the IPKF's continued stay in the island. Ranasinghe Premadasa, the Prime Minister, as well as Sirimavo Bandaranaike of the Sri Lanka Freedom Party (SLFP), the main contenders for the imminent presidential elections were pledged to sending the IPKF back. Bandaranaike wanted it to go immediately, while Premadasa wanted it to return to India as soon as possible. Both were opposed to the India-Sri Lanka agreement in substance but Premadasa was less hawkish and only wanted it replaced by an equitable friendship treaty. The third runner in the presidential contest, Ossie Abeyagoonesekara of the United Socialist Alliance, was the only supporter of the agreement.

The first presidential election in seven years in Sri Lanka saw a low voter turnout: 53.3 per cent in contrast to 81 per cent in 1982, and 86 per cent at the 1977 Parliament elections. Despite this it was hailed as a triumph for democracy even though there had been 405 killings in the Sinhala areas in the month preceding it.

The meagre voting was mainly due to the call for a boycott raised by the Janatha Vimukti Peramuna (JVP), the ultranationalist Sinhala group which was opposed to the India-Sri Lanka agreement. Because of this, despite a one-million increase in the voting strength (from 8.1 million in 1982 to 9.1 million in 1988) the voting dropped by twenty-five per cent. The winner's share dropped too, from 52.9 per cent in 1982 to 50.4 per cent against the needed 50 per cent. Premadasa edged Bandaranaike (who got 44.9 per cent) and Abeyagoonesekara polled a little over four per cent. It is interesting to note that the two contenders who opposed the India-Sri Lanka agreement got, between them, ninety-five per cent of the vote, while Abeyagoonesekara, who supported, it got less than five per cent of the vote. More significant, he got less votes than either of the main contestants in the Tamil areas, despite the call of the TULF and the Eelam People's Revolutionary Liberation Organization to support him. In effect, neither the Tamils nor the Sinhalas supported the agreement.

All that remained now was the election of a new Parliament on 16 February 1989. The main contenders were the same—the UNP and the SLFP. The India-Sri Lanka agreement and the presence of the IPKF remained the crucial issues. And the Tamil's dilemma was the same—to vote or not vote because the LTTE had given the election the thumbs down once again and even threatened every candidate with death.

Close to the nominations there was a dramatic shift in alignments in the merged north-eastern province. All the groups supporting the India-Sri Lanka agreement—the TULF which had ducked the council elections for fear of the LTTE but which yearned for a political role, the EPRLF and the ENDLF which had together captured the council, and a new ally, the Tamil Eelam Liberation Organization (TELO)—fought the Parliament elections in alliance.

It would have been a walk-over for the umbrella alliance but for the hesitant entry of the Eelam Revolutionary Organization of Students (EROS) on the scene. The EROS had neither supported nor opposed the India-Sri Lanka agreement and had managed a tight-rope walk between India and its protégés among the Tamil groups on the one hand, and the LTTE on the other.

The EROS tried to put together an alliance of all the Tamil groups. When it failed, its nominees filed nominations for all the seats in the northern districts and for most of the seats in the eastern districts. Though it had a few known LTTE functionaries on its slate, it was reluctant to campaign because of a renewed LTTE threat. Initially it limited its campaign to the eastern districts, outside the Tiger domain, but after the LTTE had signalled tacitly that it supported it, it felt emboldened to attempt house-to-house canvassing in the north. Even though this took place just before the country went to the polls, the EROS won eight of the eleven seats in the north and four in the east, and together with the bonus seat it got on the national list under the proportional representation system, it became the third largest group in Parliament with thirteen seats (after the UNP (125) and the SLFP (67) in the 225-member house).

The outcome of the election showed India in an extremely unflattering light. The TULF alliance could win only nine seats (the EPRLF seven and the TELO two). The TULF itself drew a blank in the contests but got a bonus seat. The results were clouded but not the pointers. The Tamils had rejected the old guard, moderate leadership the TULF represented, and, in a generational turnover of leadership, had voted in the militant groups new to electoral policies. The EROS, closer to the LTTE than to India, emerged the foremost Tamil group because it seemed to represent best Tamil anxieties during the traumatic transition from conflict to the political process. And, much to India's chagrin, the LTTE, which it had tried to destroy on every front, now had a pressure group in Sri Lanka's new Parliament.

The EROS decided to keep out of the new house until conditions conducive to its participation were created. These were: improvements in the devolution package, the repeal of the sixth amendment of the constitution which required members to forswear secession, the release of Tamil political detainees, and a cease-fire by the IPKF. The last demand was addressed to India and the rest to the Premadasa government in Colombo.

Besides, the EROS also stated that it stood for all-island Tamil unity (which would extend to Tamils in the plantation country outside the north-eastern province) and maintained that the India-Sri Lanka agreement could only be the basis of a broad-based, more enduring settlement, and was not the final word on the Tamil issue.

Then, in January, the LTTE found someone to speak for it in India too. The Dravida Munnetra Kazhagam which stormed back to power in Tamil Nadu, after thirteen years out in cold, made little secret of where its sympathies lay. Its Chief Minister, M. Karunanidhi, asserted his state's right to be consulted in the Sri Lanka Tamil issue (recognized by Prime Minister Rajiv Gandhi until the demise of Chief Minister M.G. Ramachandran in December 1987), and pleaded for the LTTE.

It was time, it seemed, for all those involved to recognize the fact that the LTTE (and those it supported) was the true voice of the Tamil cause. Without it nothing of any lasting nature would take place. As things stood, the emergence of the EROS as the dominant Tamil group in Parliament eroded the legitimacy of the North-Eastern Provincial Council captured by the EPRLF and its allies after a boycott-hit election. The six-week deadline President Premadasa had set for devolving powers to the provinces had gone unmet. The north-eastern council had neither the powers nor the funds to make the devolution package meaningful and Chief Minister A. Varatharaja Perumal discovered after making thirty trips to Colombo in ninety-four days that the provincial council was not working. In March he looked plaintively to India to secure the implementation of the devolution package. But now it is quite apparent that the provincial council experiment will not work without the LTTE, and by extension Tamil approval, just as the India-Sri Lanka agreement of July 1987 has not worked.

*

In early April 1989, almost two years after the India-Sri Lanka agreement, Premadasa realized that Sri Lanka could not fight two wars—one against the militant Sinhala organization, the Janatha Vimukti Peramuna (JVP) in the south and another against the LTTE in the north. The JVP's terror campaign was aimed at ending the presence of the IPKF in the island and abrogating the India-Sri Lanka agreement. Premadasa was pledged to ending the IPKF presence but ironically the continuing violence of the JVP made it impossible for him to divert forces to the north-east to fill the military vacuum that would ensue there if the IPKF left.

Finally, in a desperate gamble, Premadasa offered a unilateral cease-fire to both the JVP and the LTTE and invited them to discussions about the future of the island. The JVP, to whom the offer was primarily directed, ignored it, but the LTTE, after initial hesitation, responded.

In the process the LTTE gained new legitimacy for the Sri Lankan government was talking to it directly again after a long hiatus. Also, Premadasa was prepared to negotiate unconditionally unlike India which wanted the LTTE to surrender before talks could take place.

Premadasa's initiative was not a bad move for his interests and that of the LTTE were converging: both wanted the IPKF out; and the LTTE was particularly keen that the North-Eastern Provincial Council set-up dominated by the EPRLF be dismantled. In the negotiations which began at the end of April, the LTTE's short-term objectives included the assurance of its dominance in the north-eastern province through fresh elections, and the postponement of plans to ratify the merger of the Tamil provinces. Its long-term objectives lay in securing for the Tamils recognition of their national identity which meant a federal set-up and a degree of autonomy which would go beyond the concessions the India-Sri Lanka agreement had bought them. For his part Premadasa seemed to recognize the futility of denying the Tamil demands; the major problem he faced was how he was going to give the Tamils what they wanted without antagonizing extremist Sinhala sentiment and India. Nonetheless the fact that Premadasa and the most significant Tamil group had begun talking injected some hope into what had all along seemed an utterly hopeless situation. Now there had to be the political will and grace on both sides to make some long-term decisions and stand by them.

3

The Sinhala-Buddhist Response

Buddhism teaches that every living being is sacred and that the suffering of others is as one's own. Tolerance and compassion is its message. But, in Sri Lanka, Buddhism has acquired an edge of violence that departs from the essence of the Buddha's message.

One morning in 1959, Somarama Thero, a Buddhist monk in his thirties, appeared on the spacious verandah of Prime Minister S.W.R.D. Bandaranaike's Rosemeade Place residence in Colombo, at the head of a group of petitioners. Such deputations were a routine affair. The Prime Minister came out to meet the group and bowed to the monk in reverence. Thero whipped out a revolver and shot him dead.

Bandaranaike was an Anglican Christian convert to Buddhism. Ironically, he was one of the first victims of the Buddhist upsurge he had helped create in the island and which had swept him to office in 1956.

The Sri Lanka Freedom Party (SLFP) was founded by Bandaranaike after he broke away from the ruling United National Party (UNP) in 1951. The new party outflanked and outmanoeuvred the established power-sharing arrangement between the Sinhala and Tamil elites at the 1956 elections. In more ways than one 1956 was a turning point for Ceylon. Not only was there a new political equation at work, but there was also a new religion-state relationship. Two other events happened that year. One was the 2500th anniversary of Buddha's *nirvana*. The celebrations to mark it had marked nationalist overtones in Ceylon, a function of the strong Sinhala belief that they were the (pure Aryan) race chosen by the Buddha to inhabit the island (with the Tamil conquerors from south India mere usurpers of the northern and eastern tracts of the island).

The other was the publication of a report on the state of Buddhism in the island by the All-Ceylon Buddhist Congress, a body composed of various Buddhist societies. The report, a result of two years of work, dealt with the need for a coherent organization for Buddhism and a council to regulate it. But the real value lay in its recapitulation, with a show of authority, of the oppression of and opposition to Buddhism and its institutions by the various Christian rulers of the land.

The report recalled the story of the Buddha's three visits to Ceylon (a strongly disputed claim). Seated on a rock in India, the Buddha is believed to have surveyed the world and seen the island in the south and thought it the most suited to preserve the purity of his doctrine. He then rose to the sky and travelling along the pathway of space in the manner of the heroic lion, radiant with the infinite grace of a Supremely Enlightened One' arrived in the island to free it of its 'uncivilized and impure elements'.

Whether the report was intended as a political weapon or not, it became one thanks to the tension that prevailed in the spring of 1956. Its publication incensed the Buddhists who felt the state had treated them badly. As it was the Buddhists were caught up in a frenzy of celebration on the 2500th anniversary of the Buddha's *nirvana*. It only needed a clever strategist to turn the favour into a political asset. This the SLFP did. It examined the report of the All-Ceylon Buddhist Congress and endorsed its main finding: the policies of the western rulers had undermined the influence of Buddhism. So, to rebuild the people in the new era of independence, it was necessary to undo the injustices done to Buddhism and 'to enable the Buddhists to take fullest advantage of their religion and culture.' (However, the party's manifesto stopped short of suggesting that Buddhism be institutionalized as the state religion.) In addition to its endorsement of the report, the SLFP made the primacy of the Sinhala language (switch from English to Sinhala as the official language 'within 24 hours') its main campaign issue. The party was directing its appeal to the new strata of educated Sinhalas who resented the dominance of the English-educated elite in administration, higher education, and politics but were seeking opportunities of social advancement. In actual fact, at the time, Sinhala-educated school teachers got only half the salaries their English-trained counterparts were paid. And they had a lower status because upward social mobility was still linked to the knowledge of English. The number of educated unemployed was rising and the illusion that Sinhala in the place of English would afford greater opportunities to the new entrants to the job market was growing. Practitioners of *ayurveda* were another aggrieved group. Government medical services based on the allopathic system had marginalized them, where they had once enjoyed high social status. And, lastly, the Buddhist monks educated in Sinhala and the classical Pali, were paid lip service as the traditional protectors of Sinhala culture but were denied a say anywhere. They too longed for a place in the scheme of things.

At the beginning of the campaign, the Buddhists, who derived their inspiration from the Buddhist revival early in the century under Anagarika Dharmapala (Dharmapala had invoked myths and legends to establish the 'fact' that the Sinhalas were the original inhabitants of the island and that the Tamils were usurpers and pagans who had nearly devastated the country), asked the monks, who had now formed a front, to visit every Buddhist home to persuade the people to the right path.

The monks fanned out from house to house, held meetings and distributed pamphlets. Religious symbols were dexterously manipulated to whip up religious frenzy. The SLFP won comfortably.

The main inspiration for the spirited campaign was Buddharakkita Thero, who along with Bandaranaike had founded the SLFP. He was the country's most political monk and presided over one of the big temples. He was also well-known for his involvement in an ecclesiastical dispute which he won in court. He organized the electoral machinery for Bandaranaike.

After he came to power, some of Bandaranaike's problems, religious and political, flowed from his indebtedness to the monk who emerged as an extra-constitutional power centre (he had no official position in the government). Indeed, Thero has been compared to Cardinal Richelieu and Rasputin. Bandaranaike's 'Sinhala Only' enactment of 1956, which led to the 1958 anti-Tamil riots, was part repayment of his political debt to the monk. (When he made concessions—as a form of reparation—to the Tamils in the face of Sinhala opposition, he invited the wrath of the Buddhists. Consequently, he withdrew concessions to the Tamils on the language issue.) But that was not enough to appease the Buddhists and he was killed. Buddharakkita Thero was among those charged in connection with the Prime Minister's assassination.

Ceylon was plunged into political chaos after Bandaranaike's death. In the run-up to the March 1960 elections (the new Prime Minister Wijayananda Dahanayake could not run the government), Sinhala-Buddhist chauvinism reached a peak, though the monks (discredited by the assassination) kept a low profile. Dahanayake, who now headed the Prajatantriya Party, a splinter of the SLFP, pledged to deport Indian Tamils to the last man if returned to office. A new party called the Mahajana Eksath Peramuna (not the same as the coalition in 1956 of which the SLFP had once been part) and another new party, the Dharma Samajiya Party, together promised Buddhism its rightful place in the affairs of the state and to take over all denominational schools run by Christians.

But the elections resulted in a hung Parliament and the government formed by the UNP lasted exactly a month. There were elections again in July 1960. The impact the parties of Sinhala resurgence made at the March poll convinced the two left parties—the Lanka Sama Samaj Party (which is Trotskyite) and the Communist Party—that they could not persist with their demand for parity of Sinhala and Tamil. At these elections Sirimavo Bandaranaike, the fifty-one-year old widow of the assassinated Prime Minister (who how headed the SLFP), though a political novice, trafficked in the credulity of the Sinhala-Buddhist voters and depicted her husband as a champion of the Sinhala language and Buddhist religion. These populist strategies led to her becoming the world's first woman Prime Minister.

Once back in power, the SLFP had ho difficulty pursuing its ethnocentric policies even if it meant flouting the understanding reached with S.J.V. Chelvanayakam's Federal Party at the July poll regarding the status of Tamil. (The Federal Party had helped defeat the UNP in Parliament in March to force an election).

Among the early acts of Sirimavo Bandaranaike was the nationalization of the denominational schools despite Christian opposition. She also forced the pace of Sinhala as the official language of the country.

The Sinhala-Buddhist drive for hegemony was beginning. The link between the language and the religion was strong. The majority of the island's population was Sinhala by ethnicity and language and Buddhist by religion. (Non-Sinhala minorities formed twenty-three per cent of the population in 1981, and non-Buddhists thirty-three per cent). Indeed Buddhism is so identified with Sinhala ethnicity in Sri Lanka that it appears that one cannot exist without the other. Kumari Jayawardene, a radical historian who is a Sinhala says this ideology assumed that the island was the land of the Sinhala-Buddhists and therefore all other groups inhabiting it were 'aliens' out to exploit its people. The Sinhala-Buddhist ideology flowed from three premises: the Sinhalas were the original and true inhabitants of the island and the others were usurpers. (This premise is linked to the myth that the Sinhalas were Aryan immigrants from India's Bengal region while the Tamils were Dravidian.) Secondly, the Sinhala-Buddhist combine in its paranoia sees Sri Lanka as a beleaguered island with no one outside to look to for help, not even other Buddhists who are not ethnically Buddhist. Thirdly, they believe the Sinhalas have a special relationship to Buddhism, having been chosen and ordered by the Buddha to protect the faith.

For all these reasons, the largest non-Sinhala group, the Tamils, were seen as an immediate threat to the Sinhala identity. The Tamils had India to look to and were suspected a prioi of extra-territorial loyalty. Small wonder then that the first Sinhala swipe at the Tamils was to decitizenize and disenfranchise the plantation Tamils in 1948–49 (they were re-enfranchised only in 1989). In 1948 the Tamils had thirty-three per cent of the voting power in the legislature. With the disenfranchisement of the plantation Tamils, this proportion dropped to twenty per cent. The Sinhalas won a two-thirds majority in Parliament rendering the Tamils helpless and unable to block Sinhala policies affecting them.

The 'Sinhala Only' enactment, made possible by the Sinhala majority in Parliament, destroyed the slender chances of bilingualism which could have balanced out the various groups in the plural society that Ceylon was and is. In addition to trying to overcome the language issue through dominance (which goes against the very grain of a plural society) the Sinhalas stressed the uniqueness their own race which they held was the basis of the nation's identity.

The next step was the constitutional endorsement of the Sinhala-Buddhist drive for hegemony. Ceylon's pre-independence constitution had been drafted by Lord Soulbury, an Englishman, and had been adopted by an Order in Council and not by a constituent assembly. It had survived the transition from colonial rule to independence. In the 1950s and the 1960s there was growing Sinhala dissatisfaction with the country's constitution of foreign origin. The demand acquired new relevance with the 1966 *obiter dictum* and decision of the Privy Council in London that section 29 dealing with the rights of minorities was an entrenched provision. ('No. . . law. . . shall. . . make persons of any community or religion liable to disabilities or restrictions to which persons of any community or other communities or religions are made liable; or. . . confer on persons or any community or religion any privilege or advantage which is not conferred on other communities or religions.') This section was a built-in challenge to the Sinhala-Buddhist attempt at integrating minorities with the majority through dominance. But not until the SLFP, in alliance with two leftist parties, returned in 1970, strong enough to be able to give the country a new constitution, could this be scrapped.

With the 1972 constitution, which made Ceylon a republic and gave it a new name (Sri Lanka) section 29 was dumped. The 'Sinhala Only' enactment of 1956 acquired constitutional status through section 7. ('The official language of Sri Lanka shall be Sinhala as provided by the Official Language Act of 1956.') As for Tamil, its use was to be in accordance with the Tamil Language (Special Provisions) Act of 1958 but any regulations under this Act 'shall not in any manner be interpreted as being a provision of the Constitution'. Thus, while Sinhala had a special constitutional status, Tamil owed its limited use to Sinhala sufferance because it was treated as governed by ordinary legislation. The constitution laid down that all laws would be enacted or made in Sinhala with a Tamil translation and that 'the language of the courts. . . shall be Sinhala throughout Sri Lanka and their records . . . shall be in Sinhala.'

The 1972 constitution also accorded special privileges to Buddhism. (Section 6: 'The Republic of Sri Lanka shall give to Buddhism the foremost place and accordingly it shall be the duty of the State to protect and foster Buddhism while assuring to all religions the rights granted by Section 18 (1) (d)'.) All citizens had the right to freedom of thought, conscience and religion. But Buddhism had the 'foremost place'.

But the most flagrant act of discrimination was the distinction the new constitution made between 'persons' and 'citizens' in the matter of fundamental rights. While all persons were equal before the law (in the sense no one could be deprived of life, liberty or security except in accordance with the law) only a citizen had the rights of freedom of thought, conscience and religion, speech, publication, movement, choice of residence and the right to promote his own culture. And citizens could not be discriminated against on grounds of race, religion, caste or sex or arrested, held in custody, imprisoned or detained except in accordance with the law. The losers here were the stateless plantation workers of Indian origin who had lost their citizenship in 1948–49.

The constitution also made the unitary system immutable. Under it, the Tamils were a permanent minority with little chance of being able to change the political system.

In the 1970s amidst a phenomenal expansion of education and slow economic development (which did not generate enough jobs) the battle shifted to access to higher education and jobs and professional opportunities. The Sinhalas saw themselves as a deprived lot *vis-à-vis* the Tamils who had better access to education and could dominate the professions and services. The Sinhala majority now tried affirmative discrimination through the 'standardization' of marks to deprive the Tamils of the advantage they enjoyed, because on average they scored more marks than the Sinhalas. The standardization formula was later replaced by a quota system. In the Sinhala view this was designed to compensate for the disadvantages they were suffering from.

The negative aspects of the Sinhala-Buddhist drive for dominance, through radical integration and affirmative discrimination, alienated the Tamils in the extreme. But the Sinhala actions can be better understood if seen in the light of their fears. Since the early 1950s, the Sinhalas had seen the Tamil demand for federal autonomy as the thin end of the secessionist wedge. The concept of a Tamil homeland, which the federal demand implied, was disquieting to the Sinhalas. Once conceded it could encourage similar demands from other minorities who had territorial enclaves, like the plantation Tamils in the central highlands and the Muslims in the eastern province. So the Tamil homeland concept was sought to be defeated by among other things: the drive for the institutionalizing of the Sinhala language and religion, and the colonization by the Sinhalas of the Tamil-majority provinces to change their demographic composition. In effect, the colonization drive was seen as a twentieth century reconquest of an area once ruled by prince Dutthagamani who had defeated the Tamil king Elara of Anuradhapura in 101 BC to become the first known Sinhala to have ruled the entire island.

In the face of the government's policies, there was little the Tamils could do. Secession has always been the latent option of oppressed minorities in a plural society and the Tamils were driven to it in 1976, hardening Sinhala attitudes further.

The 1977 election was the next turning point in Sri Lanka's politics. The Tamils voted for secession. The Sinhalas rejected the SLFP and its leftist allies. The UNP was returned with a five-sixths majority and gave the island a Gaullist presidential constitution in 1978.

The new constitution only gave further legitimacy to the Sinhala-Buddhist ideology. It reaffirmed the special position Sinhala enjoyed as the sole official language though both Sinhala and Tamil were now recognized as 'national languages' and Tamil was to be the language of administration in the Tamil provinces in addition to Sinhala. Those competing for government jobs had to know Sinhala or learn it but Sinhalas were not required to learn Tamil. Thus the privileged or primary status of Sinhala was untouched.

The new constitution also reaffirmed the special position accorded to Buddhism in the 1972 constitution. It provided for the protection and fostering of the faith. It sought to protect and foster not just Buddhism but the Buddhist *sasana* (the order).

The distinction the 1972 constitution had made between 'persons' and citizens' in the matter of fundamental rights was scrapped. But the new constitution provided for sweeping Emergency provisions which could be invoked to curtail the fundamental rights of all or any section of citizens. There was an in-built arbitrariness to it. The UNP 1977 Election Manifesto had said that the Tamils had grievances and that these would be solved through an All-Party Conference. But now the party said the Tamil problem had found a fair and just solution in the 1978 constitution. (Interestingly, the TULF had no role in framing it because it kept itself out of the drafting committee.)

But most of the reforms existed only on paper—for instance, the new government scrapped the 'standardization' formula, which restricted Tamil access to higher education, but reintroduced it in new garb which did not touch the racial quota system. In employment the Tamils continued to be disadvantaged because Sinhala was the sole official language.

Colonization was another area of conflict. While the Tamils feared that state-sponsored colonization would render them a minority in their traditional homeland, the government maintained that Sri Lanka was one country and its citizens were free to live anywhere. Besides it was also necessary to shift some people to the more productive areas.

Unmet Tamil demands and the impact of the new government's 'open' economic policies—a break with the state-regulated economy under the left-of-centre SLFP rule (1970–71)—were to sharpen the ethnic conflict. Newton Gunasinghe, a Sinhala academic, has tried to establish a correlation between the open economic policy and the frequent ethnic riots. He thinks that, irrespective of who ruled the island, the island had a state-regulated economy from 1956 until 1977. The private sector came under increasing state regulation which was accompanied by a system of quotas, permits and licences—in an environment of import substitution—making state patronage vital for any venture in the private sector. The result was a system of political patronage which meant the business groups closest to political power benefited the most. Because of this a good section of middle-level Sinhala merchants and entrepreneurs and even petty traders moved up the ladder to become industrialists. It also meant an expansion of job opportunities for the Sinhala youth (because of their proximity to power) and the emergence of a new Sinhala management stratum in the growing public. sector. All this together with the stifling of democratic processes gave politics a new anti-Tamil twist.

*

Prime Minister J.R. Jayewardene became the country's first President, winning the election in October 1982. Barely two months later, the 1977 Parliament prolonged itself until 1989—an unconscionable twelve years—through a referendum. The Westminster model prime ministerial form of government had finally (and irrevocably) been replaced by a Gaullist presidential model. The 1978 constitution provides for proportional representation in the place of the British first-past-the-post system. And yet elections were not mandatory until 1989. The country had a Long Parliament, literally. Political articulation became impossible. The new economic model was foundering. And Sinhala frustration found a ready target in the Tamils seen as a threat to their national identity and economic opportunity.

The new philosophy was epitomized in a thesis propounded by Cyril Mathew, one of President Jayewardene's ministers during the July 1983 anti-Tamil massacres. Mathew controlled the ruling party's labour wing, the Jatiya Sevaka Sangamaya (National Workers Organization), which was believed to have played a leading role in the massacres.

Mathew's thesis derives its inspiration from the one associated with Mahathir Bin Mohammed, a Malaysian politician who was later to become his country's Prime Minister. Malaysia has a population which is fifty-three per cent Malay, and thirty-five per cent Chinese. Indians form a smaller percentage. Though the country had had a free enterprise system, Mohammed's thesis was that other racial groups should not be allowed to compete with the dominant ethnic group because the Malays, as the indigenous people, had some inalienable rights others could not claim. The Malay community needed protection and Islam, its religion, had to be promoted. The Malays had nowhere to go. The Chinese had China. The Indians had India.

The pernicious thesis, according to Mathew, had greater relevance and applicability in Sri Lanka than in Malaysia. The Sinhalas formed about seventy per cent of the population as against 12.4 per cent ethnic Tamils and 5.6 per cent Tamils of Indian origin. Yet the Tamils dominated everything, from the professions to trade and commerce. This could not be tolerated forever. Worse, the Tamils wanted a country of their own. According to Mathew the Sinhala people were ready to prevent the division of the country by non-violent or violent methods.

The Mathew thesis with its immense appeal to the Sinhalas helped institutionalize political violence aimed against the Tamils. The secessionist vote of the Tamils provided the alibi for the 1977 riots which were followed by more violence in 1981 and the worst-ever in 1983.

The state's response to the secessionist challenge from the Tamil militant youth was to reduce it to one of terrorism. Measures to contain it were initiated. The Prevention of Terrorism (Temporary Provisions) Act of 1979 was meant to check the growing political violence in the Tamil areas. It was made a permanent measure later. It provided for detention incommunicado for upto eighteen months without access of lawyers and without trial. People could even be detained in army camps. Confession obtained through torture was admissible evidence. If found guilty on trial, prison terms could range from five to twenty years to life.

Sri Lanka justified its Terrorism Act by pointing to other democratic countries including Canada, Australia, the United Kingdom and India who had, in similar situations, enacted similar laws. But the International Commission of Jurists found that in its sweep and arbitrariness Sri Lanka's decree was closer to the South African law against terrorism.

An 'offence' or an 'unlawful act' under the new Sri Lankan law went beyond murder, kidnapping and unlawful possession of arms to include words or signs that could cause 'religious, racial or communal disharmony or feelings of ill-will or hostility' between different communities or groups. This is close to the Terrorism Act of 1967 of South Africa's apartheid regime. The Act defines a terrorist *inter alia* as one who has attempted or committed anything that could 'cause, encourage or further feelings of hostility between the White and other inhabitants.'

In other words the Sri Lankan law could be invoked against advocacy of a separate state or criticism of perceived discrimination against Tamils. Procedurally, the Sri Lankan law violated the constitution and internationally accepted minimum standards of criminal procedure. (The constitution barred retroactive criminal offences and penalties. It also required the production of every detainee before a judge or a competent court if prolonged detention was sought.)

Beginning in July 1979, the government used its new powers with a vengeance on the Tamil militants in the northern province which was the secessionist stronghold. Arrests were indiscriminate, wanton and large-scale. Relatives were not told of the reasons for an arrest or the whereabouts of those held. Often relatives were held hostage until the wanted persons surrendered.

Under the cover of day and night curfew, government forces cordoned off whole villages. Almost every young man in the area was picked up for interrogation and torture under the 'flushing out' operations. The anti-terrorist law was used almost exclusively against the Tamils.

The abrogation of legal safeguards under the law as well as the Emergency Regulations that applied to Tamil areas made torture to extract information possible. In addition extra-judicial and arbitrary killings were a regular feature of the government's drive to crush the secessionists. After the July 1983 anti-Tamil riots, state terror became open and more widespread. Simultaneously the Jayewardene government tried another approach to resolve the escalating conflict (the Tamil militants, though sorely pressed, were giving the Sri Lankan forces an anxious time)—the classic method of using the military option and political parleys at the same time. In fact there had already been negotiations on between the government and Tamil leaders on the devolution of powers at the district level. But the riots ruled out even the moderate TULF's participation in the deliberations. In fact the Members of Parliament belonging to the party had decided to vacate their seats in Parliament but Jayewardene pre-empted them through an enactment to disqualify them if they did not subscribe to an anti-secession oath.

Inevitably the political talks failed after the riots took place so the only option left was the military one. State terror became more intense after March 1984 when Lalith Athulathmudali, who became head of the newly created Ministry of National Security, and doubled as the Deputy Defence Minister, sought the blessings of the Buddhist leadership for his war against terrorism. Unsurprisingly, Athulathmudali received their blessings and the battle against the Tamils escalated though state reprisals were in the main against the civilian population. The pattern had set itself—state terror against the civilians, guerrilla retaliation, and another wave of state terror. Thousands fled into the jungle or crossed the sea to India. The fate of Tamils if they remained was clear, because Jayewardene had declared that if Tamil terrorism continued there would be a thousand July 1983s.

India was under heavy political pressure at home to intervene militarily. In fact a contingency plan for intervention was ready and even the units were earmarked in March–April 1984 for a task force in support of the Tamil guerrillas. But the mission did not materialize mainly because of the international implications of such an action. There was also the possibility, in the event of Indian intervention, of a massacre of the Tamils outside the Tamil provinces, including the plantation Tamils of Indian origin, when Sinhala reprisals began.

It wasn't as though the Sinhalas were blind to the possibility of an Indian invasion. Jayewardene said in April: 'If India does invade us, then that is the end of the Tamils in the country. Now we have only a guerrilla war in the North. . . are you going to stop the slaughter of the Tamils in Colombo?'

The Indian forces stayed put and Jayewardene stepped up his military campaign perhaps in the hope that he would be able to negotiate from a position of strength. As the war grew, the Sri Lankan army was expanded and modernized. Friendly countries (including China, the United Kingdom, Pakistan and South Korea) pumped in sophisticated arms in addition to those being bought on the international arms trade circuit. Israeli agencies (Mossad and Shin Beth) trained the Sri Lankan forces and intelligence agencies. And the Pakistanis trained a special task force and British mercenaries (Special Air Services veterans) were recruited through a shadowy Channel Island-based firm called Keeny Meany Services.

Despite all this the government was not winning the war, especially in the Tamil provinces, which were increasingly coming under the control of the guerrillas. Jayewardene, quite desperate now, tried another tack. His government announced plans to settle Sinhalas in the Tamil provinces, especially in the strategic Trincomalee district which provided the crucial geographic link between the two provinces. 'If we do not occupy the border, the border will come to us,' he said.

But the Tamil guerrillas acted first. Dressed in army uniforms, they struck in Anuradhapura, the ancient Buddhist city which is outside the Tamil homeland. About 150 Buddhist pilgrims were massacred.

Jayewardene's threat of 'occupying' the border seemed hollow now, when even his ability to protect the Sinhala heartland was in doubt. Worse, he faced a new threat to his power because a strong Buddhist opposition was building up against him for his lapses. In the short term the government forces retaliated with fiercer reprisals against the Tamils, but Jayewardene had begun signalling frantically to New Delhi for mediation. In June he was in India for talks with Prime Minister Rajiv Gandhi. They agreed on immediate action to defuse the situation so that 'all forms of violence should abate and finally cease'.

In July 1983 Jayewardene had seen no role for India in Sri Lanka's ethnic crisis. Now he saw India as a major partner in any negotiation that would take place. A cease-fire was arranged on India's initiative to enable talks to be held directly between the Sri Lankan government and all the relevant Tamil groups—the Tamil United Liberation Front and the five major militant organizations (the Liberation Tigers of Tamil Eelam, the People's Liberation Organization of Tamil Eelam, the Eelam Revolutionary Organization of Students, the Eelam People's Revolutionary Liberation Front, and the Tamil Eelam Liberation Organization). Two round of deliberations in July–August 1985 in Thimphu, the capital of Bhutan, achieved little. But for the first time Sri Lanka was talking to the 'terrorists' across the table.

The Sri Lankan delegation of three officials, headed by Jurist H.W. Jayewardene, the President's younger brother, came to Thimphu with an aura of confidence flowing from a perception that the Tamil groups were divided. But all the six groups rejected the draft proposals for autonomy as inadequate as the basis of negotiations. They were united about the cardinal principles on which any meaningful proposals should be based. As we've seen earlier, the Sri Lankans rejected the demands when they were spelt out. One was the recognition of the Tamil national identity. Another was the Tamil right to a homeland. Sri Lanka was prepared to recognize the Tamil grievances no more. It also saw an inconsistency in the Tamil claim to be a 'distinct nationality' and their willingness to settle for something less than secession. The Sri Lankan delegation's reasoning was that the nationality of an individual signified the quality of his being the subject of a certain state and owing allegiance to it in return for protection by it. If 'distinct nationality' meant separateness from other communities and racial groups by virtue of a difference in the obligation of their allegiance, it meant the Tamils wanted a state of their own. The 'homeland' concept implied the break-up of the island and the denial of the right of others to live in it—this violated the fundamental rights and freedoms enshrined in Sri Lanka's constitution. The third condition was the recognition of the Tamil right to self-determination. As far as it implied the right to secession, it was unacceptable.

The fourth principle (citizenship rights for all the Tamils who had made Sri Lanka their homeland) assumed that the ethnic Tamil groups represented at Thimphu could speak for the 'stateless' plantation Tamils of Indian origin. Sri Lanka would not recognize the right of these groups to represent the plantation Tamils who had their own organization, the Ceylon Workers Congress, whose leader, S. Thondaman, was a minister in the Jayewardene government.

There was little common ground at Thimphu. Sri Lanka, it was clear, was just buying time through the June cease-fire and the July–August 1985 negotiations. And, most duplicitously, the government forces resumed their offensive even as the Thimphu talks were on, massacring Tamil civilians (211 of them at Vavuniya and twenty-five to thirty in Trincomalee), as they ostensibly hunted the guerrillas.

Sri Lanka came up with another set of proposals at the end of August after consultations with Indian experts.

The TULF also drew up an alternative set of proposals in December. But the long-drawn-out negotiations, steered by the mild-mannered, excessively decorous approach of the Indian mediators, robbed the deliberations of clarity, purpose and direction; they soon proved inconclusive.

At the beginning of 1986, Sri Lanka's immediate objective was to re-assert its authority in the Jaffna peninsula, controlled by the guerillas, and, in particular, Jaffna city which was the symbol of Tamil militant authority and power.

The preparation for the Sri Lankan offensive began with the 'notification' of a one-kilometre-radius security zone around every one of the sixty-odd military camps that dotted the northern and eastern provinces. The new provision gave the armed forces powers to search people and vessels and arrest or shoot at anyone without provocation within the designated zone. The measure was ostensibly to prevent guerrilla mortar attacks on the camps (and mainly the garrison in the Jaffna fort), but in actual fact it was used to inflict heavy civilian casualties and destroy property. The government was not too apologetic at the resulting uproar. 'Anywhere in the world, the army has no choice but to retaliate when attacked. . . . When you fight a battle you do not give territory. You take territory,' said Athulathmudali.

Several small towns were within the security zone limit because the Jaffna peninsula is densely populated and were therefore vulnerable to sniper fire by the troops. Worst affected was Jaffna because under the shadow of its fort was the city's most congested quarter, with hospitals, churches and temples, all within the mortar range of the garrison.

The guerrillas tried to pin the government forces down to their camps by mining the approaches to prevent the movement of convoys. The government forces retaliated with bombing raids on civilian targets in Jaffna city. The aerial attacks were actually a desperate measure to overcome the guerrillas on the ground because the armed forces had failed miserably on this score despite the advantage the security zones gave them.

By April 1986 Jayewardene was appealing to India for a new initiative because the Aid Sri Lanka Consortium was to meet in a few weeks to decide the year's package and it was unlikely to endorse the military drive. (When the Consortium met in June it pledged an aid increase but voiced concern over the adverse effects of the continuing conflict on the economy and urged an early political settlement of the ethnic issue).

While seeking renewed Indian mediation Jayewardene was also blaming India for the conflict. 'They accuse Pakistan of helping Sikh terrorists', he said, alluding to the secessionist problem in India's Punjab state. 'We have accused India (of helping the Tamil terrorists) and they have not denied it. We know (Indian help) is there, we can prove it is there', he stormed and added, 'We must have a military solution to a military problem. What is Rajiv (Gandhi) doing in Punjab?' Jayewardene's tirades amounted to charging India with dishonesty: urging a political solution while helping Tamil militants with arms, training and sanctuaries.

Jayewardene came up with another set of proposals in June and said this was 'the decisive phase in the achievement of a political solution.' However, the provincial councils he was offering in this package as the unit of devolution, was only the minimum demand of the Tamils and not the maximum. But it was a start: the President was recognizing for the first time that Sri Lanka was a multi-racial and multi-religious society.

Obviously at India's instance, the TULF resumed negotiations with Colombo and there was some agreement on the grounds for discussion but there was no settlement. India tried to keep the dialogue going and in the process Sri Lanka gained time. To not much avail, as it turned out, for by November, the Sri Lankan troops were losing on every front to the guerrillas of the LTTE. Jayewardene quickly changed his stand. As a first step he made his participation in the South Asian Association for Regional Co-operation (a seven-nation regional grouping) summit in Bangalore conditional to a political solution of the Tamil problem. This had some effect for India put pressure on the LTTE (the other groups were not pressurized) and its leader Velupillai Prabhakaran to come to the negotiating table and work out an agreement. But Prabhakaran ruled out a compromise, went to Jaffna from Madras and the guerrillas stepped up their campaign.

Jayewardene offered a new package, known as the '19 December proposals,' but he reneged on this as well saving the Tamil groups the trouble of rejecting it.

Meanwhile, the decision of the LTTE to take over civil administration in the Jaffna peninsula from 1 January 1987 was used by Sri Lanka to impose an economic blockade of the area and launch a new military offensive. This was planned as a five-pronged drive on the Jaffna peninsula. The LTTE effectively controlled all the other districts of the northern province—Vavuniya, Mannar, Kilinochchi and Mullaitivu—and hoped to extend its hold to the eastern province (where it had had to compete with the EPRLF in November–December 1986). The Sri Lankan offensive, which began in February 1987, aimed to narrow down the area of the guerrillas' operation and finally eliminate them. The armed forces succeeded in forcing the guerrillas to abandon their bases in the eastern province. The government forces also managed to clear the area south of the Elephant Pass—which provides the tenuous link between the northern mainland province and the Jaffna peninsula. Here they set up a network of fortified camps. Alongside they began another offensive in the northern province. The plan was to advance on a triple trajectory path and destroy all guerrilla bases *en route* and establish new camps while strengthening the old ones. Eight thousand troops already stationed in the province along with a further ten thousand supported by armoured vehicles, artillery and air support began the operation—a push across the four districts of the provinces which would be a prelude to the assault on the Jaffna peninsula. Sia-Marchetti planes and Bell helicopter gunships bombed and strafed areas followed by artillery and mortar shelling to drive the civilian population out. The guerrillas were helpless against the assault because they possessed only low-calibre weapons. Their mortar and artillery fire was unable to check the offensive. Gradually they were driven into the Jaffna peninsula and the Sri Lankan forces regained the four mainland districts of the northern province with minimum military and civilian casualties.

Now it was a matter of taking Jaffna. 'Just one week is enough,' a military analyst in Colombo said in April. But the high political cost of the option appeared to inhibit the Jayewardene government and it refrained from the decisive assault. In retrospect, there seems to be no doubt that the Sri Lankan forces could have taken Jaffna then if they had pressed their advantage—so heavily did they outnumber and outgun what was still a small, ill-equipped force. From July 1983, when the army was only 12,000 strong and mainly occupied with ceremonial duties, it now had 70,000 men under arms including the Pakistani-trained Special Task Force and paramilitary forces. Its weapons systems had been upgraded and mobilized and the men manning them were well versed in their operation. The other side had an estimated 2,000 guerrillas of the LTTE, with 3,000 to 4,000 skilled helpers to support them. Victory would have been fairly certain for Sri Lanka if it had made the final push for Jaffna then. However, Sri Lanka dithered and Indian mediation efforts, which had been suspended in February, because Sri Lanka was unrelenting over its economic blockade of the peninsula and was going ahead with its military offensive, were resumed in late March. India told Sri Lanka that the militant groups based in Madras were willing to talk peace on the basis of the 19 December proposals if the climate for it—the lifting of the blockade, a properly observed cease-fire and the release of political prisoners—was created.

Unrelated to India's suggestion, but aimed at strengthening it, Sri Lanka announced a ten-day unilateral cease-fire to coincide with Sinhala and Tamil festivals in April. But the massacre of 127 Sinhala civilians on Good Friday (blamed on the LTTE which disowned it) ended the cease-fire abruptly. Four days later, on 21 April 1987, a car bomb explosion in Colombo's busy Pettah commercial quarter left 150 dead.

Military operations, including the bombing of civilian and suspected terrorist areas, began again as the cease-fire collapsed. Now, if nothing else, Sri Lanka could tell the world that the Tamil guerrillas preferred a military solution even if India was earnest about a political settlement. And, given the way matters were evolving, the responsibility of bringing the major militant group to the conference table soon devolved upon India.

On the eve of the short-circuited April cease-fire, Athulathmudali had said that if the proposed round of talks ('the final one') failed, Sri Lanka would have only the military option. After the cease-fire Jayewardene said his government could destroy the whole of the Jaffna peninsula (with a population of over 800,000 people) in a day if it wanted to.

Beginning 25 May 1987 a pincer movement on Jaffna city (of under 200,000 people) began. Air strikes were launched against suspected guerrilla hide-outs (in Sri Lankan double-speak this meant civilian targets). But again Sri Lanka stopped short of taking the city. Athulathmudali said later: 'We (didn't take it because we) knew that the Indian concern was over Jaffna town.' But this was not the only reason.

The other major reason for Sri Lanka's reluctance to take Jaffna was the high military cost involved. Jayewardene's own military advisers had told him that it was a hopeless war, and trying to take the city would have meant a long military involvement with no hope of success.

But the decisive reason was probably the risk of rousing India's ire, for any assault on Jaffna would have resulted in heavy civilian casualties which would have prompted India to act—it had already tried to tell Colombo, through a paradrop of food and other relief material over Jaffna on 4 June 1987, that its inaction should not be taken for granted and it would not allow the city to fall. Besides the demands in India for immediate military intervention to prevent the imminent genocide in Jaffna, there would also be a sharp international reaction to the bloody episode that the battle for the city would have meant—Sri Lanka had to take all this into account.

A surprise India-Sri Lanka agreement on 29 July to end the ethnic conflict broke the uneasy military stalemate that prevailed.

The agreement, in retrospect, should not have surprised anyone for it was the only practical way out of a messy situation for both India and the Jayewardene government. Of the several compulsions (that lay behind the actions of both sides) that led to the agreement, the first was political. India's airdrop of supplies, in clear violation of Sri Lanka's airspace, was an open challenge to Sri Lanka and a warning that India could not be ignored with impunity by countries within its sphere of influence. For his part, next to the Anuradhapura massacre by Tamil militants in early 1985 (which forced him to seek Indian mediation), the paradrop was the biggest setback to Jayewardene's credibility at home. His ability to win the war was in doubt and if he wanted a political solution his skill as a negotiator was seen as even more doubtful.

The second compulsion in terms of the Sri Lankans was that the predominantly Sinhala armed forces were ill at ease with the idea of fighting the Tamil guerrillas in their terrain, amidst an unfriendly civilian population. It would mean getting bogged down in a never-ending operation. And Jayewardene had every reason to fear a coup by an army unwilling to fight a war with little chance of success and every likelihood of heavy casualties.

The third reason was economic. After its 1977 election victory the UNP ended the left-of-centre populism of the Sirimavo Bandaranaike-led United Front (1970–77). The island lurched rightward, opting for a liberalized policy regimen which pleased the World Bank. Soon Sri Lanka was the model of a Third World country developing without tears, thanks to foreign aid backing and 'open' policies to promote export-led growth.

A policy crisis was inevitable but the heavy military burden imposed by the ethnic conflict hastened it. The long-term effects of the war since 1983 are difficult to estimate. The Gross Domestic Product grew normally by six per cent a year until 1983. It dropped by one per cent in 1984 and by another percentage point in 1985. This taken together could mean there was a ten to fifteen per cent downslide in the country's growth potential.

In May 1986, Finance Minister Ronnie de Mel had projected a Gross Domestic Product growth of 4.5 per cent a year for the next five years (1986–90) because of the escalating defence spending—ten per cent of the total budget in 1985 against 4.5 per cent in 1984 and 3.5 per cent in 1983. The budget for 1986 had projected defence spending to continue at ten per cent but it turned out to be fifteen per cent. A confidential World Bank Report in 1986 underlined the difficulties of keeping government spending in check. More tellingly, the country's budget deficit had risen from Rs 21.5 billion in 1985 to Rs 29.8 billion in 1986, and was projected at a marginally lower Rs 28.5 billion for 1987—again largely due to the growing expenditure on defence. Sri Lanka's aid-donors grew wary of pumping funds into its economy in order to release domestic resources to fight a war which by all indications would be near impossible to win. All of them favoured a political solution.

Also, the economic crisis compounded social and political tensions. The Janatha Vimukti Peramuna (JVP), the ultra-left Sinhala youth group was active again, though it had been declared illegal since 1983 and its leader Rohana Wijeveera was still underground. By mid-1987 Jayewardene was under siege on every side. The Tamil militants controlled the north with the armed forces trying somewhat ineffectually to overcome them. The Sinhala youth challenge was building up in the south. There were dissensions in his own party. The gestures from across the Palk Straits were menacing. And his plea for support from other nations, including the United States and China, did not fructify; instead he was told to seek a *modus vivendi* with India and settle the ethnic issue. The absence of the United States condemnation of India's 4 June 1987 blandishment must have been particularly galling but Jayewardene finally got the message and the 29 July India-Sri Lanka agreement was born.

The agreement (which had been hastily cobbled together) had political, military and strategic components. It called for a limited devolution of power to the Tamil areas—this was Jayewardene's responsibility. In return India would secure Tamil consensus in favour of the agreement and overcome any military opposition to it. In effect India was required to demilitarize the conflict by means of a peace-keeping role.

The agreement secured some of India's strategic interests. Sri Lanka was to deny the use of the Trincomalee harbour to any third country to the detriment of India's interests. The oil tank farm near Trincomalee was to be developed jointly by Sri Lanka and India keeping other countries out. The involvement of foreign agencies and elements in the anti-guerrilla operations would end.

Sinhala acceptance of the agreement was taken for granted; at any rate it was assumed that Jayewardene would secure its political acceptance at home. However, the vast mass of Sinhalas, egged on by the Buddhist clergy and the JVP, reacted violently to the agreement and it could only be signed after an island-wide curfew had been clamped down and censorship on news imposed.

The opposition to the agreement had two key elements. The first was that the proposals for the unification of the two Tamil provinces (though subject to a referendum in the eastern province) and the powers sought to be vested in the united province were seen as a 'sell-out' to the Tamils, since they were to be given a virtual Tamil Eelam. This Sinhala opinion could not reconcile itself to, for in its view the Tamil provinces would have to be colonized to achieve a population ratio corresponding to that which obtained in the rest of the island—about seventy per cent Sinhala and twenty-six per cent others. The Sinhalas also resented the vast powers being vested in the provincial councils which would in effect make the Tamils a privileged minority, even if the merger of the two provinces was not translated into a long-term reality.

The second major aspect of the opposition was to the new pattern of Sri Lanka-India relations the agreement tried to institutionalize. The imminent arrival of the Indian Peace-Keeping Force in the Tamil provinces was seen by the Sinhalas as compromising national sovereignty (with some of India's security concerns being met through voluntary limits on Sri Lanka's sovereignty). And the bright lights of the two Indian Navy frigates anchored off Colombo harbour to act in the event of a coup was a disturbing early warning that India's role could grow beyond merely keeping the peace and demilitarizing the ethnic conflict.

However, Jayewardene capitalized on the confusion among the Buddhist clergy which, though spearheading the opposition to the agreement, was unsure about the means of protest it should use. (The elder Mahanayakas counselled moderation and restraint but the younger monks were less inhibited and forged links with the JVP.) To add to the incertitude among those opposing the agreement, the Sri Lanka Freedom Party, the main Sinhala opposition force, was not too sure that any campaign it launched would not strengthen the extremist JVP (which saw in the agreement the vindication of its stand that Indian 'expansionism' was the real threat and that democratic functioning was impossible in Sri Lanka).

However, the respite Jayewardene gained, by the initial confusion and antagonism among those opposing the agreement, soon ended. The initiative passed to the JVP which thrived on the opposition to the Indian military presence, a feeling which cut across political, ethnic and ideological lines. Soon the SLFP backed it and most members of Jayewardene's UNP began endorsing the anti-agreement campaign in private. Jayewardene, with his captive four-fifths majority in Parliament[*] could certainly endorse the agreement but it was obvious he had failed to convince the Sinhala majority, particularly the youth, that he had not given India a permanent caveat on the island's sovereignty. His time had come.

*

The Queen's Club on Colombo's elegant Buller's Road once used to be rendezvous of the island's planters when tea was king in the high noon of the British Empire. In 1972 one of its panelled halls provided the incongruous setting for a sedition trial. Armoured personnel carriers guarded the entrance, while inside, the manacled Rohana Wijeveera, a drop-out of Moscow's Patrice Lumumba University and the leader of the Janatha Vimukti Peramuna (JVP), charged along with others of spearheading the 1971 'Che Guevarist' insurrection, thunderously

---

* In a slick move the President had legitimized the four-fifth's majority his party had won in the December 1982 election by holding a referendum, two months after he took office, to extend the life of Parliament by six years. In fact, a number of Sri Lanka's problems in later years flowed from the fact that Jayewardene could bulldoze his way through most of the issues the country faced with his brute majority, paying little heed to the vestigial opposition.

denounced the system, trying to turn the accuser (the state) into the accused.

The JVP had been organizing clandestinely since the mid-1960s but was heard of vaguely only during the 1970 elections when some of its members were held by the United National Party (UNP) government on the charge of plotting to disrupt the elections that year. (Actually, at the time, the JVP cadres were campaigning actively for the Trotskyite and Communist candidates against the UNP.)

The 1971 JVP insurrection that failed was one of the many instances of the growing social and economic discontent finding expression in a rash of strikes and demonstrations outside the structures of the traditional left—Trotskyite and Communist (which had sought accommodation within the system by participating in the government resulting from the 1970 elections).

In an attempt to dispel the discontent, the United Front government (which was to rule the island until 1977) carried out land reforms but these were limited and applied mainly to the plantations leaving the landlord and rich-peasant-owned rice farms untouched. The government also nationalized some banks, transport services and the Colombo port, started a few industries and imposed stringent foreign exchange controls and licensing procedures, but ultimately proved unable to control the growing incidence of unemployment.

Despite its knowledge of the unhappiness in the nation, the government, the opposition and many other sections of opinion were stunned when the 1971 JVP insurrection did take place in a nation that had never known armed struggle or political violence. The uprising threw the traditional left into a turmoil because the challenge to the system came from militant youth described by the media as 'Che Guevarist' (a term the JVP never applied to themselves). The insurrection, in variance to the many myths that surround it, was an ambitious and organized attempt at seizure of power by a left-oriented cross-section of the underprivileged youth, caught up in a system alien to their lives, and under pressure to achieve ends which they could not identify with. It coincided, too, with the birth of militancy among the Tamil youth of the north who were also plunged into the despair of unemployment. But the two movements were unrelated.

Though it claimed to be Marxist-Leninist, the JVP's political understanding at the time seemed limited. Neo-colonialism and its appendages in Ceylon (it was not Sri Lanka yet) was its professed target. It was also opposed to 'Indian expansionism' which, in Ceylon's context, reflected the Sinhala-Buddhist hatred of the plantation Tamils.

The JVP's membership comprised Sinhala youth, Buddhist as well as Christian, of the post-independence generation, in the age-group 15–25, from the low country as well as the Kandyan highlands. The group's members had grown up in an environment of Sinhala nationalism, promoted by official educational and cultural policies. They were mostly first-generation-educated, jobless school-leavers (there was only a sprinkling of graduates and undergraduates in the JVP then) who had rejected the ideology of the traditional left and saw little use in the parliamentary system and electoral processes. Their immediate disillusionment was with the broken promises of the United Front government.

But the insurrection, which began with attacks on police stations, mostly in the south-west, was destined to fail because it lacked a social base and its influence was limited to the central and southern regions of the country. The trade unions were impervious to the group's aspirations, as were the well-organized Tamil-speaking workers of the plantation sector. The JVP also did not reckon with the state's ability to get military help from countries as politically disparate as India and China. For all these reasons, the insurrection did not last more than two weeks. But, however short-lived it may have been, it showed up the vulnerability of the system. In the aftermath, the armed forces panicked and resorted to mass arrests, torture and summary execution. At least 8,000 youth were killed, though some estimates put the total number of deaths at 15,000.

Though the brief-lived insurrection was quickly over, the causes that had provoked it remained. Fifteen years later the JVP was again a major force, led by the same man, Rohana Wijeveera, but composed of a new generation of youth motivated by a more strident Sinhala-Buddhist ideology in the context of the exacerbated ethnic conflict. In mid-1983 when the anti-Tamil riots broke out, the JVP was an open political party; however it was soon proscribed for its alleged complicity in the riots which were sought to be depicted as part of an elaborate foreign conspiracy (no foreign country was identified) to overthrow the Jayewardene Government. (Also proscribed were the Nava Sama Samaj Party, which is Trotskyite, and the Communist Party, though the proscription of the JVP alone continued till early 1988.)

The situation in the wake of the July 1983 riots strengthened the anti-Tamil stand of the proscribed party. Its current ideology on the ethnic question, propagated through a pamphlet and a cassette tape is broadly this: the objective reasons for the conflict are the geographical location of Sri Lanka (and the influence of the contradictions that obtain in the Indian sub-continent), the conflict between the Sinhala and Tamil national entities (which have a distinct origin as well as language and culture-based differences) and the island's proximity to the Indian mainland; the subjective reasons are successive invasions from south India in the past and the British policy of treating the nationalities in Sri Lanka as separate groups to ensure their own dominance of the island.

In addition the JVP sees another factor as crucial to the situation—i.e. the region is vital to the strategic interests of the United States against the Soviet Union. Since India is seen as partial to the Soviet Union, the United States, charged with supporting the Assam and Punjab separatist movements in India, wants India's Tamil Nadu to secede and incorporate Sri Lanka's northern and eastern provinces into it. And who wants Tamil Eelam besides the United States? The JVP's answer is: 'The capitalist class in Tamil Nadu, the racist Tamil capitalist class and the racist Tamil petit bourgeois of Sri Lanka.'

The JVP in sum represents the typical extra-constitutional challenge that arises when governments have made a hash of political solutions to a country's problems. In Sri Lanka, developments since 1977—cycles of repression and resentment and the deflection of democracy—have unfortunately conferred a premium on extra-constitutional alternatives like the one represented by the JVP.

*

Ironically, the India-Sri Lanka agreement aimed at solving the island's ethnic conflict only helped revive the Janatha Vimukti Peramuna (JVP) through a Sinhala backlash. The agreement might have found limited Sinhala acceptance had not the Indian Peace-Keeping Force (IPKF) run into difficulties trying to marginalize the Liberation Tigers of Tamil Eelam (LTTE). This reinforced the Sinhala apprehension that India was deliberately not achieving its military objective because it wanted to prolong its stay indefinitely.

The first swipe at President J.R. Jayewardene, from within his government, came on the last day of 1987, when the IPKF's drive against the LTTE was barely eleven weeks old. His Prime Minister Ranasinghe Premadasa, a known critic of the India-Sri Lanka agreement said in one of his public speeches: 'Why should the neighbour be brought to scold our quarrelling children?' Another critic of the Indian military involvement was the hawkish National Security Minister, Lalith Athulathmudali, 'The people want the IPKF to go,' he said, and added: 'Let's face it. The experience all over the world is that external forces come to a country to pursue their own ends.'

Gamini Jayasuriya, the Minister for Food, was the first minister to quit the government over the accord. He said ninety-five per cent of the ruling party's MPs were unhappy but stayed on because they did not want to relinquish power. He was followed by the high-profile Ronnie de Mel, the Finance Minister, initially an ardent supporter of the agreement but now a disillusioned man. But the crowning irony was that President Jayewardene was the chief guest at India's Republic Day festivities in the last week of January despite the sharp Indian Tamil reaction (by now the IPKF's role had become an issue at home, even in the ruling Congress Party and the government) to the invitation.

As Jayewardene began his final year in office, the general Sinhala mood was one of betrayal and the uneasy feeling that his inability to fight the LTTE had compromised Sri Lanka's sovereignty in the form of the IPKF presence. The proximity of the presidential and parliamentary elections (due by early 1989) forced this issue to the fore and made Jayewardene's position very shaky.

The Sri Lanka Freedom Party (SLFP), which aspired to replace the United National Party (UNP), saw in the criticism of Jayewardene an opportunity and began befriending the JVP, now in the ascendant again, as the antipathy to Tamil aspirations hardened. Interestingly, in 1971, the year of its failed insurrection, the JVP had recognized the Tamil people as a nation and victims of the Sinhala majority oppression. The JVP had held then that the Tamils were entitled to self-determination, including the right to secede. Over a decade later, in his 1982 presidential campaign, its candidate, Wijeveera, ducked the issue, maintaining silence.

Then, after it was driven underground, the JVP opted for the rhetoric of Sinhala extremism which opposed any concession to the Tamils. Tamil activities were denounced as part of an imperialist plot to break up Sri Lanka. Wijeveera now said the only way to resolve the ethnic conflict was to dilute the concentration of Tamils in the northern and eastern provinces by dispersing them across the country so they had no 'homeland' to claim.

The new-look JVP directed its appeal to the younger Buddhist clergy, to students, and the unemployed youth. It captured student unions in most campuses, infiltrated the armed forces and the civil services and trained its cadres for violent activities when the government was fully occupied with fighting the Tamil guerrillas.

Until the 1987 India-Sri Lanka agreement, the JVP's terror campaign was limited to eliminating the dissidents in its ranks or picking off cadres of leftist organizations competing with it for influence among the Sinhala youth. However, just before the India-Sri Lanka agreement was bloodied in the Tamil areas, the JVP had already begun stoking Sinhala opposition to concessions to the Tamils. Its battle-cry in the new role it had found for itself was, 'Motherland or death!' The main enemy was India and its war was directed at all those responsible for the 'surrender' to India—and this naturally meant all those who supported the agreement. Since the SLFP was not among them, it was an ally, though its leader, Sirimavo Bandaranaike, had been the Prime Minister who crushed the 1971 insurrection.

When a young naval rating made an attempt on the life of the Indian Prime Minister the day after the India-Sri Lanka agreement, the JVP hailed the rating as a patriot. Later, it claimed the credit for the bomb explosion in Parliament House that was aimed at eliminating President Jayewardene and his colleagues.

Now that it had found a popular issue the JVP was encouraged to spread its own brand of violence. A systematic assassination campaign began—among the victims were Harsha Abeyawardene, President of the UNP, and Vijaya Kumaranatunga, the film-star son-in-law of Sirimavo Bandaranaike and President of the Sri Lanka Mahajana Party. A good number of its victims were Communist functionaries.

With the JVP succeeding in its effort to destroy the politicians who supported the agreement, Jayewardene's isolation was near complete. And his effort to convince the people was made even harder by the attitude of many of his party followers who sympathized with the JVP cause. At this point Sri Lanka was more explosive than ever before: not only had Jayewardene failed to sell the agreement to the Sinhalas but India was having a hard time getting the Tamils to see its merits as well.

Yet, putting a brave face on the matter (he really didn't have an option, with India breathing down his neck and having committed himself), Jayewardene enacted the legislation to create councils in each of the nine provinces. Power was to be decentralized through provincial councils. The SLFP abstained from the provincial elections because it wanted a new Parliament elected first and was opposed to the councils in principle. The main contest in the seven Sinhala majority provinces was therefore between the UNP and the four-party United Socialist Alliance (of the Sri Lanka Mahajana Party, the Communist Party, the Lanka Sama Samaj Party and the Nava Sama Samaj Party). The JVP went all out to disrupt the elections, with a campaign of terror to back its boycott call. However, there was a good voter turnout in the first four provinces that went to the polls to elect their councils (in April 1988) and this was interpreted as a rebuff to the JVP. But the turnout was less impressive in the next three provinces to vote, and despite an aggregate of sixty-three per cent for the seven provinces, it was a miserable thirty per cent in the southern province, a JVP stronghold. There were no elections in the Tamil provinces because India could not ensure conditions conducive to their taking place. The completion of the elections (in the seven Sinhala provinces between April and June) showed the irony of the situation—the councils had been devised to meet Tamil demands, and to transfer power to them as part of a devolution package (which incidentally was to benefit the non-Tamil provinces too), but what really happened was the Sinhalas got the councils while the Tamil provinces remained as mired in conflict as ever.

However, the UNP victory in all the seven Sinhala provinces was claimed as a triumph for Jayewardene and the India-Sri Lanka agreement. But then the only other contender in the polls, the United

Socialist Alliance, was no opponent of the agreement either, and for all the trumpeting it was obvious the UNP would have to come up with some very good ideas to end the conflict if it wanted to remain in power.

*

The run-up to Sri Lanka's presidential election began well before the amalgamated Tamil-majority north-eastern province finally elected its council in November. The United National Party had chosen Prime Minister Ranasinghe Premadasa as its candidate against the Sri Lanka Freedom Party's predictable choice of Sirimavo Bandaranaike. Premadasa fired the first shot in the campaign on 28 September by demanding a friendship treaty (between India and Sri Lanka) in the place of the India-Sri Lanka agreement. It was quickly obvious that relations with India would be the key issue on which the elections would be lost or won.

On 23 October 1988, the JVP launched a campaign for the dissolution of Parliament, backing it with strikes and demonstrations. Four leading Mahanayakas (Buddhist high priests) joined the fray demanding that presidential and parliamentary elections be held simultaneously under a caretaker government. Jayewardene responded with a conditional offer to dissolve Parliament, if the JVP abjured violence.

On 6 November, Jayewardene met Sirimavo Bandaranaike to seek her help out of the 'national crisis'. A day later he was desperate and threatened that India would come to his help if the JVP tried to topple his government.

By now the island was virtually crippled by the strikes and demonstrations that had swept it. Shoot-at-sight orders were issued on 10 November. The next day the government proclaimed that illegal strikes would be punished with death and decreed a state of Emergency. The army was given wide-ranging powers to tackle the unrest. The near-civil-war conditions that prevailed showed how far Rajiv Gandhi's adventurism had isolated Jayewardene and sharpened the ethnic polarization in the island. All shades of opinion had united against India's military involvement in the island.

*

Belying all expectations, the presidential election on 19 December 1988 did not reflect the polarization evident in the run-up to the election. If anything the polarization was arrested as allies drifted apart and clashed with each other. For instance, it had first seemed that Sirimavo Bandaranaike, a friend of the left until 1977, had united the non-left opposition, including the as yet untested JVP, behind her candidature.

During the year that preceded the presidential poll, the UNP cadres had been the target of the JVP violence and the SLFP, known for its anti-India posture, its undeclared ally.

After demonstrating its prowess at disturbing elections in the Sinhala provinces (which chose their councils between April and June 1988) the JVP declared that it was willing to participate in the presidential elections but only on its terms: it wanted the India-Sri Lanka agreement scrapped, the IPKF sent back and President Jayewardene out of office before the poll so that he would not be able to rig the election. The farthest Jayewardene could go was to announce elections to Parliament on 16 February 1989. The JVP also rejected Jayewardene's offer of an interim government, conditional on its participation in it, and called for the elections to be boycotted.

The JVP-SLFP parted ways at this stage. There had been a marriage of convenience between the two at the time of the council elections in the Sinhala provinces—the SLFP had abstained from them and the JVP had tried to enforce its boycott. But in the presidential election Sirimavo Bandaranaike did not want to lose her last chance of a political come-back after her party's 1977 rout and over a decade in the political wilderness.

This only strengthened the JVP's determination to disrupt the election because it was keen on weakening the SLFP (whose social base overlapped its own) in the hope of replacing it as the alternative to the UNP. The JVP directed its violence not only against the UNP and the SLFP but also against the third contender, Ossie Abeyagoonesekara of the United Socialist Alliance (comprising his Sri Lanka Mahajana Party, the Communist Party, the Lanka Sama Samaj Party, and the Nava Sama Samaj Party), because he supported the India-Sri Lanka agreement unconditionally (Premadasa wanted it replaced by a treaty and Bandaranaike wanted its abrogation).

It was a bizarrely abnormal campaign for a country that had won independence without a shot being fired. Most people were not sure the voting would take place to schedule on 19 December. It was rumoured that Bandaranaike would bow out of the contest because of the violence that had accompanied the campaign. But the election did take place and Bandaranaike was still in the running as the country went to the polls.

It is still a matter of speculation as to who lost the most because of the low voter turnout caused by the JVP disruption—a mere fifty-five per cent in a country proud of its political consciousness. This was a sharp drop from the eighty-one per cent at the 1982 presidential elections and the eighty-six per cent at the 1977 parliamentary elections. In fact, Premadasa just managed to squeak past the requisite fifty per cent of the vote, which is required in Sri Lanka, to avert a second-count. He polled 50.43 of the vote against Bandaranaike's 44.95 and the distant third runner Abeyagoonesekara's 4.63 per cent.

Although the JVP's terror campaign did not extend to the Tamil province, the turnout there was lower than the national average pointing to the alienation of the Tamils who had little stake in the presidential contest. Even so, it is significant that Abeyagoonesekara, the sole candidate supporting the India-Sri Lanka agreement, got fewer votes than either of his rivals, despite the backing he got from two pro-agreement Tamil groups (the Eelam People's Revolutionary Liberation Front which dominated the North-Eastern Provincial Council, and the moderate Tamil United Liberation Front).

The season of elections was not over yet. Sri Lanka had to choose a Parliament. In the face of the threat to the parliamentary system itself—from the JVP in the Sinhala areas and the LTTE in the northeast—stability emerged as *the* issue of the elections. The prospect of a hostile Parliament—of the SLFP ranged against Premadasa, the President, who belonged to the UNP, was not something the average Sinhala looked forward to; the UNP played on this and projected itself as the only party that could provide political continuity and avoid chaos.

The UNP's job was made relatively easier because, after its debacle at the presidential election, the SLFP was a demoralized party. Long years out of power since its defeat at the 1977 elections had debilitated its lack-lustre leadership. But it still believed that the voter would live up to the Sinhala tradition of not giving any party a second consecutive term. (Since 1956, it had been 'out with the scoundrels' at every election.)

The atmosphere of violence in which the election took place was awesome. Each of the 1,393 candidates was entitled to two revolvers for self-defence. In addition, each candidate was provided with six armed bodyguards. And yet several candidates were killed. The island-wide toll of those killed between 11 and 16 February was 433, including seventy on the day of voting.

There were several interesting aspects to this election. First, the voter turn-out, at sixty-five per cent, was better than at the presidential contest. Second, it was the first election to Parliament in over eleven years, and so a large proportion of the voters had been enfranchised during a period of chaos and conflict. It was also the first election under the proportional representation system in place of the first-past-the-post elections at which the winner took all. At the 1977 elections, the UNP, with 50.9 per cent of the vote, had had a four-fifths majority in the house, while the SLFP, with 29.7 per cent, had ended with a miserable eight in the 168-member Parliament. Confident of victory, Premadasa had been asking for a two-thirds majority—needed to get vital enactments past the Parliament. But with a 50.7 per cent vote the UNP could now only get a simple majority (125 in a house of 225) while the SLFP, whose vote had dropped from 44.95 per cent at the presidential elections to 31.82 could get only sixty-seven seats.

The election had brought Sri Lanka a new President who promised stability, but Premadasa did not have the advantage of his predecessor—a four-fifths majority, though he inherited all Jayewardene's problems. One was building a Sinhala consensus on the ethnic issue within the constraints of the India-Sri Lanka agreement (which had polarized Sinhala opinion against new concessions to Tamils). The other was the JVP's terrorism which primarily was in response to the perception that the agreement was an imposition from without in furtherance of India's expansionist and hegemonistic designs.

Where the Tamils were concerned, the government had to contend with the resurgence of the extremist-moderate divide in Tamil opinion (this had shown up in the results of the elections to Parliament in the north-eastern province). The moderates had been weakened and the LTTE's pressure group, the EROS, had emerged the main political group of the Tamils. (The EROS is for narrowing the gap between the absolute minimum—devolution of powers on a limited scale through the provincial councils—and the absolute maximum—a sovereign Tamil Eelam—in Tamil expectations. It sees the limited devolution proposals as the starting point for talks and wants the package enlarged into a broad-based and enduring settlement. Its concept of Tamil unity extends to the plantation areas inhabited by immigrant Tamils.)

Premadasa has had to a walk a tightrope between the Tamil and Sinhala demands: he cannot concede Tamil demands without alienating the Sinhalas and vice versa. Besides even if he had the political will and courage to take some necessary, if unpopular, steps to resolve the various issues he would be unable to do much because he does not have the requisite two-thirds majority in Parliament that he would need to enact legislation on his own. For the same reason he is vulnerable to hard-liners in own party. Adding to Premadasa's problems is the SLFP, which frustrated over its successive electoral setbacks, has decided to opt for a more strident anti-Tamil stance to match the ultranationalism of the JVP with which it has to compete for support. Premadasa therefore has to devise a package that would not only meet Tamil aspirations but would also find Sinhala endorsement. He cannot seek dissolution of Parliament and a fresh mandate for a year.

The immediate problem he faces is the ratifying of the merger of the Tamil provinces by the people of the eastern districts. The merger, as we've seen, was a last ditch attempt by Jayewardene to save the India-Sri Lanka agreement by conciliating the Tamils. (In addition he promised that Tamils would receive recognition as an official language on par with Sinhala and English; 'stateless' Tamil plantation labour of Indian origin would receive citizenship; and Tamil political detainees would be released.) But the mounting JVP violence in the first half of

1989 made Premadasa come up with the idea of a referendum, by the people of the eastern provinces, to legitimize the merger of the Tamil provinces; this measure to appease Sinhala sentiment was thought necessary because the majority of the Sinhalas felt that the merger of the two provinces was a concession in principle to the Tamil demand for a homeland. (The referendum was initially fixed for 5 July 1989.)

Unsurprisingly the ethnic Tamils in general, and the LTTE in particular, objected strenuously to the idea of the referendum (the ethnic Tamils form only forty-two per cent of the eastern province which is also twenty-five per cent Sinhala and thirty-three per cent Tamil Muslim. The Tamils are concerned that the Tamil Muslims who hold the decisive vote might not opt in favour of the merger — for fear of being swamped by the ethnic Tamils which would render them a minority within a minority) for if the merger was rejected it would mean a shrunken homeland (the northern province and the Tamil-dominated districts of the eastern province). Premadasa's position became even more difficult because if he bowed to Tamil pressure and cancelled the referendum there was bound to be a Sinhala backlash.

There was only one issue all the groups coincided on — they all wanted India to leave, though Premadasa, always an opponent of the Indian presence, had begun to realize that it was only because of the IPKF bottling up of the LTTE in the north-east that he was free to use his army to fight the JVP revolutionaries. If the IPKF left there was simply no way the Sri Lankan army could handle both the LTTE and the JVP.

Trapped in a crisis that defied easy solutions, Premadasa tried to sue for peace. Early in April, realizing the futility of a military answer to the Tamil problem or his inability to overcome the Sinhala backlash, he made a 'make-or-break' attempt at political reconciliation. He offered representation in Parliament to the JVP (whose ultimate aim is to capture state power) and the LTTE (which had, like the JVP, opted out of the election), if they laid down arms and entered into a political dialogue with him.

The JVP responded with an effective one-day strike to mark the anniversary of the 1971 insurrection. Colombo, the capital, was pitifully paralyzed and major provincial towns in the Sinhala south were 'ghost towns' by sundown. 'Such was the spread of the silent, insidious and sweeping authority of the JVP that the press and the opposition had started to talk of "the JVP writ" and "parallel government" ', a Sri Lankan columnist wrote.

Premadasa followed up this offer with a unilateral cease-fire for a week from 12 April 1989 which both the JVP and the LTTE rejected.

Then, surprisingly, the LTTE agreed to hold talks in May. Its demands were: it wanted the IPKF out; it wanted the present north-eastern council dissolved and fresh elections held; it wanted the referendum dumped. Premadasa didn't reject the demands outright but agreed to work out an equitable solution.

Why has the LTTE agreed to talk? Indian army officers believe it is a tactical manoeuvre on the part of the LTTE to gain some breathing space in which to replenish supplies and its depleted ranks. But Premadasa has no option but to take the LTTE on good faith and hope he can sort out the Tamil problem with it. However, for there to be a chance for a lasting settlement he will also have to work out how exactly the JVP is to be tackled. Stop-gap measures like the call for the IPKF to leave will not work in the long run. But that action on the part of Premadasa shows he recognizes the fact that in the future the JVP (which is totally against the presence of the IPKF) given its effective use of terror (one such instance was the terror psychosis it induced in Indian businessmen and businesses in Colombo when it demanded that they all leave immediately, failing which they would be exterminated), and the latent (and often vocal) support for it by the majority will soon be the major group to be wooed. The only alternative is to wipe out its cadres completely, but this will take a long time (the JVP has an estimated 20,000 cadres and 3,000 trained combatants). And ironically, to tackle them militarily with any degree of success, Premadasa needs the IPKF to hold off the LTTE.

In the final analysis, however, Premadasa would have invited a barrage of criticism if he had agreed that he needed the IPKF (this was in part—he also needed to placate the JVP and the LTTE—why he announced in June that the IPKF should be totally withdrawn by 29 July 1989, the second anniversary of the India-Sri Lanka agreement). In any case by this time Rajiv Gandhi had announced that most of the troops of the IPKF would return home soon. Whatever the other implications of this development, Premadasa knows that unless he handles things right, the eventual departure of the IPKF will plunge the country into an internecine war more bloody than anything that has gone before. The only hope in this increasingly gloomy scenario is that the LTTE will probably enter the political process. If it does, Premadasa will need to muster every ounce of his political acumen to see that the JVP does so as well. Otherwise the extra-constitutional and violent forms of struggle that have taken the place of political process in the country, since 1983, will continue.

4

The View From Point Calimere

In 1981, the unguarded, desolate, palmyrah-palm-fringed Ramanathapuram coast, south of Point Calimere, came alive with armed men as Sri Lanka's Tamil secessionist guerrillas shifted to India. Gradually, the narrow stretch of sea, that separates the two countries, was dotted with speed-boats as organized gun-running and the training of new recruits began on a large scale after 1983.

Point Calimere (the Calligicium of Ptolemy), which juts out like a thumb into the Indian Ocean, is just forty miles away, across the Palk Straits, from the picturesque little town of Point Pedro in Sri Lanka's Jaffna peninsula. Geologists believe the northern reaches of Sri Lanka were once part of the Indian mainland.

Tamil is the language of more than ninety per cent of the people in the Jaffna peninsula. But the people of Jaffna speak a language not readily understood by the fifty million Tamils (most of whom live in Tamil Nadu) in India. In their manners, customs, ceremonies and food habits they have more in common with the Malayalis of another state in south India, Kerala, and the Sinhalas who make up over seventy per cent of Sri Lanka's population.

This is because the Jaffna Tamils were removed enough from the larger home of Tamil culture to develop a distinctive culture of their own. Jaffna, like the rest of Ceylon, was ruled as a Crown Colony by the British—initially from Madras in India.

But the Jaffna Tamil did not look to India for economic opportunity. He looked to the rest of the island and faraway British colonies like Malaya. If anything the Jaffna Tamil had contempt for the Indian Tamil who provided cheap labour for the British plantation economy—the ethnic Ceylon Tamil and the dispossessed Kandyan farmer looked upon such employment with disdain.

At the political level, Indian interaction with the Tamils in Ceylon was with the immigrant plantation Tamil and not with the ethnic Ceylon Tamil. Even when there were secessionist stirrings among India's Tamils (in the Madras Presidency), the Jaffna Tamil was insulated from such tendencies.

And yet the Sri Lankan Tamil secessionist demand evoked sympathy in India's Tamil Nadu state. It compelled Indian involvement which eventually resulted in military intervention. This is not just a result of mere cultural affinity or even geographic proximity. The Indian Tamil empathy with the Jaffna has its roots in something far deeper and complex—the siege mentality these two communities have acquired as a result of being language 'nationalities' in nations where other languages dominate.

The Tamil diaspora stretches from Guyana in the Caribbean to South Africa and Mauritius and Malaysia in the Indian Ocean to Fiji in the Pacific. But nowhere outside India and Sri Lanka do Tamils have a concentrated majority with territorial enclaves of their own which they call their homeland. Unlike the ethnic Tamils of Sri Lanka and India, Tamils in the other British colonies were immigrants and were dispersed spatially. Today, they are language minorities and not language nationalities.

It is for this reason, that simplistic arguments over India's involvement—such as the one which holds that the spill-over of Sri Lanka's ethnic conflict into India, in the form of a refugee influx which touched the 100,000 mark after the 1983 flare-up, is why India was forced to intervene—need to be discarded. A simple example will prove the point. India has a long border with China, mostly with its Tibet province. After the unsuccessful Lama revolt in 1959, the Dalai Lama, the god-king of six million Tibetans fled, along with thousands of his followers, to India. But India treated the Tibetan issue as an internal problem of China, choosing not to claim a *locus standi* in the problem because there were over a 100,000 Tibetan refugees in India.

Similarly India has had successive waves of refugees from Bangladesh, belonging to the Chakma tribes of the Chittagong hill tracts. The Chakma tribals are Buddhists fleeing the terror accompanying the Muslim colonization of their sparsely populated homeland. And even though the Chakma refugees, like the Dalai Lama's presence, is an irritant in India's relations with neighbours Bangladesh and China, these have never been major issues in bilateral relations. As regards the other obvious refugee problem that India had to contend with in the past—that of Bengalis from what was then East Pakistan and is now Bangladesh—the reason India went to war with Pakistan was for geo-political and domestic strategic reasons, though the refugee problem and the aspirations to independence of East Pakistan's Bengalis were ostensible issues mentioned at the time.

India's involvement in Sri Lanka's ethnic conflict should therefore be traced to the cross-national ethnic tensions endemic to not a few post-colonial Third World countries. Once the struggle against alien rule was over, religious and ethnic tensions came to the fore in several Asian and African countries stirring up dormant conflicts. India had to contend with secessionist demands in its north-east (which is the nation's

Mongoloid fringe) and from the Tamil-speaking people in its south and later from the Sikhs in Punjab in the north. This in addition to lesser conflicts and tensions. Other countries of the region have had to face similar problems. We have already examined such situations in Pakistan and Bangladesh but there has also been ethnic tension in countries like Malaysia, and the Philippines. In Africa, Kenya, Nigeria and Sudan have witnessed fierce ethnic struggles.

It is true of course that Sri Lanka's conflict has little in common with these movements but it does share some parallels with India's own Tamil secessionist demand, which now obtains in a subdued form as a movement that stresses the Tamil identity within the Indian framework. More important, the Tamil quest for identity in India has had a direct bearing on Sri Lanka—via the immigrants of Indian origin in the island, who are mostly Tamil-speaking.

Soon after it gained freedom, Ceylon deprived the Indian immigrants of citizenship and disenfranchised them through legislative fiats in 1948–49. Ceylon's political leadership contended that, despite their long residence in the island, the immigrants did not belong to it and had a live interest in the country of their origin and were therefore aliens. But India thought they were or ought to be Ceylon nationals.

Between 1951 and 1962, only 132,312 persons of Indian origin had been granted Ceylon citizenship and only 35,411 persons had been recognized as Indian citizens in 1963 out of the island's 1,122,850 strong population of Indian origin. In 1964, the Indian and the Ceylon governments estimated that there were 975,000 'stateless' persons in the island. To resolve this problem, the Prime Ministers of the two countries, Lal Bahadur Shastri of India and Sirimavo Bandaranaike of Sri Lanka, entered into an agreement in October 1964.

The salient feature of the Lal Bahadur Shastri–Sirimavo Bandaranaike agreement was that Ceylon and India would divide the 'stateless' persons in a 4:7 proportion. It meant that for every four persons accepted by Ceylon, India would take seven back. In effect Ceylon was to give citizenship to 300,000 persons and their natural increase while India would accept 525,000. The status of the 150,000 left out in the sharing exercise was to be decided later.

The agreement was reached by the two countries without consulting the people most affected by it—the Tamils of Indian origin living in Ceylon. The Ceylon government's enactment to implement the agreement took effect in 1968 and following this the two governments invited applications for citizenship. While 700,000 opted for Ceylonese citizenship (the agreement provided for Ceylon accepting only 300,000), only 400,000 sought Indian citizenship despite India having committed itself to taking 525,000 back as repatriates. Ceylon insisted on following the 4:7 ratio and took only 225,000 of the 700,000 who had opted for Ceylonese citizenship while India accepted all the 400,000 who had opted for its citizenship. (The fate of most of those Tamils who opted for Indian citizenship and were lodged in miserable conditions in resettlement camps is beyond the scope of this book; suffice it to say they found India was not a hospitable environment.) So, in addition to the 150,000 stateless people whose fate had not been decided when the agreement was signed, there were a further 200,000 for whom there was no place in either country. Adding to the problem was the fact that though the 1964 estimate had put the number of stateless people at 975,000, in actual fact the number of applications the two governments received for citizenship totalled 1.1 million (it is of course possible that some of the stateless people applied for citizenship in both countries hoping they would not be left out when the counting began).

In 1974, Sirimavo Bandaranaike, the world's first woman Prime Minister and her Indian counterpart, Indira Gandhi, the world's second, signed another agreement that would decide the fate of the 150,000 who, it had been officially stated, at the time of the 1964 deal, would be looked after in a supplementary agreement. The 1974 agreement decided the 150,000 would be divided equally between the two countries.

But these agreements and enactments did not solve the problem of the other stateless Tamils (in the main, those who had opted for Ceylon in 1964 and had been denied) who numbered, according to Sri Lankan admission, 500,000 in 1986. The position after an enactment in 1986 was that Sri Lanka would accept 469,000 and India 506,000 and any person of Indian origin, lawfully resident in the island and stateless, would get Sri Lankan citizenship. (While on the surface it seemed the issue had been settled, there still remained the fact that the Sri Lanka Freedom Party (SLFP) of Sirimavo Bandaranaike was opposed to the 1986 law. Nothing would prevent it from repealing the enactment if and when it won power or shared power. All action under the 1986 could thus be nullified through such a repeal. But this will with luck remained a distant problem.)

In theory the major problem between India and Sri Lanka—the problem of the stateless persons—had been resolved. But the issue of the 'stateless', like the refugee overflow, was only a surface indication of the real compulsions behind India's involvement in Sri Lanka's ethnic conflict. This becomes clearer when we see that the stateless were not a party to the secessionist demand of the ethnic (Sri Lankan) Tamils, even though they were the victims of the discriminatory policies of the Sinhala-dominated government.

The real reasons for India's involvement had more to do with its domestic political compulsions on one hand and its geo-strategic concerns on the other. Indian Tamil sympathy for the Sri Lankan Tamil secessionist cause was the domestic compulsion. And New Delhi had no real option but to try and satisfy its Tamils given the history of conflict between the two. This strain which resulted in the Indian Tamils' demand for secessionism (which peaked immediately after independence) was the result of a collision between the Tamil identity and the ethos that dominated India's nation-building process after independence.

The language conflict which propelled the Tamil secessionist demand preceded the partition of India by the British at the time of independence to create a Muslim majority Pakistan. The British paid very little attention to the Tamil demand because they were not interested in working out an equitable language policy—this was because they were not interested in building the linkages between the centre and the periphery. But the emergence of a national political authority signalled the need for participative national communities.

*

Like the Jaffna Tamils, the Indian Tamils and others who lived in the polyglot Madras Presidency and the Bengalis of the east had dominated the services and professions because of their proficiency in the English language which was a passport to the professions and other positions of high status under colonial rule.

However, the reason language became the issue in India cannot be simply attributed to a matter of access to higher learning and employment opportunities. Myron Weiner, an American political scientist, feels that beyond the practical and political considerations of cleaving to a particular language, lie deeply held convictions which intensify the opposition of many non-Hindi speakers to the adoption of Hindi as the sole official language: 'It is feared that the Hindi-speaking area views itself as the Prussia of India with its intention of politically and culturally dominating other regions. In contrast, the non-Hindi people view India as a country of divergent regions, each of which has the right to develop its own culture and traditions'.

Long before independence, in the 1920s, the Indian nationalist leadership (represented by the Congress Party founded in 1885) which was predominantly from the Hindi region was opposed to any language nationality finding its own identity through language-majority administrative units. Though still in the process of evolving into a language nationality, the Hindi-speaking people already had language-majority states of their own. They were the United Provinces, Behar (now Bihar), and the Central Provinces and Berar. Evidently the leaders from the Hindi areas feared that if other language groups got their own language-majority provinces, their languages would develop faster than Hindi. And they would not submit meekly to Hindi hegemony when India became free.

That the Hindi belt's fears were not unfounded quickly became apparent when the Tamil secessionist demand began a couple of decades before India became independent. The demand was encouraged by the British who were masters in the art of dividing a people among themselves. Just as they had found a much-needed counterpoise in Ceylon in the ethnic Tamils, in the Madras Presidency they found one in the Justice Party, which represented the elitist non-Brahmin caste, and fought against the domination of the professions and services by the minority Brahmin caste of priests who were atop the social hierarchy.

However, the struggle in the Madras Presidency against Brahmin domination was not limited to electoral representation in a system based on educational and property qualifications (and not on adult franchise which Ceylon got in 1931 and India only in 1952). Nor was it for just a share in educational opportunities and government jobs. The conflict extended to the control of the Congress Party.

The Madras Presidency was a multilingual unit comprising Telugu, Tamil, Malayalam and Kannada-speaking tracts but the Justice Party was strongest in the Tamil-speaking districts.

As early as 1916, the Dravidian Association, which tried to assert the non-Brahmin identity (it regarded the Brahmins as Aryan), aimed at political power. It declared that a 'Dravidian State' under British rule, 'a government of, by and for the non-Brahmin' was its goal. More significant than this was the *Non-Brahmin Manifesto* of the South Indian People's Association formed to propagate the non-Brahmin Hindu cause. It voiced the demands of the narrow social elite which aimed at non-Brahmin advancement in the face of a perceived Brahmin dominance of education, the professions, and government services. It was a call for the rediscovery of non-Brahmin 'self-respect'.

The group's manifesto was an attempt at checkmating the challenge to non-Brahmin interests implicit in the support by Brahmins all over India to the Congress Party's demand for Home Rule. The non-Brahmin liberals of the Madras Presidency, like the Jaffna Tamil leadership, had to turn collaborationist, because the Brahmins, like the Sinhalas of Ceylon, were keen to be seen in an oppositionist role.

The Justice Party, formed a year after the 1916 manifesto, drew its leadership from devout but anti-Brahmin Hindus. In 1919, the party sent its own delegation to the London parleys of the Joint Parliamentary Committee on Constitutional Reforms and won the demand for separate non-Brahmin representation in the Presidency as part of an all-India award through the Montague-Chelmsford reforms of 1919.

But as in Ceylon, the situation bristled with contradictions created by the British. Muslims, Europeans, Anglo-Indians and Indian Christians were a minority in relation to the Hindu majority and were given separate electorates to protect their interests. But the Hindu non-

Brahmins were a majority *vis-á-vis* the Brahmin minority. It was an extraordinary phenomenon, the majority seeking protection against minority.

Though the British had found a counterpoise in the Justice Party, its elitist character was to render the party irrelevant as the tide of anti-imperialism swelled. The non-Brahmin masses were not only anti-Brahmin; they were anti-British too and for this reason they soon began to feel the Justice Party, which was rapidly acquiring a negative image in the midst of the nationalist fervour sweeping the country, was not good for them.

But one of the leaders of the non-Brahmin Tamils, E.V. Ramaswami Naicker, a former leader of the Congress Party, soon gave them a positive boost by describing the non-Brahmin people as Dravidian—the assumption being Brahmins were Aryans and therefore anti-Brahminism meant being anti-Aryan and by extension anti-Hindu (because Hinduism was seen as the religion of the Aryans). Naiker held that the non-Brahmin opposition should extend to the whole Hindu order which institutionalized discrimination and untouchability on the basis of caste status at birth.

Naicker's Dravidian movement had little appeal to Ceylon's ethnic Tamils though they were the linear descendants of the Dravidians who had inhabited India's southern tracts from antiquity.

In the late 1930s, when the Congress Party ruled Madras Presidency under a limited self-rule arrangement, Hindi was used as a language for study in state-run schools—a prelude to the imposition of Hindi after independence. Naicker saw in this a calculated affront to the Tamil language and culture and lashed out at Hindi which he saw as Brahminism's weapon for the future, when the British left and English had to be replaced. An agitation in 1938 forced the retreat of Hindi. It was to be taught now only as an optional language.

While the Indian Tamils' search for identity found specific expression over Hindi, seen as an instrument of cultural domination of the Dravidians by the Aryans, the Ceylon Tamils' search for an independent destiny began only after their failure to roll back S.W.R.D. Bandaranaike's 1958 enactment making Sinhala the sole official language in the place of English.

In both countries, however, the movements eventually became racist, with differing interpretations. Naicker asserted that the non-Brahmins of the south were Dravidian by race and therefore ethnically distinct from the Aryans of the north. In Ceylon, the Sinhalas asserted their superiority by virtue of their Aryan descent and looked down upon the Tamils whom they regarded as Dravidian.

With ethnic distinctions coming into play, the Tamil movement in India entered a new phase—the secessionist phase. Naicker had no difficulty getting the Justice Party to demand a Dravidian state separate from the rest of India, even if it had to be ruled by the British. In 1939 Naicker called a conference to demand a homeland for the Dravidians (which effectively meant the Tamils). He reiterated this demand in 1940, while pledging support to the Muslim League's demand for Pakistan (realized at India's independence in 1947). Thus the first demand for India's break-up came not from the Muslims who wanted Pakistan but from the Tamils who wanted a Dravidian homeland.

The demand was vague and contradictory. The term Dravidian was used loosely to denote anything Tamil. Consequently, it was assumed that the Tamils were distinctly more Dravidian than the other groups which spoke other Indo-Dravidian languages (Telugu, Kannada and Malayalam). The Naicker-inspired demand also ignored the areas speaking Indo-Dravidian languages outside the Madras Presidency—the Mysore, Travancore and Hyderabad states ruled by native princes.

Naicker forced a split in the Justice Party in 1944 and reorganized the larger faction into the Dravida Kazhagam which proclaimed an independent, sovereign Dravidian republic, a federal union of people speaking the four Indo-Dravidian languages but coterminus with the Madras Presidency, excluding Dravidians outside it.

As the freedom struggle moved to its climax before the end of the Second World War, the Dravida Kazhagam realized that the British were in no mood to concede their homeland demand even if they had to quit India. So its campaign now hammered the point that India's independence had no meaning as long as the Brahmin and north Indian domination of the south continued.

After independence, the Dravida Kazhagam's main target was Hindi. The party split in 1949, the younger elements asserting the basic Dravidian objectives and forming the Dravida Munnetra Kazhagam. The birth of the new party coincided with a breakthrough in education and a sharp fall in employment opportunities in Madras state (as the Madras Presidency of yore came to be known after 1950). The fear of imposition of Hindi added to the frustration of the non-Brahmin middle classes. In 1954, the Telugu-speaking people of the state won a language-majority state of their own after an agitation which had begun long before independence. In 1956, India reorganized its states on the basis of language and only a residuary Tamil-speaking Madras state was left.

The Dravida Munnetra Kazhagam which had kept out of India's first adult franchise elections in 1952 made its debut at the 1957 polls and entered the state legislature and the federal Parliament. It improved its electoral showing in 1962 and abandoned its secessionist plank in 1963 to overcome an electoral law requiring contestants at elections to swear allegiance to the constitution (which meant no secession). It now wanted an autonomous Dravidian union of the four southern states within the Indian Union. This drew a meagre response from the other three states so the Dravida Munnetra Kazhagam's relevance was limited to its anti-Hindi role. As the deadline for replacing English (26 January 1965) approached, the Dravida Munnetra Kazhagam called an anti-Hindi agitation. A young party functionary burnt himself in Madras city leaving a note which said: 'This is my peaceful way of protest against alien Hindi. My body belongs to the earth. My soul to Tamil.' The state exploded into violence and would thenceforth never trust the Congress or New Delhi.

The electorate of the state of Madras, to become Tamil Nadu later, threw the Congress Party out of office at the 1967 elections over the Hindi issue. New Delhi's weak assurances that English would be used as an additional official language as long as the non-Hindi people wanted it had little effect on the voters. The state has defied the national pattern since, electing the Dravida Munnetra Kazhagam again in 1971 and 1988 and its splinter the All-India Anna Dravida Munnetra Kazhagam (born in 1972) in 1977 and 1984. The Tamil identity in India had asserted itself with a vengeance.

*

India's Tamil secessionist movement and the separatist sentiment later had little impact on Ceylon. But successive Ceylon governments feared a fallout of this disaffection among the Tamil plantation workers. A small 'Dravida Munnetra Kazhagam' (disowned by the party of the same name in India) was active among them but Prime Minister Sirimavo Bandaranaike banned it in 1962. When the ban lapsed in 1967 she prevailed upon her successor Dudley Senanayake to reimpose it. After she regained office in 1970, she barred the visit of the Dravida Munnetra Kazhagam Chief Minister M. Karunanidhi of Tamil Nadu and deported an Indian politician visiting Sri Lanka. She curbed and eventually banned the entry of Tamil newspapers from India. But all this had little to do with the aspirations of Sri Lanka's ethnic Tamils whose secessionist demand was not to crystallize before 1976.

The Sinhala intolerance of the Tamil quest for national identity reached a high point in 1974. The International Conference on Dravidology and Linguistics (better known as the World Tamil Congress) was held in Jaffna after similar conferences in Kuala Lumpur (1966), Madras (1968), and Paris (1970). To the Jaffna Tamils the 1974 conference they were hosting was of immense significance because it underlined their identity in Sri Lanka. Naturally, the government was opposed to it; the last day's session was broken up by policemen who lobbed teargas shells at the audience before attacking it.

The first links between the Jaffna Tamils and the Indian Tamils were forged in the wake of this outrage. Seven years later, after the 1981 anti-Tamil riots, the guerrilla groups found sympathy for the Sri Lankan Tamil cause was building in Tamil Nadu. Chief Minister M.G.

Ramachandran of the All-India Anna Dravida Munnetra Kazhagam (AIADMK) and former Chief Minister M. Karunanidhi of the Dravida Munnetra Kazhagam (DMK) were among the sympathizers. Soon the militant groups found sanctuary in Tamil Nadu and Madras became the political headquarters of the militant groups. In 1982, Liberation Tigers of Tamil Eelam (LTTE) leaders Velupillai Prabhakaran and Uma Maheswaran exchanged gunfire on a busy Madras street, proclaiming a split in the organization. Both were held by the police but were freed soon. Also, the Tamil Nadu government refused to deport the Tamil offenders President Jayewardene wanted to try at home. After the July 1983 battle in Sri Lanka, the presence and activities of the guerrilla groups was more open in Tamil Nadu. All the significant groups functioned from Madras city with the covert and open support of the state government and the two Dravidian parties. They had offices, telephone numbers that were not secret and even wireless sets for communication with Jaffna. (This was in violation of the Indian law.) They carried unlicensed arms, again in violation of the law. They could commute to Jaffna and back without travel documents by (what was nicknamed in Madras 'the Eelam Shipping Service') boats that left the Ramanathapuram coast and returned eluding Sri Lankan naval surveillance—this was easy as the Indian Coast Guard turned a blind eye to the guerrillas' boats. Early in 1983 *India Today* magazine reported the existence of guerrilla training camps in Tamil Nadu, and one right in the vicinity of Madras airport. India never admitted to this.

In actuality, what was happening was that the Tamil guerrillas were building up their forces—the aim was to raise a force of 5,000—before launching a decisive military campaign. Ironically, India which once feared Tamil secessionism in its south, and has had other secessionist challenges in the north-east (of the Nagas and Mizos), was now permitting secessionist activity aimed at a friendly country. India had done this once before, when it provided sanctuary to Bangladesh guerrillas in 1971, but that had been primarily for strategic reasons. This time (in the early 1980s at any rate), domestic compulsions were the major reason for India's benevolence.

Prime Minister Indira Gandhi's Congress Party which lost Tamil Nadu in 1967, owed its shrunken survival to the AIADMK which ruled the state. This party, in turn, owed its primacy to the Tamil separatist sentiment. Neither the government at the centre, nor the one in the state could ignore the fact that the Tamils of India sympathized with the secessionist cause across the Palk Straits.

That was the major reason, but it wasn't the only reason. India had reason to apprehend that the convergence of its and Sri Lanka's foreign policy interests had ended with the defeat of the Sirimavo Bandaranaike left-of-centre government in 1977. India had been quite happy with Bandaranaike, believing her foreign policy was progressive and non-aligned, like its own. (Not that there were no irritants. She did not support India over the border dispute with China, leading to the 1962 war. Again, in 1971, though India had helped the regime in Colombo against the Janatha Vimukti Peramuna insurrection, Bandaranaike provided Pakistan transit facilities for aircraft from Pakistan's western wing to the eastern wing—which later was to become Bangladesh—because they could not overfly Indian territory which separated the two wings).

Bandaranaike's successor, Jayewardene, had his own reasons for moving away from India: in his thinking New Delhi was using the Tamil issue to destabilize the island. So it was not surprising when, in the wake of the 23 July 1983 riots, a western news agency reported that Sri Lanka had sought military assistance from the United States, the United Kingdom, Pakistan and Bangladesh apprehending an invasion from an unspecified quarter. That India was suspected can be inferred from the fact that Jayewardene did not appeal to it for help.

Also, the situation in 1971 when Ceylon had asked India for help was different from the one in 1983 in several respects. In 1971 Ceylon had wanted to contain a domestic challenge from the Sinhala youth. The Tamils were not part of the insurrection. As Ceylon's immediate neighbour India had a stake in the island's political stability.

In 1983, Sri Lanka's appeal for external help was against a perceived threat of invasion in the context of the anti-Tamil flare-up and the strong reaction to it among India's Tamils across the Palk Straits.

India reacted to the situation immediately. It had to do so because of the strength of domestic opinion which favoured support to Sri Lanka's Tamils. But it had to tread carefully, for it had to convince the world that it was a stickler for the ground rules of the non-aligned movement[*] (of which it was the reigning chairman). Also, India had to make sure it didn't appear hypocritical given that it had been alleging Pakistan's complicity in its Sikh secessionist problem.

What it was determined to do, notwithstanding the various diplomatic hazards it had to steer clear of, was to keep the countries Sri Lanka had appealed to for help out of the region. The diplomatic and strategic initiative India came up with at this time later came to be known as the India Doctrine or India's Monroe Doctrine. As spelt out in private to these countries, it was: India had vital interests in the stability of South Asian countries; any instability in the region could affect India because it might spill over into it. *Ergo*, any assistance to meet such a threat should be in consultation with India and the other South Asian countries, keeping powers that did not belong to the region out.

There was another strand to the doctrine: there should always be a

---

[*] Basically non-alignment means non-interference in another country's domestic affairs.

one-to-one relationship between India and its South Asian neighbours, which meant issues had to be resolved bilaterally with no mediation by powers of the region or from outside the region. The doctrine aimed at asserting India's primacy and its right to a decisive say in the matters of the region.

The doctrine was spelt out to pre-empt any direct outside involvement in Sri Lanka. In contrast all the foreign powers that had extended help to Ceylon against the JVP in 1971 (except India) were not from the region. They included the United States, the United Kingdom and China.

India's public posture now was that if Sri Lanka needed India's help, that was another matter. The two could stay in touch and India would act with due regard to the natural concern of its people and to the obligations of a good neighbour.

Under the pressure India was exerting, President Jayewardene sent his brother, H.W. Jayewardene, as his special envoy to India to explain the situation. The envoy later visited eight Asian capitals, including Beijing, but significantly gave Islamabad the miss. Prime Minister Zhao Ziyang told the visitor in Beijing, in what in retrospect looks a caveat to the Indian Doctrine, that China had told all South Asian countries (which axiomatically should have included India) that relations among them should be harmonious and that 'the big country should not bully the small, and the small should not oppress the weak', and that all countries were equal.

The Indian Doctrine forestalled for a while a military alliance between Sri Lanka and some other country or direct foreign military involvement in the ethnic conflict. India's interests had been served.

*

The timing of the India Doctrine suggested that India's strategic interests were at stake in Sri Lanka. In geographic location, the pearl-shaped island 500 miles north of the equator straddles the Gulf-Far East oil route and there is no appreciable landmass south of it until one reaches Antarctica. Amidst the great distances of the Indian Ocean (28,362,200 square miles), Trincomalee, on Sri Lanka's east coast, is among the world's best natural harbours. It can accommodate about a hundred ships and berth around thirty large vessels of any size including aircraft carriers and nuclear-powered submarines because of its unlimited draught.

During the Second World War, when it was pushed out by the Japanese, the British navy retreated from Singapore to Trincomalee. The port became the headquarters of the South-East Asia Command (SEAC) under Lord Louis Mountbatten of Burma (who after the war was to become India's last Viceroy). The British built an airbase and an oil storage facility in the vicinity of the harbour.

When the British gave Ceylon independence in 1948, the two countries saw the advantage of a naval base at Trincomalee for different reasons. The British were waning as a major world power and could do with a foothold in the Indian Ocean and Ceylon's leadership saw in the British presence in Trincomalee a bulwark against a feared Indian push. A United Kingdom-Ceylon defence agreement was signed a few months before independence. However, in 1956, S.W.R.D. Bandaranaike's Sri Lanka Freedom Party (SLFP) government, committed to a non-aligned foreign policy, ended the agreement. In 1964, his wife Sirimavo Bandaranaike barred all foreign navies from Trincomalee.

Meanwhile, India feared that the United States was eyeing Trincomalee harbour as a potential naval base to expand its influence in the Indian Ocean and link its Atlantic and Pacific blue-water navies. This was not all fancy, for during the 1971 India-Pakistan war the United States sent a task force of its Seventh Fleet, led by the aircraft carrier *Enterprise*, into the Bay of Bengal to intimidate India.

India responded immediately by bombing Chittagong harbour. The message was clear: United States interference in the war would not be tolerated. Backing India's response was its treaty ally, the Soviet Union, which had strengthened its Indian Ocean fleet to counter the United States manoeuvre.

When it because clear to the US that it was not going to get Trincomalee without a prolonged political battle with India, it began developing the Indian Ocean island of Diego Garcia as a military base. Diego Garcia is just 1,600 kilometres from India and is close to Sri Lanka.

The defeat of Sirimavo Bandaranaike's Party in 1977 meant not only the end of the left-of-centre populist domestic policies she and her allies represented but a sharp turn in the foreign policy. Jayewardene's United National Party (UNP) government lifted the ban on foreign naval vessels calling at Trincomalee. An agreement to provide rest and recreation facilities to United States military personnel in Trincomalee was also signed.

Other developments added to the suspicion that the United States had not given up its interest in Trincomalee. In 1981, the Coastal Corporation of Bermuda, associated with United States interests, obtained a lease to develop the disused oil tank farm in Trincomalee much to India's discomfiture. Jayewardene had called for global tenders to develop the oil tank farm and the Coastal Corporation had won it, inviting Indian and Soviet protests. Fresh tenders were floated and India's bid turned out to be the most competitive. Sri Lanka could not decide. Another bid was floated and this time a Singapore-based consortium (also believed to be a United States front) won it.

Another irritant was the renewed agreement over the location of the Voice of America transmitter in Sri Lanka. An agreement in 1952 had

122 / Sri Lanka: The Fractured Island

provided the United States government broadcast system relaying facilities in the island. This was renewed every five years. In 1983, the renewal came at the end of a 105-minute refuelling stop in September by the United States Defence Secretary, Caspar Weinberger, who had a meeting with Jayewardene. Weinberger's visit was followed by that of General Vernon Walters, special envoy of the United States President, in November 1983.

India alleged that the renewed VOA agreement provided for facilities beyond normal relaying and covered electronic monitoring and the directing of nuclear missiles to their targets. It said that now the USA, besides normal military communications in the Indian Ocean region, would be able to monitor all vital communications within India because the facility had an effective range of 3300 kilometres and covered even submarine communication.

India's fears of outside interference were compounded by other developments. The response of powers outside the region to Sri Lanka's request for assistance, after the 1983 disturbances, was disconcerting. Help came directly or by proxy. Tamil militant groups say the United States arranged military help through Israel with which the Sirimavo Bandaranaike government had snapped diplomatic relations in 1971. Mossad, Israel's external intelligence agency, and Shin Beth, its counter-insurgency agency, were believed to have been advising Sri Lankans since 1982. In 1984, an 'Israel interest section' was set up in the United States embassy in Colombo allegedly to channel United States military assistance.

The United Kingdom did not help directly, but succour came through the Channel Island-based Keeny Meany Services, a security firm which comprised Special Air Services veterans of the Rhodesian war. The mercenaries were apparently involved in operations against the Tamil guerrillas. Also, Pakistan helped train the Special Task Force to combat the guerrillas while China sold arms to Sri Lanka. Arms also came from South Africa and South Korea in addition to what could be bought in the international arms bazaar.

India's apprehension grew at these signs of increased external involvement in Sri Lanka's ethnic conflict. Believing its geostrategic interests threatened (and fearing especially a threat of invasion at the very least instability on its southern flank) India prepared a blueprint for containing the Sri Lankan situation. Units for intervention were ear-marked in early 1984 but the plan was called off. It was disclosed in connection with the Coomar Narain spy scandal in India that a position paper advocating military intervention in Sri Lanka, prepared by New Delhi's Research and Analysis Wing, had reached Washington and was made available to Colombo which confronted New Delhi with the tell-tale document. The plot, as they say, was thickening.

*

'India is not just another country', Prime Minister Indira Gandhi said, a bare week after the July 1983 riots. She said most countries in the region were multi-racial and multi-religious but she did not specify what India proposed to do about the conflict in Sri Lanka. A few days before the riots, India sent a note (leaked out in Colombo) protesting the ordinance passed by the Sri Lankan government permitting the disposal of unidentified bodies without an inquiry. Sri Lanka rejected India's protest.

In 1981, India had held that the anti-Tamil riots were an internal matter of Sri Lanka. This time it thought differently; its messages to Sri Lanka, however, remained veiled and vague. While the riots continued, a handpicked Indian force was readied for a peace-keeping role if sought. But Jayewardene refused to heed India's offer. In his view, India had no role in the matter though New Delhi communicated its concern at the prospect of a million refugees entering its shores. (Interestingly, India had welcomed ten million refugees from Pakistan's eastern wing.)

Indira Gandhi sent her External Affairs Minister P.V. Narasimha Rao to Colombo while the massacres were still going on. Sri Lanka viewed this as an unusual step, yet another manifestation of India's attitude that nothing in its vicinity could be decided without its knowledge and approval. Rao's mission, India claimed, helped end the anti-Tamil riots. Then India provoked Colombo further by inviting, without waiting for Sri Lanka's response, A. Amirthalingam, leader of the Tamil United Liberation Front, for talks. A question asked in Colombo was: 'Can Pakistan invite Jagjit Singh Chauhan?' (Chauhan, proponent of the Sikh secessionist cause in India's Punjab, is an expatriate living in the United Kingdom.)

India's strategy was slowly becoming clear. In its essence, the Indian response to the conflict across the Palk Straits was two pronged: one was support to Tamil aspirations, short of endorsing the secessionist demand; the second was support to the militant activity aimed at secession.

By now, Sri Lanka was more than convinced that despite India's vehement denials, its Tamil Nadu state was harbouring the Tamil guerrillas and aiding them. In May 1982, five LTTE activists had been held in Madras after Sri Lanka had produced voluminous evidence in support of its charges against them of murder and other terrorism-related offences. But the Tamil Nadu government freed them on bail within forty-eight hours. Two jumped bail and the other three were rearrested only to be freed again in short order.

Despite all this, India's ostensibly high-minded efforts for ending the conflict (on one level) began to pay off. Sri Lanka agreed to consider India's proposals to solve the ethnic issue. Indira Gandhi named G. Parthasarathi as her envoy to mediate between the Tamil groups and the Sri Lankan government. Parthasarathi, a Tamil who had started as a journalist, drew on his experience as a diplomat. He had handled India's Kashmir dispute, cause of three wars with Pakistan. (The Jammu and Kashmir state enjoys a special autonomous status denied to others in India's federal set-up.) He also drew on his experience of the Mizo ethnic secessionist demand, and the conflict in Vietnam of which he had direct experience. His substantive achievement was a set of proposals known as Annexure C, for the devolution of power to the regional councils (this was regarded as adequate to meet Tamil aspirations within the Sri Lankan set-up).

But Parthasarathi's set of proposals collapsed because Jayewardene (its co-author) reneged on it, blaming Sinhala opposition for his volte-face. However, the fact that there was a political vacuum in India, following the assassination of Indira Gandhi on 31 October 1984, and turmoil in Tamil Nadu with Chief Minister M.G. Ramachandran away in the United States for medical treatment, may have also encouraged Jayewardene to go back on his commitments.

*

After Rajiv Gandhi legitimized his succession, winning the elections with a massive majority, India's attitude to the ethnic conflict in Sri Lanka changed once again. Parthasarathi, who headed the foreign policy planning committee of the government, was being overshadowed by Romesh Bhandari, the new external affairs secretary. Bhandari went to Colombo in May 1985 to assure Jayewardene, who was under heavy military pressure from the guerrillas, that India would tighten the screws on the Madras-based Tamil militant groups.

After the Anuradhapura massacre of Sinhalas by Tamil militants, Jayewardene rushed to New Delhi in June for a summit meeting with Rajiv Gandhi. The two leaders agreed on immediate action to diffuse the situation and to attempt a political solution acceptable to 'all concerned' and within the framework of Sri Lanka's unity and integrity. The key concern of the talks was that 'all forms of violence should abate and finally cease'. For the first time India, which under Indira Gandhi had tried coercive diplomacy with Sri Lanka, was equating the Sinhala state terror against the Tamil civilian population with the defensive violence of the guerrillas.

India, as a consequence of its role as peace-maker, began getting tough with the Tamil guerrillas. Rajiv Gandhi began saying he would not permit a Tamil Eelam in Sri Lanka. He also initiated steps to ensure that Indian territory would not be used as a staging point by the guerrillas. The groups were told they could not ferry material and men across the Palk Straits. A ship-load of arms (estimated value: US $ 4 million) meant for the People's Liberation Organisation of Tamil Eelam was intercepted and seized at Madras harbour to get this message across to the groups.

India then arranged a cease-fire to enable direct talks between the Tamil groups (which were forced to participate in them, under the threat of deportation of their leaders) with the Sri Lankan government. The talks failed.

India was now committed, under the new dispensation, to a much more involved role in the resolution of the issue. Consequently it began to lend balancing support to Sri Lanka, playing off the moderate Tamil United Liberation Front against the militants, and one set of militant groups against the other.

In late 1986 when the guerrillas were militarily on top and the Sri Lankan forces were in a hapless position, India acted to mount pressure on the LTTE to force a negotiated settlement. There was a crackdown on all the groups. Their arms were seized and even their wireless communication equipment was taken away. India was now firmly involved. Two factors probably propelled India into this precipitate course of action. One, an anxiety to save Jayewardene from being toppled (by the pressure of Sri Lankan political opinion) for his failure to win the war. Another, the fear of foreign involvement to save Jayewardene which would mean new security concerns for India.

When the LTTE leader Velupillai Prabhakaran turned down the idea of a settlement, he was warned that the United States Seventh Fleet might intervene in the island if the conflict continued. As the year was drawing to an end Jayewardene offered a new devolution package known as the '19 December proposals' but he reneged on these as well.

The LTTE threat to set up a Tamil Eelam government on New Year's Day (this was not carried out thanks to India's pressure) was used by Sri Lanka to impose an economic blockade on the Jaffna peninsula in the north and mount a major military offensive in the Tamil areas. By the end of March, the Sri Lankan forces had regained control of the northern province, except the Jaffna peninsula, and were poised for a final assault on the Tamil secessionist stronghold.

While all this was going on, the onus of getting the LTTE to talks had devolved on India. In an attempt to make the path of the 'peace process' run smoother, Sri Lanka announced a unilateral cease-fire in April 1987, but this was cut short by the massacre of Sinhala civilians on Good Friday and a bomb explosion in Colombo two days later.

It was war again, including aerial attacks on targets in the Jaffna peninsula. After a three-week military lull, Sri Lanka announced, on 26 May, its 'Operation Liberation' to take the Jaffna peninsula. The preparations for this assault had begun early in May and a Sri Lankan spokesman was to say later that it would not have been necessary had the LTTE not torpedoed the April cease-fire.

To kick off Operation Liberation, Sri Lankan Air Force planes whirred over Jaffna city dropping leaflets announcing a forty-eight hour curfew and asking civilians to move away from the bunkers and shelters of the Tamil militants. Within two hours, 20,000 troops moved out of their camps in three columns towards the city. Planes and helicopters provided them cover and naval strikes backed the operation. Turbo-prop civilian planes, improvized for a military role, dropped fifty-pound bombs and fired unguided 75 mm rockets while the infantry used 120 mm mortars and 105 mm field guns to pound guerrilla bunkers in heavily populated areas.

It was meant to be a short and swift operation but the initial success of the government forces was blunted by fierce guerrilla resistance, heavy mining and booby traps. However, the guerrillas were sorely pressed and they rapidly withdrew to Jaffna city where they dug in. The government forces consolidated their positions around it.

On the eve of the April cease-fire, National Security Minister Lalith Athulathmudali had said that if the next round of talks ('the final one') failed, Sri Lanka had only the military option which meant the decisive battle for Jaffna. After the cease-fire was declared, Jayewardene had said, the government could destroy the Jaffna peninsula in a day if the guerrillas did not surrender.

But the government forces did not move on Jaffna for fear of what India might do. And India was almost certain it should not allow the assault on Jaffna city because of the political fall-out of the action in Tamil Nadu, especially if the civilian casualties were high. At the same time India was not prepared to intervene militarily just yet because the international implications of such an intervention could be serious; this took on added importance because of the precedent of the 1971 India-Pakistan war, when India had objected to the role of the United States navy. If it was not to appear hypocritical, and more important, forestall foreign military intervention, India would have to stay out of Sri Lanka.

There were other complications too. Political opinion in Tamil Nadu was demanding Indian intervention citing the Bangladesh analogy. But Indian intervention in Bangladesh had followed two steps: the announcement of a joint command of its forces with the Mukti Bahini (the liberation army) and the recognition of the fictitious Bangladesh government. India was not willing to act along these lines again for obvious reasons. Nor could it give the impression of being a helpless bystander. India's diplomacy it appeared had reached a dead-end, but then South Block came up with a clever move.

India announced that it would send humanitarian aid (food and medicine) in boats flying the Red Cross flag in the next forty-eight hours and Sri Lanka would be expected to co-operate with the mission. Sri Lanka was not so keen and said that it had to first discuss the modalities of the offer. Eventually the idea was turned down.

India decided to send an unarmed and unescorted relief mission anyway.

The loading of the aid, destined for the beleaguered Jaffna populace, was to be in the presence of foreign and Indian media persons. When it was done, a flotilla of over a score of mechanized fishing boats, led by a 1,000-tonne Indian Coast Guard vessel, *Vikram*, sailed out of Rameswaram on 3 June 1987. It was turned away from Sri Lanka's territorial waters after negotiations over the radio (that dragged on for four hours) between an Indian official and the commander of a Sri Lankan patrol vessel. The return of the Indian fleet was a humiliating anti-climax to the Indian initiative. 'Lanka stands firm, flotilla goes back,' proclaimed a gleeful headline in a Colombo daily. The Sinhalas burst crackers to celebrate the victory. Gloom descended on the External Affairs Ministry's offices in faraway New Delhi. Opposition leaders demanded that India act decisively immediately. A hurriedly called meeting of the cabinet committee began at one in the morning.

The next day the civilian plane bringing the media back from the Rameswaram fiasco had already taken off from Madurai when it was diverted to Bangalore where, it was announced, an important message was awaiting the press. Within minutes of landing, the media people were hustled into five AN-32 transport planes laden with food and medicines for Jaffna. Eagle Mission-4 was taking off, escorted by two Mirage-2000 fighter aircraft, with instructions to down any resistance.

A radio message from the lead plane of Eagle Mission-4 did not get any response from the Colombo airport control tower and the planes headed deep into Sri Lankan airspace. The mission did not have the sanction of the Red Cross or any other relief organization, and was an airforce operation. For all these reasons it was a flagrant violation of the Sri Lankan skies. In effect, India was rolling up a dubious victory to overcome the humiliation of the day before, and Sri Lanka (which has no air defence system) was being told that India could bomb it any time it wanted to.

The mission also meant that Sri Lanka could not move on the ground or water without taking into account India's presence: the relief mission had already broken the Sri Lankan naval blockade of the Jaffna peninsula and it would be a simple step from there to blockade Sri Lanka's two main ports—Colombo on the west and Trincomalee on the east—so that the military offensive against the guerrillas did not last long.

Predictably Sri Lanka reacted bitterly over the assault on its sovereignty. India immediately began playing down the affair:

diplomats in New Delhi were told that it was a one-off mission. Despite the reassurances, India's purposes had been served, and the Sri Lankan government turned amenable: the modalities of relief were discussed and the military operations in the Jaffna peninsula began slowing down.

In a last show of defiance Sri Lanka bombed Jaffna for two weeks after the paradrop and did not allow a kilogram of relief material to reach Jaffna until after the modalities were settled. But it was clear that these were only a means of saving face. From now on, Sri Lanka had to reckon with the fact that India could and would intervene militarily if it had sufficient reason to. Sri Lanka's other options too were disappearing. The United States had failed to denounce the paradrop. On the contrary, when approached for military assistance, the US asked Sri Lanka to find a *modus vivendi* with India and find a political solution. (India was kept informed by the US of its deliberations with Sri Lanka.) Pakistan insisted on a treaty as a precondition for military assistance.

In addition, to all these developments at the political level, the crippling effect of the war on Sri Lanka's economy, the despair in his own party over his failure to solve the ethnic issue, and demoralization in the armed forces at having to fight an unwinnable war (and there were reports of a possible military coup) totally unmanned President Jayewardene. He had no one to turn to but India.

*

India had its own compulsions to find an early solution to the problem. It realized that it had failed in its attempts to get the Liberation Tigers of Tamil Eelam (LTTE) to negotiate, which meant that it had failed overall, for as the principle guerrilla force the LTTE had the veto on any formula for a settlement.

It was not as if India had not tried every resource at its disposal (even M.G. Ramachandran of Tamil Nadu, whose patronage the LTTE enjoyed, could not persuade its leader Velupillai Prabhakaran to negotiate in November 1986 when Jayewardene was desperate); the problem was that the LTTE proved an extremely irrational and obdurate party to deal with. Prabhakaran was finally told that if he did not want a settlement and wanted to continue with the guerrilla campaign he should shift to Jaffna. Prabhakaran left taking his fighters and weapons leaving only political cadres behind in Madras.

The LTTE's intransigence had a lot to do with the assumption that it could hold out militarily until the end of 1988 when it felt it could get a better bargain out of any settlement, if only because all the parties involved would be pretty desperate by then. What it did not reckon with was the fact that things would go badly for it militarily. The fall of the strategic town of Vadamarachi, after a three-day battle in May, upset the

LTTE's strategy.

Then, the Sri Lankan forces began closing in on Jaffna city. As unhappy as the LTTE was with this situation, India felt worse: if the battle for the city was joined and heavy civilian casualities ensued, India would have to intervene militarily for fear of a violent reaction in Tamil Nadu. But if it did intervene, it could mean a divided Sri Lanka with a new country, a Tamil Eelam, across the Palk Straits, which could revive dormant secessionism in Tamil Nadu.

The only way out of the impasse would be to get the LTTE to sit down at the negotiating table with the Sri Lankan government and negotiate a political settlement. An unofficial message was sent to Jayewardene that India did not mind the LTTE emasculated militarily. In the past the LTTE had provided India its leverage with Sri Lanka for a two prong strategy—mediation and support to the militant groups. But now, so far as India was concerned, peace within Sri Lanka and India-Sri Lanka relations should no longer be hostage to the obduracy of the LTTE. More immediately India feared active Pakistani involvement because a Pakistani military expert was believed to have drawn up the blueprint for the final phase of the Sri Lankan army's operations to take Jaffna city, the symbol of Tamil resistance.

*

Once it became clear in New Delhi's mind that peace would be better for everyone than a no-win war, things began happening fast. Jayewardene, who was thoroughly demoralized, jumped at Rajiv Gandhi's latest peace plan (which was in effect the India Doctrine in a different guise, and whose end-result would be to establish India's supremacy in South Asia).

It is conjectured that Jayewardene only accepted the Indian peace plan when a last minute appeal to the US did not yield positive results. Whatever the 'real' reasons, on 29 July 1987 India and Sri Lanka signed the India-Sri Lanka accord to end the ethnic conflict, an accord hailed as a triumph of Indian diplomacy. And Indian troops, to enforce the military aspect to the accord, began arriving in Sri Lanka a day after the accord was signed. In a week there was an entire division in Jaffna (the 54 Air Assault Division).

When the Indian Peace-Keeping Force landed in Sri Lanka it was welcomed both by the Tamils and Jayewardene—for different reasons of course. The Tamils, including the LTTE, felt they had an ally that would keep the Sri Lankan forces at bay and Jayewardene was comforted by the fact that he would have a superior army to tackle the Tamil guerrillas if they got belligerent.

The sentiments of the Tamils and the Sri Lankan government aside, the IPKF had a clearly defined role in terms of the India-Sri Lanka agreement. This was, in brief, to disarm the guerrillas and ensure they participated in the political processes envisaged by the agreement to resolve in the ethnic issue once and for all, without loss of blood. In effect the IPKF was to be what its name connoted—a force that kept the peace.

India is not new to the peace-keeping job. Indian contingents have participated in such missions, either to repatriate prisoners or to monitor cease-fire arrangements in Korea, Indo-China, Lebanon, Egypt, Cyprus and Congo. All of these were under the United Nations flag, and did not involve India being part of local power equations. But there have been other instances, where India was an active participant in another country's issues: in 1950 Indian troops intervened in Nepal at the King's request when his rule was threatened by a movement for democracy; in East Pakistan in 1971 India helped in the creation of Bangladesh.

Likewise, in Sri Lanka, at Jayewardene's invitation the IPKF was expected to be involved (if only in a supporting role) in ending the conflict.

All went well, until the LTTE went back on its promises and retreated into the jungles to take up arms again in October 1987 (the ostensible reason for its action was that India had decided to turn over seventeen LTTE militants it held to the Sri Lankan authorities; the seventeen had threatened to commit suicide if this happened but India stood by its decision—twelve of the militants died by swallowing cyanide, and the LTTE took up arms and went to ground in Jaffna city, accusing India of betraying them).

From then on the IPKF found itself carrying out an increasingly unpopular chore. It took Jaffna for Sri Lanka with heavy casualties, and cleared Batticaloa and the adjoining areas of the Tamil militants; pushed through elections in the north-eastern provinces despite an LTTE boycott; stood guard while parliamentary and presidential elections were carried out in the Tamil provinces and is currently engaged on two fronts: flushing out the Tamil militants and propping up the north-eastern council, dominated by the EPRLF and the ENDLF—both groups that would be destroyed utterly by the LTTE if the IPKF wasn't around. The IPKF's stay in Sri Lanka (at one stage, there were 70,000 IPKF men in the country) has been marked by heavy casualities (nearly 900 men killed and over 2500 wounded) and it is obvious, as the months wear on, that it will be virtually impossible for it to eliminate the guerrillas as support for the LTTE and hostility for the IPKF grows in the countryside.

Besides, Sri Lanka now has a President, Premadasa, who has from the beginning been opposed to the India-Sri Lanka agreement and who therefore would like India to minimize its role in his country and have the IPKF leave as soon as possible. Further, the parliamentary elections in the country brought a pro-LTTE group, the EROS, to power and they would like the IPKF out as well. Finally, the JVP, the Sinhala extremist organization, which killed nearly 3000 people in 1988–89 alone, would like India to withdraw immediately.

Setting the seal on the almost universal distaste for the IPKF, the India-Sri Lanka agreement and India, was the LTTE's agreeing to talks with the Sri Lankan government in April 1989. The LTTE's demands included the abolition of the 'phoney' north-eastern council, the holding of fresh elections in the Tamil provinces, the complete cessation of Sinhala colonization of the north and the east, no referendum to ratify the merger of the Tamil provinces, the legitimizing and recognizing of the Tamil identity, and the ejecting of the IPKF from the island.

The first round of talks between the Premadasa government and the LTTE adjourned in May 1989 on a promising note. Both the sides, and also the JVP (not a party to the talks), found their interests converging on an immediate end to the role of the IPKF. On 1 June 1989, Premadasa declared that the island had had enough of Indian peace-keeping. He described the IPKF as a 'foreign' army, and wanted it to pack up by 29 July 1989. India was taken by surprise by this development. Premadasa's call, followed by a frenzied anti-India campaign by the JVP, was a conclusive proof of the failure of the accord.

Even as India tried to equivocate on the demand to pull out the IPKF (sometimes pleading logistical problems about meeting the short deadline, and sometimes linking the withdrawal to the implementation of the accord), Premadasa reiterated his call on 16 June. This time his tone was more firm and his references to the IPKF less complimentary. He said that the only condition for withdrawal of the IPKF, namely the decision of the Sri Lankan President on whose invitation it was sent, had been met.

It was apparent that India's options had shrunk: either it could withdraw and jeopardize the north-eastern council set-up, claimed to be the most tangible gain of the accord (the EPRLF which dominated the council underwritten by India threatened to return to the jungles to wage armed struggle for Tamil Eelam if it was ditched at this stage); or the IPKF could stay put and further deepen the ethnic conflict. If India chose to police the whole island, its eventual withdrawal would expose the Indian and Sri Lankan Tamil interests, that would survive, to a bitter revenge. An extreme option was to review its commitment to the integrity and unity of Sri Lanka (which ruled out Tamil secession). An Indian daily, *The Times of India,* said ominously on 21 June that India should prepare itself for a 'Cyprus solution' in Sri Lanka (which meant a break-up of the island at India's bidding), 'regardless of the costs involved'.

Nothing had been resolved as the accord, which has no time limit, approached its third year. The island lay fractured.

Tragic Destiny

The India-Sri Lanka agreement of July 1987 was an attempt at a short-term management of the island's ethnic conflict, in the hope a solution could be found. Unfortunately, India's intervention aggravated the conflict in geometrical progression, polarizing the island as never before. As a result there were several wars being fought instead of one—India against the Tamil militants and Sri Lanka against the Sinhala militants, and all the other Sinhala and Tamil groups—with no end in sight to either conflict.

This situation arose because neither India nor Sri Lanka had studied the problem deeply enough before positing solutions. So where did the problem begin? To answer this we have to go back to the time of the British rule. The British failed to prepare the nation for self-rule when they left it in 1948 by not recognizing adequately enough its separateness in terms of national and cultural components. And successive governments in free Sri Lanka compounded the problem by ignoring the realities of the country's composition exactly as the British had done. Sri Lanka, today, is a continuation of the political union the British left behind.

With independence, Ceylon became a nation-state, which, as understood by western liberal scholars, is a political unit transcending ethnic, religious and linguistic differences. Each group holds by its own religion, culture, language and ideas with different sections of the broader community living side by side but separately within a single political unit. A nation-state is an institution with a date of inception.

However, as is the norm, the independence of Ceylon (which meant a transition from a Crown Colony to a Dominion in the British Commonwealth) implied the right to self-determination which is based on the belief that each nation has the right to its destiny. (In a union of more than one nation, each of the constituents has the option to become an independent state, enter a federal relationship, or secede from the union.) Ceylon was soon to realize that the transition from an independent state to a fully fledged nation would not be an easy one. This was particularly true in its case because it was a political union from above. The ethnic Tamils, who are distinct from the Tamil-speaking plantation Tamils from India, saw the very framework of

Ceylon as false because they saw themselves as forced to be part of the union by the British. As a nation is a more democratic entity than that of a colony, ruled from afar, people have a greater say in the deciding of their own destinies: it is only after the demands of all its citizens have been weighed, accepted (or compromised on) and assimilated can a nation-state (or any other political entity) truly become a nation.

The evolution towards nationhood can begin before the initiation of a nation-state. India's Muslim minority demanded a nation of its own long before the British thought of giving India independence—and as a result of this the British partitioned India to create a Muslim-majority Pakistan before leaving the South Asian mainland. The process can continue after decolonization. Pakistan's Bengali-speaking eastern wing broke away from the west in 1971 to form the independent nation of Bangladesh.

Thus the process of nation formation has little to do with the nation-state which is a political imposition. And in contrast to the readymade political structure of a nation-state which is imposed from above, self-determination is a process from below, where the initiative is left to the people, to permit a process of elimination and accommodation of identifiable differences of language, culture, race and other historical distinctions.

Historically, cultural unity has followed rather than preceded national unity. The present-day United States, for instance, is a melting pot of cultural and ethnic identities and has been so for 200 years (unlike Canada which is a mosaic, with the French-speaking Quebec province recognized as a distinct entity). Similarly, Malaysia, with its multi-ethnic, multi-cultural, and multi-lingual attributes, holds together as a nation despite its Islamic orientation. (Immigrants of Indian origin rank number three as an ethnic group, after the Malays and the Chinese and hold the balance between the two. The ethnic groups are spatially dispersed, with neither of the minorities able to claim a contiguous territory of its own to be able to assert its right to self-determination.) But in Ceylon, the Tamils were a cultural nation before the island became independent, even though they constituted a union with the Sinhala majority, and with minorities like the Burghers, Malays and the immigrant Tamils from India. The ethnic Tamils had a territory of their own and a history as old as that of the Sinhalas. And unlike the immigrant Tamils, they could not be deprived of citizenship rights or rendered stateless and sought to be deported to the country of their origin—the short-term solution dreamed up by the Sinhalas to solve the problem of minorities in the country.

The tendency among the Sinhalas has been to assume the desirability, or even the inevitability, of identifying the political state (which Sri Lanka in its present form is) with the cultural nation which, in the island's context, is the majority Sinhala nation. The tendency was also to assume that the larger cultural nation, if not a state already, was capable of becoming one.

Once the ideal identification of a cultural nation and the political state is accepted, the state in its own defence begins acting as if it is a single and united cultural nation. And if it is not, it tries to bring the facts into focus with the ideals regardless of the rights of the other nationalities or minorities.

The majority drive in this regard began immediately after Ceylon became independent with the disenfranchisement and decitizenization of the immigrant Tamils who had been the backbone of the island's plantation economy since the early nineteenth century. And from 1956, the drive for the Sinhala-Buddhist supremacy was further heightened— through language, educational, religious, land-colonization and other policies, all designed to marginalize the Tamils.

*

The British could hold the ethnic balance in the island. But India, Sri Lanka's giant neighbour across the Palk Straits, was not seen by the Sinhala majority as a threat. And so it went about its hegemonistic plans without fear of being chastized. Why were the Sinhalas so determined to blank out the Tamils? The answer might seem obvious, but it is worth spelling out.

The Sinhalas were gripped by a fear complex and felt they had to seek a new identity, when the British left South Asia, for two reasons. First, though in a majority in the island, the Sinhalas felt they were a minority in the South Asian region with no one to identify themselves with. So, they believed, they had to carve out an identity of their own and where better to do this than in their own country. Secondly, a movement for Tamil secession (in India's Madras Presidency) had predated independence in 1947. There were justified Sinhala fears of a link-up between the island's Tamils and the Tamils in peninsular India. The Sinhalas have long had a vision of the island being invaded by Dravidian armies from across the Palk Straits. All this in addition to the historical antipathy the Sinhalas have had for the Tamils. (Sinhala mythology has it that their hero-king Dutthagamani gave them a sovereign identity some hundred years before Christ by defeating a Dravidian ruler in the island.)

When the Sinhala onslaught on Tamil identity began in 1956, the Colombo-based upper, Vellala, caste Tamil leadership from Jaffna responded feebly and half-heartedly, and held that it was willing to enter power adjustment pacts with the majority. They were not the only ones lacking in initiative.

As we have seen earlier, unlike in India, where the Muslim demand for a religion-based Pakistan, and the Tamil demand in Madras

Presidency for secession, predated independence there was no Tamil demand for self-determination in Ceylon. The ethnic Tamils were not even asking for devolution of power to the northern and eastern provinces which they began to claim as their traditional homeland. (Interestingly, the first practical demand for devolution was by the Kandyan* chiefs who went to the Donoughmore Constitution Commission (1928–29) to demand a system of government that recognized the need for devolution of power—for a federal dispensation with the north and east as a federal unit, the central province, as now, constituted as another and the southern and western provinces as the third. The Kandyan demand was a prelude to their demand for 'home rule'.)

When the Kandyan chiefs were demanding federal accommodation, there was no such demand from the Tamils for federal autonomy though they were also interested in negotiating 'home rule'. The Tamil demand for federal autonomy followed, and did not precede, independence, and only happened when it did (in 1949) because the plantation Tamils had been disenfranchised and rendered homeless.

Even at this point, the Tamils, though a cultural nation, showed no political aspirations. It was only after the Tamils had failed to arrest the Sinhala drive for majority domination—a process that destroyed the pluralism that obtained at the island's independence—that the Tamils began the secessionism demand.

Had there been a Tamil demand for secession before independence, the British might have been obliged to work out a federal arrangement as a concession to the Tamils before leaving the island as in India where the British offered a federal set-up (to avoid the partition of the country).

*

Even as the Tamils were being marginalized, the Sinhala leadership comprising largely the upper caste (Goyigama) elite, hoped the Colombo-based Tamil elite from Jaffna would keep their countrymen in check.

The turning point came in 1971 with the advent of the left-of-centre Sri Lanka Freedom Party led government headed by Sirimavo Bandaranaike, who had to face the insurrection of the Sinhala militant organization, the Janatha Vimukti Peramuna (JVP). Though she was able to put it down, the example set by the restive Sinhala youth, denied access to economic opportunity by the westernized elite, gave the equally deprived Tamil youth, who were also dissatisfied with their circumstances and the elite upper caste Tamil Vellala leadership, ideas.

* Sinhala highlanders

The Tamil youths' demand soon became secession and not just devolution of power or federal autonomy anymore, crystallizing into the demand for a sovereign homeland in 1976. The Tamil United Liberation Front (TULF), though led by moderates, was obliged to seek a mandate for secession at the 1977 elections.

The Tamil secessionist demand coincided with major changes across the world. Liberation movements in Latin America, South Africa and the Arab world were seeking the armed overthrow of existing state apparatuses to advance the cause of national self-determination. Encouraged by this Sri Lanka's Tamil youth backed the demand for secession with armed guerrilla struggle. The state responded to it with its own brand of terror.

Meanwhile, the JVP, despite its failure in 1971 (and its being consigned to the political wilderness thereafter), was coming back among the Sinhala youth in the south. This time it was more than a lower caste movement against the elite Sinhala leadership, but rather a national populist upsurge with a crudely defined ideology that bristled with all the inconsistencies inevitable in a heady mix of Buddhism, anti-casteism, ethnic chauvinism and a weird brand of Marxism.

Common to the LTTE in the north and the JVP in the south was the non-elite educational background of their leaders who, though marginalized from the power structure, had a mass following.

Neither the Tamil nor the Sinhala youth had any use for the Reaganite economics that had shaped the United National Party's 'open' policies since 1977—marking a break with the left-of-centre populism of Sirimavo Bandaranaike—geared to making Sri Lanka a show-case of free-enterprise, and export-oriented growth, an alternative to ritzy Singapore. So the government was now faced with a twin challenge—from the LTTE and the JVP, both of them anti-systemic.

Over the next decade, the ethnic conflict built up and the July 1983 ambush of Sinhala soldiers was followed by retaliatory anti-Tamil pogroms in Colombo and elsewhere. The moderate Tamil leadership fled to the safety of Madras in India and looked plaintively to New Delhi for support while the Tamil guerrillas stepped up their struggle. The conflict had finally escalated to total civil war.

*

India's involvement in the ethnic conflict began after the July 1983 flare-up but its support to the Tamil cause was selective and calculated. India never supported the demand for secession but it proclaimed sympathy for Tamil aspirations (primarily because the Tamils in India supported the Eelam demand). India helped the guerrillas with sanctuaries, arms and training while playing off one group against the other. It did not want the guerrillas to lose; it did not want them to win either. As a young Sinhala intellectual put it, India's role was one of regional bonapartism, relatively autonomous to the contending forces, tilting towards one side now and the other later, in an effort to ultimately impose a settlement to its advantage. India was 'helped' in this endeavour by President J. R. Jayewardene who was also trying to balance between the Sinhalas and the Tamils, as well as between factions of his own party and between the left and the right.

India's role, at once mediatory and interventionist-hegemonistic, would not have been necessary had the United National Party attempted an honest dialogue with the Tamil groups. It did not.

Jayewardene turned to India in sheer despair when no one else was prepared to bail him out of his losing war against the Tamil Tigers. More than a diabolical design to draw India into a war he could not win, it is more likely that Jayewardene acted out of an instinct for political survival. Jayawardene's appeal came at the right moment for India was keen to end the war to its strategic advantage and was not averse to liquidating the Tamil Tigers. Followed the India-Sri Lanka agreement which was 'imposed' on the Tamils, who were not a party to it, and on the Sinhalas whose government had outlived its mandate and was in office for the tenth year. After the agreement, Jayewardene was left with a hostile Sinhala sentiment even as India's Indian Peace-Keeping Force (IPKF) was fighting a hopeless war, picking up where he had left off.

Despite the initial welcome the IPKF got from all sections of Tamils who wanted the conflict to end, India's involvement did not build a Tamil consensus. This was a function of India's strategy which went through various stages. First, it began arming diverse Tamil groups against the LTTE. Then, it tried to revive the political processes in the Tamil areas around a Tamil United Liberation Front–People's Liberation Organization of Tamil Eelam combine. Next, when it failed to subdue the LTTE militarily and politically, and the credibility of the India-Sri Lanka agreement was at stake during the delayed elections to the North-Eastern Provincial Council, it promoted the Eelam People's Revolutionary Liberation Front (whose base is limited to the east) as an alternative to the LTTE which dominates the north. After the farcical elections staged by the IPKF, India began underwriting the EPRLF-dominated North-Eastern Provincial Council which lacked legitimacy. Thus India was actively contributing to the distortion of the Tamil electoral will. Far from uniting and winning over the Tamils, India deepened the differences among them.

Outside the Tamil areas, India's involvement activated dormant Sinhala-Buddhist nationalism and thereby promoted a cohesion of the anti-Indian forces which fear that Sri Lanka will become a semi-client of a hegemonistic neighbour.

The credibility of President Ranasinghe Premadasa's government lay in getting the IPKF out of the island even if it meant buying peace with the LTTE to be able to appease Sinhala sentiment. He realized that India, by intervening, had gained its strategic objectives, while the conflict within his country remained as vexed as ever. For this reason he made overtures to both the LTTE and the JVP. The LTTE seized the opening, for its interests lay in getting the IPKF out and having the India-backed North-Eastern Provincial Council set-up demolished. The interests of Premadasa and the LTTE were converging.

A political settlement through direct talks with the LTTE presupposes a greater measure of autonomy for the Tamils than the India-Sri Lanka agreement provides for. But can the Sinhala-oriented nation-state, that Sri Lanka is, provide the framework for the solution of a conflict which has its origins in the drive for Sinhala-Buddhist supremacy to marginalize the Tamils? To resolve this issue successfully will require a much tougher stand than various Sri Lankan governments have taken upto the present.

*

The India-Sri Lanka agreement tried to solve the conflict within the framework of the Sri Lankan nation-state which entrenched the supremacy of the Sinhala majority. The agreement tried to determine the quantum of autonomy the Tamils should get and proposed the modalities for ensuring it. But it left the issue of Tamil-Sinhala relations and the future of the plantation Tamils (of Indian origin) untouched, which was a major lacuna, for the Tamil demand is not limited to a provincial council and parity for Tamil with Sinhala as the official language.

Indeed, Tamil aspirations reflect a right to self-determination but Sri Lanka's constitution does not recognize the reality of two nations within the present nation-state. The plural character of Sri Lankan society, though mentioned in the India-Sri Lanka agreement, is not reflected in the constitution which is self-sealing: its entrenched clauses rule out amendments except through a referendum which the Tamils cannot win except with the consent of the Sinhala majority.

As opposed to the Tamil view, the Sinhalas, this far, have not budged from their historical perception of Sri Lanka as a haven of the Sinhala language and the Buddhist religion; this is reinforced by the belief that Sri Lanka was consecrated by the Buddha himself (therefore the Sinhalas see themselves as the defenders of the Buddhist faith).

The Sinhala majority has all along thought that any Tamil demand can be met only at the cost of its own interests, a zero-sum game. And, exacerbating the friction between the two groups is the fact that the Sinhala majority is not reconciled to even the limited concessions the Tamils were given under the India-Sri Lanka agreement. It thinks devolution of power is the sinister prelude to secession and the merger of the northern and eastern provinces (which the Tamils regard as non-negotiable) is the legitimization of secessionism because it implies a recognition of the Tamil right to a homeland.

To cut across these basic differences any solution to the ethnic conflict needs to be radically different and needs to have as its foundation a recognition of Sri Lanka's reality—that it comprises two nations.

In order to work such a solution the Sinhala majority needs to be neutralized on the Tamil demands and persuaded to recognize the Tamil right to their national identity as the price of the keeping the nation-state together. The Canadian constitution, amended after the June 1987 agreement, laid the French secessionist ghost to rest by recognizing the French-speaking province of Quebec as both a distinctive national and linguistic entity. Something on these lines in Sri Lanka would be a significant improvement on the India-Sri Lanka agreement (which recognizes the Tamils as a linguistic and ethnic group, but not as a nationality).

The recognition of the Tamil national identity with the right to self-determination and the right to their homeland will have to be built into a federal constitution that would not permit majority dominance and would ensure reasonable autonomy for the Tamils. In return the Tamils might have to reconcile themselves to a territorially smaller homeland that would exclude non-Tamil enclaves.

A solution that recognizes the Tamil national identity need not *per se* lead to Tamil secession though no union is voluntary without the right to secede.

The ruinous alternative to such a solution is renewed ethnic war and the tragedy of intervention, by invitation or without, to prevent or undo secession.

Appendix I

India-Sri Lanka Agreement to Establish Peace and Normalcy in Sri Lanka

The President of the Democratic Socialist Republic of Sri Lanka, His Excellency Mr J.R. Jayewardene and the Prime Minister of the Republic of India, His Excellency Mr Rajiv Gandhi, having met at Colombo on 29 July 1987.

Attaching utmost importance to nurturing, intensifying and strengthening the traditional friendship of Sri Lanka and India, and acknowledging the imperative need of resolving the ethnic problem of Sri Lanka, and the consequent violence, and for the safety, well-being and prosperity of people belonging to all communities in Sri Lanka.

Have this day entered into the following Agreement to fulfil this objective.

In this context,

1.1 Desiring to preserve the unity, sovereignty and territorial integrity of Sri Lanka;

1.2 Acknowledging that Sri Lanka is a multi-ethnic and a multi-lingual plural society consisting, *inter alia*, of Sinhalese, Tamils, Muslims (Moors), and Burghers;

1.3 Recognizing that each ethnic group has a distinct cultural and linguistic identity which has to be carefully nurtured;

1.4 Also recognizing that the Northern and the Eastern Provinces have been areas of historical habitation of Sri Lankan Tamil speaking peoples, who have at all times hitherto lived together in this territory with other ethnic groups;

1.5 Conscious of the necessity of strengthening the forces contributing to the unity, sovereignty and territorial integrity of Sri Lanka, and preserving its character as a multi-ethnic, multi-lingual and multi-religious plural society, in which all citizens can live in equality, safety and harmony, and prosper and fulfil their aspirations;

2. Resolve that,

2.1 Since the Government of Sri Lanka proposes to permit adjoining Provinces to join to form one administrative unit and also by a referendum to separate as may be permitted to the Northern and Eastern Provinces as outlined below:

2.2 During the period, which shall be considered an interim period, i.e. from the date of the elections to the Provincial Council, as specified in para 2.8 to the date of the referendum as specified in para 2.3, the Northern and Eastern Provinces as now constituted, will form one administrative unit, having one elected Provincial Council. Such a unit will have one Governor, one Chief Minister and one Board of Ministers.

2.3 There will be a referendum on or before 31st December, 1988 to enable the people of the Eastern Province to decide whether:

(a) The Eastern Province should remain linked with the Northern Province as one administrative unit, and continue to be governed together with the Northern Province as specified in para 2.2, or

(b) The Eastern Province should constitute a separate administrative unit having its own distinct Provincial Council with a separate Governor, Chief Minister and Board of Ministers.

The President may, at his discretion, decide to postpone such a referendum.

2.4 All persons who have been displaced due to ethnic violence, or other reasons, will have the right to vote in such a referendum. Necessary conditions to enable them to return to areas from where they were displaced will be created.

2.5 The referendum, when held, will be monitored by a committee headed by the Chief Justice, a member appointed by the President, nominated by the Government of Sri Lanka; and a member appointed by the President, nominated by the representatives of the Tamil speaking people of the Eastern Province.

2.6 A simple majority will be sufficient to determine the result of the referendum.

2.7 Meetings and other forms of propaganda, permissible within the laws of the country, will be allowed before the referendum.

2.8 Elections to Provincial Councils will be held within the next three months, in any event before 31 December 1987. Indian observers will be invited for elections to the Provincial Council of the North and East.

2.9 The Emergency will be lifted in the Eastern and Northern Provinces by 15 August 1987. A cessation of hostilities will come into effect all over the island within 48 hours of the signing of this Agreement. All arms presently held by militant groups will be surrendered in accordance with an agreed procedure to authorities to be designated by the Government of Sri Lanka. Consequent to the cessation of hostilities and the surrender of arms by militant groups, the army and other security personnel will be confined to barracks in camps as on 25 May 1987. The process of surrendering of arms and the confining of security personnel moving back to barracks shall be completed within 72 hours of the cessation of hostilities coming into effect.

2.10 The Government of Sri Lanka will utilize for the purpose of law enforcement and maintenance of security in the Northern and Eastern Provinces the same organizations and mechanisms of government as are used in the rest of the country.

2.11 The President of Sri Lanka will grant a general amnesty to political and other prisoners now held in custody under the Prevention of Terrorism Act and other Emergency laws, and to combatants, as well as to those persons accused, charged and/or convicted under these laws. The Government of Sri Lanka will make special efforts to rehabilitate militant youth with a view to bringing them back into the mainstream of national life. India will co-operate in the process.

2.12 The Government of Sri Lanka will accept and abide by the above provisions and expect all others to do likewise.

2.13 If the framework for the resolutions is accepted, the Government of Sri Lanka will implement the relevant proposals forthwith.

2.14 The Government of India will underwrite and guarantee the resolutions, and co-operate in the implementation of these proposals.

2.15 These proposals are conditional to an acceptance of the proposals negotiated from 4.5.1986 to 19.12.1986. Residual matters not finalized during the above negotiations shall be resolved between India and Sri Lanka within a period of *six* weeks of signing this Agreement. These proposals are also conditional to the Government of India co-operating directly with the Government of Sri Lanka in their implementation.

2.16 These proposals are also conditional to the Government of India taking the following actions if any militant groups operating in Sri Lanka do not accept this framework of proposals for a settlement, namely,

    (a) India will take all necessary steps to ensure that Indian territory is not used for activities prejudicial to the unity, integrity and security of Sri Lanka.

    (b) The Indian Navy/Coast Guard will co-operate with the Sri Lanka Navy in preventing Tamil militant activities from

affecting Sri Lanka.

(c) In the event that the Government of Sri Lanka requests the Government of India to afford military assistance to implement these proposals, the Government of India will co-operate by giving to the Government of Sri Lanka such military assistance as and when requested.

(d) The Government of India will expedite repatriation from Sri Lanka of Indian citizens to India who are resident there, concurrently with the repatriation of Sri Lankan refugees from Tamil Nadu.

(e) The Government of Sri Lanka and India will co-operate in ensuring the physical security and safety of all communities inhabiting the Northern and Eastern Provinces.

2.17 The Government of Sri Lanka shall ensure free, full and fair participation of voters from all communities in the Northern and Eastern Provinces in electoral processes envisaged in this Agreement. The Government of India will extend full co-operation to the Government of Sri Lanka in this regard.

2.18 The official language of Sri Lanka shall be Sinhala. Tamil and English will also be official languages.

3. This Agreement and the Annexure thereto shall come into force upon signature.

IN WITNESS WHEREOF we have set our hands and seals hereunto.
DONE IN COLOMBO, SRI LANKA, on this the twenty-ninth day of July of the year One Thousand Nine Hundred and Eighty Seven, in duplicate, both texts being equally authentic.

Junius Richard Jayewardene

President of the Democratic
Socialist Republic of Sri Lanka

Rajiv Gandhi

Prime Minister of the
Republic of India

Annexure to the Agreement

1. His Excellency the President of Sri Lanka and His Excellency the Prime Minister of India agree that the referendum mentioned in paragraph 2 and its sub-paragraphs of the Agreement will be observed by a representative of the Election Commission of India to be invited by His Excellency the President of Sri Lanka.

2. Similarly, both Heads of Government agree that the elections to the Provincial Council mentioned in paragraph 2.8 of the

Agreement will be observed by a representative of the Government of India to be invited by the President of Sri Lanka.

3. His Excellency the President of Sri Lanka agrees that the Home Guards would be disbanded and all para-military personnel will be withdrawn from the Eastern and Northern Provinces with a view to creating conditions conducive to fair elections to the Council.

   The President, in his discretion, shall absorb such para-military forces, which came into being due to ethnic violence, into the regular security forces of Sri Lanka.

4. The President of Sri Lanka and the Prime Minister of India agree that the Tamil militants shall surrender their arms to authorities agreed upon to be designated by the President of Sri Lanka. The surrender shall take place in the presence of one senior representative each of the Sri Lanka Red Cross and the Indian Red Cross.

5. The President of Sri Lanka and the Prime Minister of India agree that a joint Indo-Sri Lankan observer group consisting of qualified representatives of the Government of Sri Lanka and the Government of India would monitor the cessation of hostilities from 31 July 1987.

6. The President of Sri Lanka and the Prime Minister of India also agree that in terms of paragraph 2.14 and paragraph 2.16 (c) of the Agreement, an Indian Peace Keeping contingent may be invited by the President of Sri Lanka to guarantee and enforce the cessation of hostilities, if so required.

Letter from Mr J.R. Jayewardene
   (President of the Democratic Socialist Republic of Sri Lanka)
To Shri Rajiv Gandhi
   (Prime Minister of the Republic of India)

Excellency,
Please refer to your letter dated the 29th July 1987, which reads as follows:

   Excellency,
   Conscious of the friendship between our two countries stretching over two millennia and more, and *recognizing* the importance of nurturing this traditional friendship, it is imperative that both Sri Lanka and India reaffirm the decision not to allow our respective territories to be used for activities prejudicial to each others unity, territorial integrity and security.

   2. In this spirit, you had, during the course of our discussions,

agreed to meet some of India's concerns as follows:

(i) Your Excellency and myself will reach an early understanding about the relevance and employment of foreign military and intelligence personnel with a view to ensuring that such presences will not prejudice Indo-Sri Lankan relations.

(ii) Trincomalee or any other ports in Sri Lanka will not be made available for military use by any country in a manner prejudicial to India's interests.

(iii) The work of restoring and operating the Trincomalee oil tank farm will be undertaken as a joint venture between India and Sri Lanka.

(iv) Sri Lanka's agreements with foreign broadcasting organizations will be reviewed to ensure that any facilities set up by them in Sri Lanka are used solely as public broadcasting facilities and not for any military or intelligence purposes.

3. In the same spirit, India will:

(i) Deport all Sri Lankan citizens who are found to be engaging in terrorist activities or advocating separatism or secessionism.

(ii) Provide training facilities and military supplies for Sri Lankan security forces.

4. India and Sri Lanka have agreed to set up a joint consultative mechanism to continuously review matters of common concern in the light of the objectives stated in para 1 and specifically to monitor the implementation of other matters contained in this letter.

5. Kindly confirm, Excellency, that the above correctly sets out the agreement reached between us.

Please accept, Excellency, the assurances of my highest consideration.

Yours sincerely,
Sd/-
(*Rajiv Gandhi*)

His Excellency
Mr J.R. Jayewardene,
President of the Democratic Socialist Republic of Sri Lanka,
Colombo

This is to confirm that the above correctly sets out the understanding reached between us.

Please accept, Excellency, the assurances of my highest consideration.

Sd/-
(*J.R. Jayewardene*)

His Excellency
Mr Rajiv Gandhi,
Prime Minister of the Republic of India,
New Delhi

Appendix II

The Liberation Tigers of Tamil Eelam View of the India-Sri Lanka Agreement

The 'we love India and the people of India' speech of Liberation Tigers of Tamil Eelam leader V. Prabhakaran on 4 August 1987 at the Sudumalai Amman temple in the vicinity of Jaffna town is an interesting political exposition. This translation from Tamil was made available by the LTTE.

My beloved and esteemed people of Tamil Eelam:

Today there has taken place a tremendous turn in our liberation struggle. This has come suddenly, in a way that has stunned us, and as if it were beyond our power to influence events.

Whether the consequences of this will be favourable to us, we shall have to wait and see.

You are aware that this Agreement, concluded suddenly and with great speed between India and Sri Lanka, without consulting our people and without consulting our people's representatives, is being implemented with expedition and urgency. Until I went to Delhi, I did not know anything about this Agreement. Saying that the Indian Prime Minister desired to see me, they invited me and took me quickly to Delhi. The Agreement was shown to us after I went there. There were several complications and several question marks in it. The doubt arose for us whether, as a result of this Agreement, a permanent solution would be available to the problems of our people. Accordingly, we made it emphatically clear to the Indian government that we were unable to accept this Agreement.

But the Indian government stood unbudging on the point that whether we accepted or did not accept the Agreement, it was determined to put it into effect. We were not taken by surprise by this stand of the Indian government. This Agreement did not concern only the problem of the Tamils. This is primarily concerned with Indo-Sri Lankan relations. It also contains within itself the principles, the requirements for making Sri Lanka accede to India's strategic sphere of influence. (An alternative translation of this sentence, closer perhaps to its literal meaning, would be: 'It also contains within itself the stipulations for binding Sri Lanka within India's big power orbit'.) It works out a way for preventing disruptionist and hostile foreign forces from gaining footholds in Sri Lanka. That is why the Indian government showed such an extraordinary keenness in concluding this Agreement. However, at the same time, it happens to be an Agreement that determines the political future and fate of the people of Tamil Eelam. That is why we firmly objected to the conclusion of this Agreement without consultations without people and without the seeking of our views. However, there is no point in our objecting to this. When a great power has decided to determine our political fate in a manner that is essentially beyond our control, what are we to do?

This Agreement directly affects our movements and our political goals and objectives. It affects the form and shape of our struggle. It also puts a stop to our armed struggle. If the mode of our struggle, brought to this stage over a fifteen year period through shedding blood, through making sacrifices, through staking achievements and through offering a great many lives, is to be dissolved or disbanded within a few days, it is naturally something we are unable to digest. This Agreement disarms us suddenly, without giving us time, without getting the consent of our fighters, without working out a guarantee for our people's safety and protection. Therefore we refused to surrender arms.

Under such circumstances India's Honourable Prime Minister Mr Rajiv Gandhi, invited me for a discussion. I opened my mind and spoke to him of our concerns and our problems. I pointed out to the Indian Prime Minister the fact that I did not response the slightest faith in the Sinhala racist government and did not believe that they were going to fulfil the implementation of this Agreement. I spoke to him about the question of our people's safety and protection and about guarantees for this. The Indian Prime Minister offered me certain assurances. He offered a guarantee for the safety and protection of our people. I do have faith in the straightforwardness of the Indian Prime Minister and I do have faith in his assurances.

We do believe that India will not allow the racist Sri Lankan state to take once again to the road of genocide against the Tamils. It is only out of this faith that we decided to hand over our weapons to the Indian Peace-Keeping Force.

What ardent, immeasurable sacrifices we have made for the safety and protection of our people! There is no need here to eleborate on this theme. You, our beloved people, are fully aware of the character of our passion for our cause and our feelings of sacrifice. The weapons that we took up and deployed for your safety and protection, for your liberation, for your emancipation, we now entrust to the Indian government.

In taking from us our weapons—the one means of protection for Eelam Tamils—the Indian government takes over from us the big responsibility of protecting our people. The handing over of arms only signifies the handing over, the transfer of this responsibility.

Were we not to hand over our weapons, we would be put in the calamitous circumstance of clashing with the Indian Army. We do not want this. We love India. We love the people of India. There is no question of our deploying our arms against Indian soldiers. The soldiers of the Indian Army are taking up the responsibility of safeguarding and protecting us against our enemy. I wish very firmly to emphasize here that by virtue of our handing over our weapons the Indian government should assume full responsibility for the life and security of every one of the Eelam Tamils.

My beloved people.

We have no way other than co-operation with this Indian endeavour. Let us offer them this opportunity. However, I do not think that as a result of this Agreement; there will be a permanent solution to the problem of the Tamils. The time is not very far off when the monster of Sinhala racism will devour this Agreement. I have unrelenting faith in the proposition that only a separate state of Tamil Eelam can offer a permanent solution of the problem of the people of Tamil Eelam. Let me make it clear to you here, beyond the shadow of a doubt, that I will continue to fight for the objective of attaining Tamil Eelam.

The forms of struggle may change, but the objective or goal of our struggle is not going to change. If our cause is to triumph, it is vitally necessary that the wholehearted, the totally unified support of you, our people, should always be with us.

The circumstance may arise for the Liberation Tigers of Tamil Eelam (LTTE) to take part in the interim administration or to contest elections, keeping in view the interests of the people of Tamil Eelam. But I wish firmly to declare here that under no circumstances and at no point of time will I contest elections or accept the office of Chief Minister.

The Liberation Tigers yearn for the motherland of Tamil Eelam!

Select Bibliography

Political Transition

Coomaraswamy, Radhika, *Sri Lanka: the Crisis of Anglo-American Constitutional Traditions in a Developing Society*, New Delhi: Vikas, 1984.

De Silva, K.M., *A History of Sri Lanka*, New Delhi: Oxford University Press, 1981.

De Silva, K.M. (ed.), *Sri Lanka: A Survey*, Hamburg: The Institute of Asian Affairs; London: C. Hurst, 1977.

De Silva, K.M. and Wriggins, Howard, *J.R. Jayewardene of Sri Lanka: A Political Biography* (Vol. 1: the first fifty years), London: Anthony Blond, 1988.

Fernando, Tissa & Kearney, Robert N. (eds.), *Modern Sri Lanka: a Society in Transition*, Syracuse NY: Maxwell School of Citizenship and Public Affairs, 1979.

Jacob, Lucy M., *Sri Lanka: From Dominion to Republic*, New Delhi: National, 1973.

Kearney, Robert N., *Communalism and Language in the Politics of Ceylon*, Durham NC: Duke University Press, 1967.

Phadnis, Urmila, *Religion and Politics in Sri Lanka*, New Delhi: Manohar, 1976.

Roberts, Michael (ed.), *Collective Identities, Nationalisms and Protests in Modern Sri Lanka*, Colombo: Marga Institute, 1979.

Suryanarayana, P.S., *The Peace Trap: an Indo Sri Lankan Political Crisis*, New Delhi: Affiliated East West Press, 1988.

Warnapala, W.A.W. & Hewagama, Dias L., *Recent Politics in Sri Lanka: the Presidential Election and Referendum of 1982*, New Delhi: Navrang, 1983.

Wijetunga, W.M.K., *Sri Lanka in Transition*, Colombo: Wesley Press, 1974.

Wilson, A.J., *Politics in Sri Lanka 1947–73*, London: Macmillan, 1971.

Wilson, A.J., *The Gaullist System in Asia: the Constitution of Sri Lanka*, London: Macmillan, 1979.

Wriggins, Howard W., *Ceylon: Dilemmas of a New Nation*, Princeton: Princeton University Press, 1960.

The Ethnic Conflict

Amirthalingam, Appapillai, 'Self-Determination and National Minorities', *Logos*, Vol. 16, No. 4, December 1977, pp. 73–4.
Appathurai, Edward, 'Communal Politics and National Integration in Sri Lanka', Israel, Milton (ed.), *National Unity: the South Asian Experience*, New Delhi: Promilla, 1983, pp. 209–33.
Balasuriya, Stanislaus Tissa Fr. O.M.I., 'Our Crisis of National Unity', *Logos*, Vol. 16, No. 3, September 1977, pp. 41–96.
Balasuriya, Stanislaus Tissa, Fr. O.M.I., 'Race Relations: A Spiritual Challenge to the Nation', *Logos*, Vol. 16, No. 14, December 1977, pp. 75–87.
Centre of Society and Religion, *Race Relations in Sri Lanka*, Colombo, 1978.
Colombo Study Circle, *Sri Lanka: Region of Terror in Jaffna*, Colombo: Kumaran Press, 1981.
De Silva, Chandra Richard, 'The Sinhalese-Tamil Rift in Sri Lanka', Wilson A.J. and Dennis, Dalton (editors), *The States of South Asia, Problems of National Integration*, London: C. Hurst, 1982, pp. 155–74.
De Silva, Chandra Richard, 'The Tamils and the Constitution of the Second Republic of Sri Lanka (1978)', *Sri Lanka Journal of Social Sciences*, Vol. 3, No. 1, June 1980, pp. 9–17.
Dubey, Swarooprani, 'National Integration and Constitution in Sri Lanka', *South Asian Studies*, Vol. 11, Nos. 1 & 2, January–December 1976, pp. 120–5.
Jacob, Lucy M., 'Challenges to National Integration in Sri Lanka: Some Perspectives on Tamil Problems', *South Asian Affairs*, Vol. 1, No. 1, January 1982, pp. 1–15.
Jacob, Lucy M., 'Constitutional Development and the Tamil Minority in Sri Lanka', *South Asian Studies*, Vol. 13, No. 2, July–December 1979, pp. 66–79.
Jacob, Lucy M., 'Regionalism in Sri Lanka', *South Asian Studies*, Vol. 15, Nos 1–2, January–December 1980, pp. 173–84.
Jayawardene, Kumari, 'Class Formation and Communalism', *Race and Class*, Vol. 26, No. 1, Summer 1984, pp. 51–62.
Kearney, Robert N., 'Language and the Rise of Tamil Separatism in Sri Lanka', *Asian Survey*, Vol. 18, No. 5, May 1978, pp. 521–34.
Manor, James, 'Sri Lanka: Explaining the Disaster', *World Today*, November 1983, pp. 450–9.

Michael, Robert, 'Ethnic Conflict in Sri Lanka and the Sinhalese Perspective: Barriers to Accommodation', *Modern Asian Studies,* Vol. 12, No. 3, July 1978, pp. 353–73.

Siriweera, Wi. I., 'Recent Developments in Sinhala–Tamil Relations', *Asian Survey,* Vol. 20, No. 9, September 1980, pp. 903–13.

Thambiah, Stanley Jeyaraj, 'The Politics of Language in India and Ceylon', *Modern Asian Studies,* Vol. 1, No. 3, July 1967, pp. 215–40.

Wilson, A.J., 'Tamil Federal Party in Ceylon Politics', *Journal of Commonwealth Political Studies,* Vol. 4, No. 2, July 1966, pp. 117–37.

Wilson, A.J., 'Cultural and Language Rights in a Multinational Society', *Tamil Culture,* Vol. 7, No. 1, January 1958, pp. 22–32.

Wriggins, Howard W., 'Impediments to Unity in New Nations: the Case of Ceylon', *American Political Science Review,* Vol. 55, No. 2, June 1961, pp. 313–20.

Index

H

'Home Rule' 115,135
Hindi 113,115,116
Hinduism 115
Hindu order 115
Hyderabad 116

I

Immigrant Tamils
33,106,109,111,133,134
India, hegemonistic plans 134
India Doctrine (India's Monroe
Doctrine) 119,120
India-Pakistan War 121,126
India Today 118
Indian and Pakistani Residents Act of
1949 36
Indian expansionism 37,98
Indian National Congress 34
Indian Ocean 120,121,122
Indian Peace-Keeping Force, IPKF 17,
20, 26, 29, 30, 69, 96, 107, 131,
137: arrival of 16,60; fires on
Tamil mob in Mannar 18:
marginalizes LTTE 100: takes
Jaffna 20, 130
Indian Tamil 110
Indira Gandhi–Sirimavo agreement
112
Indo-Dravidian languages 116
Ireland 18,31
Israel 89,122
'Israel interest section' 122

J

Japanese 120
Jaffna peninsula
90,91,94,109,125,126,127:
attack by Sri Lankan forces 92:
battle for 13: population 13
Jaffna 21, 22, 26, 27, 28, 29, 32, 43,
46, 53, 61, 68, 70, 91, 92, 94,
109, 110, 113, 117, 118, 125,
126, 127, 129, 130, 131, 135:
conquered by Portuguese 48: elite
of 47; library burnt 51
Jammu and Kashmir 124
Janatha Vimukti Peramuna, JVP 16,
20, 21, 28, 30, 23, 43, 75, 95,
96, 97, 98, 101, 102, 103, 104,
106, 107, 108, 119, 120, 130,
135, 136

Jatiya Sevaka Sangamaya (National
Workers Organization) 86
Jayasuriya, Gamini 100
Jayawardene, Kumari 82
Jayewardene, H.W. 120,90
Jayewardene, J.R. 14, 15, 17, 19,
20, 22, 23, 26, 27, 28, 40, 53,
60, 63, 71, 89, 92, 97, 100, 103,
106, 118, 119, 120, 121, 122,
123, 124, 125, 126, 128, 129,
130, 137 country's first President
86: his govt's approach to resolve
conflict 88: seeks Indian
mediation 91
July 1983 anti-Tamil pogrom/riots
16,31,32,52,55,86,88,118,119,
136
Justice Party 114,115

K

Kankesanthurai 48
Kukbukkan Oya 49
Kumana 49
Karunanidhi, M. 77,117,118
Kandy 32,40
Kandyan chiefs 135
Kandyan farmer 33, 109
Kandyan highlanders 98
Kannada 114,116
Kashmir dispute 124
Kaula Lumpur 117
Keeny-Meany Services 89,122
Kenya 111
Kerala 109
Kilinochchi 70,74,92
Korea 130
Kotelawala, John 38
Kotte 32,33
Krishna Kumar, Sadasivam (Kittu)
26,27,71,73
Kumaranatunga, Vijaya 22,101
Kumarappa 19

L

Lal Bahadur Shastri–Sirimavo
agreement 111
Language conflict 113
Lanka Sama Samaj Party, LSSP
37,38,43,44,81,102,104
Latin America 135
Lebanon 130
Left-of-centre politics 38,44,85,121

Tamil Nadu 25, 28, 59, 65, 72, 109,
117, 118, 123, 126, 128
Tamil New Tigers 47
Tamil secessionism 14, 42, 48, 54,
85, 87, 90, 117, 125, 134, 135,
136, 139: Indian Tamil sympathy
for 112; in India 113, 118;
parallels with India 111
Tamil-Sinhala parity issue 38,44,75
Tamil United Front 47
Tamil United Liberation Front, TULF
23, 29, 42, 48, 49, 52, 54, 57,
59, 61, 88, 89, 92, 104, 123,
125, 135: talks with Jayewardene
50, 56
Telugu 114,116
The Bridge on the River Kwai 34
Thero, Buddharakkita 81
Thero, Somarama 79
Terrorism Act of 1967 of South
Africa's regime 87
Thileepan, Amirthalingam 18,66
Thimpu 57,58,59,89,90
Third World countries 95,110
Thondaman, S. 37,90
Travancore 116
Trincomalee 19, 50, 53, 58, 74, 89,
90, 96, 120, 121

U

Unemployment problems 46,47
Unitary system 35
United Front 44,95,98
United Kingdom 87,89,119,120,122
United Kingdom–Ceylon defence
agreement 129
United Nation 130, 131
United National Party (UNP) 17, 43,
50, 52, 79, 82, 97, 100, 102,
103, 104, 105, 121, 137:
formation of 35; 'open' policy

136; 1977 Election Manifesto
85;
United Provinces 113
United Socialist Alliance
24,75,102,104
United States 95, 99, 119, 120, 121,
122, 124, 125, 126, 127, 133
Universal adult franchise 34,35,36
Untouchability 115

V

Vadamarachi 128
Vadukkodai 42,48
Vavuniya 49,70,73,74,90,92
Vellala caste 134,135
Vietnam 124
Vijaya 32
Viplavakari Lanka Samaj Party 39
VOA transmitter 121,122

W

Wallouve 49
Walters, Vernon 122
Washington 122
Weerasinghe, Jayadasa 15
Weinberger, Caspar 122
Weiner, Myron 113
Wijeveera, Rohana 95,97,99,101
Wijawardane, Wimala 40
World Tamil Congress (International
Conference on Dravidology and
Linguistics) 117

Y

Yogeswaran, V. 51

Z

Ze-dong, Mao 67
Ziyang, Zhao 120